CHANGING LANES

CASSANDRA DARDEN BELL

CHANGING LANES

sepia™

CHANGING LANES

ISBN-13: 978-1-58314-710-8
ISBN-10:   1-58314-710-1

www.kimanipress.com

Printed in U.S.A.

Dedicated to my dad

Ronald M. Darden

Acknowledgments

Using the television news arena as the backdrop for *Changing Lanes* is my way of paying tribute to the hundreds of thousands of journalists who give of themselves each day to bring news and information into our homes. Special thanks to all my friends in the business. My life is richer for having known and worked with you all...News Directors—Roy Hardee and Neal Fox, General Manager—Ed Adams, News Anchors and reporters—Alan Hoffman, Roseanne Haven, the late Jim Woods, Rex Rowland, Speight Williams, Claudine Chalfant, Phillip Williams, Brian Bowman, Chris Stansbury, John Spence, John Moore, Nicole Jenkins, Lynnette Taylor and Deborah Carey, Producers—Robin Phyilaw and Tracey Bennett, Technical Staff—Stephanie Blow, Norm Collins, John Wilson, Luther Williams and Dave Brown.

Additional thanks to my editor, Glenda Howard, for her tireless effort to always help me put my best foot forward. To my agent, Sha Shana Crichton, for being an excellent negotiator, advocate and friend. To Linda Gill and all the staff at Kimani Press for continuing the vision of bringing forth compelling stories by and for the African-Americans.

And to my husband, Larry, and children, Lauryn, Ariel, and Jordan...may I never take your love and devotion for granted.

CHAPTER 1

"Don't touch that tape."

"But I need—"

"I said, don't touch the damn tape."

Andrea Shaw laughed at the near growl in the voice, the intensity of the struggle. The voices rang out from behind her. She couldn't see their faces, but her mind flashed a memory of her two children when they were just toddlers…fighting over a toy.

In this case, the voices behind her were not children. They were professional news broadcasters. The tape to which they referred was not some child's toy, but rather the lead story for Baltimore's highest-ranked newscast.

Still, Andrea laughed. The investigative story she had fought tooth and nail to get exclusively and spent several late nights piecing together, had been reduced to what sounded like a mere juvenile power struggle.

"Fifteen minutes, Ms. Shaw."

A lanky production assistant yelled over her shoulder as he dashed past her desk, the breeze from his movement ruffling papers and Andrea's nerves. She didn't bother to look up at him, just slapped a hand down to steady the papers, and closed her eyes for a five count to recenter herself. No matter the noise level or the number of bodies scurrying around her desk, she would not let their pandemonium ruffle her feathers.

Andrea didn't bother to yell and scream in response to the eager assistant about his frantic announcement, not because she didn't want to, but primarily because she didn't know his name. During her years at the station she had witnessed one production staff member after another work a few months, and then move on either to greener broadcasting pastures or out of the business altogether. She reasoned that this guy would be like the rest and have moved on before she'd have a name logged in her memory bank well enough to recall it on command.

Andrea glanced at her desk clock. Production guy was right. Time was short for WVTR Baltimore's star news anchor. But she didn't flinch at the notion of time. It wasn't as if they would start the show without her. As competent as her coanchor, Dave, was, there was something about the two of them on the news set that made the effort complete. At least in Andrea's mind that was the case.

She was certain that it was the dual force that made the WVTR's six o'clock evening newscast the highest rated show in their market. Calmly, deliberately, Andrea continued sipping a cup of piping hot orange pekoe tea, and watched the others sweat and rush about as if on the brink of disaster.

The evening producer, Nancy Sanchez, glanced in Andrea's direction as if half expecting her, like any normal news anchor, to jump up and rush off to the news set. But Nancy knew better. Anyone who had been around the newsroom for more than a few months knew better. Andrea wouldn't budge until she had consumed at least half of her tea, popped open the top button on her skirt, and perused the news copy the associate producer had plopped onto her desk just seconds earlier.

"Ever thought of a cold beverage?" Nancy asked as she snatched a tape from Christy Tyler, one of the newest reporters on the scene.

Christy, who had just hours earlier been sharing a cigarette with Nancy, now jerked her head around, giving the evening producer an evil eye roll before grabbing a makeup bag and rushing out the back door. They had gone from chums to enemies just ten minutes earlier when Nancy had insisted that Christy change a line of dialogue in her script.

It was pretty much the same at most news outlets. At the start of a news day, the powers-that-be handed out assignments, made preliminary newscast rundowns and then everyone jumped into their day with optimism and enthusiasm. But then somewhere during the six or seven hours that followed, something sinister happened. No one could quite explain it, but the once-well-made-up fashionably dressed, professional men and women lost all decorum. The pressure of getting every aspect of their story wrapped up in time for presentation made tempers flare, turning those formerly perfect communicators into monosyllabic persons uttering phrases like *stop, don't* and *move,* with enough passion to frighten the fainthearted.

By five o'clock, when the early newscast started, ear-piercing noise from phones and police scanners provided the background, while the foreground was full of no-longer-calm men and women scurrying in every direction yelling and screaming both requests, instructions and a few obscenities. Reporters, photographers, producers, all hell-bent on the idea that their job was the most important and crucial to getting a top-notch newscast on the air. All willing to give a hefty piece of their mind if anyone stood in their way. All except Andrea, who sat sedately at her desk, sipping hot tea.

"Cold beverage," Andrea said in response to Nancy's question. "Not good for the vocal cords. They'd tighten and you don't want me to sound like Daffy Duck, now do you?"

Nancy pushed air through her tightly clamped lips and continued running down her list for the show. Andrea knew Nancy could care less what she sounded like, as long as she got it right, and it didn't make any of the off-camera folk look bad. And for the record, Andrea always did get it right. Calm, calculated perfection was what they paid her to do. Worrying was what they paid Nancy to do. And in Andrea's opinion, she did it well.

Nancy slid one partially polished fingernail across her rundown list to near midway and stopped, letting her hand rest on her tiny waist. Not that Andrea could see that waist. Although Nancy was as slim as a beanpole, she covered herself from head to toe in clothes two sizes too large.

This particular day, the white oxford shirt could have belonged to an extralarge man. And probably did. Nancy's husband, no doubt. Her brown skirt swung wide and long, making a perfect tepee around a set of well-worn Keds tennis shoes. Without an ounce of concern for fashion, Nancy leaned over the front of Andrea's desk close enough for her to hear over the hysteria around them.

"Who was that call earlier, the one you didn't take?"

"A guy I went out with once."

More tea sipping.

Nancy went back to the list before continuing her interrogation. And she would continue. Andrea knew that much. Both women had started at the station around the same time, both minorities, married with kids and eager to rise through the ranks. Andrea and Nancy had become fast friends. There wasn't much that happened with either woman that the other wasn't aware of. When Andrea had gotten the six o'clock news anchor spot five years ago, she had requested Nancy for the show producer.

"Which guy?" Nancy asked, not bothering to whisper.

Andrea gulped before answering, still unaffected by the mounting chaos around her. A sweaty photographer had just sprinted through the door screaming that he needed an editing bay ten minutes ago. His eyes communicated that he might hurt anyone who stepped in his path or tried to divert his editing needs.

"Body odor," Andrea finally answered.

Nancy shrieked as if she could smell the guy. Andrea had gone out with the well-connected accountant only once and the entire time there was an odor that wouldn't go away. She wasn't sure it was body odor or something in the air. He had looked clean and well-groomed, but she couldn't really be sure. Every time he leaned into her personal space, the smell nearly choked her. What was she to think? She had assumed that beneath the polished veneer was a real stinker and she didn't want to subject her olfactory glands to another date.

"Line one," the news department receptionist yelled across the room to Andrea.

Andrea's brow crinkled, her eyes locked on the girl. What was her name again, Cara or Carla? She couldn't remember which as she blinked the smelly date from her mind and continued sipping her tea.

Before Andrea could refuse the call, the phone on her desk was beeping. Cara had forwarded it despite Andrea's request for no phone calls prior to the newscast. A request she'd worked long and hard to earn. Nearly ten years to be exact, starting as a producer for the early-morning show, then some field reporting and finally the coveted Prime-time News Anchor spot. A quick leap up the ladder, but leaps she'd labored for and according to her colleagues, had deserved. However, none of that mattered as the phone beeped again, minutes past the time she was due on set.

"He said it was urgent," Cara explained as Andrea held back the need to roll her eyes at the girl.

That was the most she would do if angry at work...roll her eyes. No harsh words like the rest of her news family. For her, a tarnished reputation was not worth the pleasure of mouthing off at a coworker.

"Thanks, Carla," Andrea growled.

"It's Cara!" the girl shouted, as if Andrea had committed an unpardonable sin.

Andrea's lips parted with the need to apologize, but

Cara was already on another line. Andrea sipped again before reaching for the phone.

"Another one of your dates," Nancy scowled.

"Not likely. Probably the ex. Cara said, *he* and *urgent.* That usually spells Ronald."

Nancy had glanced at her watch during Andrea's speech, which drew the need for explanation.

"I really should take this, Nancy."

In the chain of command and pecking order, Andrea was Nancy's boss, but observing the current interaction between the two, an outsider would have suspected the opposite. Nancy stopped in her tracks as Andrea's hand rested on the beeping phone. A snarl formed at Nancy's mouth and spread over the rest of her olive-toned face.

"No way. As good as you are at multitasking, this is a no-no. Ten minutes, Andrea. Which means you should have been on set five minutes ago," Nancy yelled, as if Andrea were one of her four kids.

Four kids, two cats, a ferret, a one-foot-in-the-grave dog and a husband who also worked at the station. An engineer. He was one of those techie types who avoided the news-people like the plague. Nancy's specialty, however, was jumping right into the madness—something that newspeople are known for. It was as if she was born to rush through life putting out other people's fires. And Andrea had given her plenty of opportunities to do just that.

"Promise, Nance. I'll be there," Andrea said, for the first time feeling a tiny bit anxious.

Andrea knew her tone sounded convincing, but she could see Nancy's brain churning with a plan to lead the coanchor Dave into the show without her. Nancy rushed out of the newsroom and Andrea grabbed the phone. On the fifth or sixth beep, she slapped the receiver against the side of her head.

"Andrea Shaw, how may I help you?"

She crossed her fingers and hoped it wasn't Ronald, but rather the missing interview for her next investigative story. She had just wrapped up one of two hot pieces that might send a couple of university officials to the big house.

"Mrs. Shaw, this is Hal Pimpkins, Amber's school principal."

Principal Pimpkins paused as if Andrea should be expecting his call. She wasn't. She stopped breathing.

Only ten minutes...no make that nine minutes to showtime...and she was on the brink of a phone call that couldn't possibly go in a positive direction. How many times does a parent get a call from her teenager's school with news praising the youngster? Andrea fought to control her emotions, but she could feel her heartbeat in her ears as she tried to sound professional and unaffected by the call.

"Yes, Mr. Pimpkins, what can I do for you?"

"I realize you're about to be on television, but I wanted to make sure that you were aware of our decision concerning Amber's disciplinary issues."

He couldn't have possibly been aware that she was about to be on television or he wouldn't have called. Not minutes before the show.

Andrea managed to control the anger and frustration that was rising in her chest. The clock was ticking and her brain was doing laps around her thirteen-year-old daughter's most recent escapades.

Amber had been in a fight several weeks earlier, and then she was caught smoking on the school bus. Both incidents, according to Amber's telling, were not her fault. The fight had kept Amber home for a few days. Mostly TV and relaxation time. Andrea had complained about the backward school-suspension policy. What kind of punishment is unsupervised time at home? The smoking incident, however, had gotten Amber kicked off the school bus, and forced Andrea into involuntary taxi service.

"The smoking or the fight?" Andrea asked.

She glanced at the clock while waiting for Mr. Pimpkins to reply, but there was no need. By now, everyone in the newsroom had stopped their own panicked activities and was staring back and forth from the newsroom monitors to her.

The five o'clock news anchor, Carol Manning, was wrapping up her hour-long show with teasers for what Andrea and Dave had coming up at six. However, the remarkable Andrea Shaw was not on the news set, but rather sitting board stiff, news copy in one hand, telephone receiver in the other…and a half cup of lukewarm tea still sitting on her desk.

Andrea had been calmly ready to deliver the latest news and information into the homes of tens of thousands of viewers, but in a matter of seconds all of that changed; she was still sitting at her desk, with less than eight minutes to airtime.

At best, she could run to the studio, slide the microphone up the front of her jacket and straighten herself just in time for a winded news open. But only if she hung up on Amber's principal at that very second.

"Tell Dave to go on without me. Family emergency. I'll try to get there in time to pitch my piece at the end of the first block," she yelled toward one of the sets of eyes glued to her...an intern from one of the universities in the city.

Interns were worse than the actual employees. They only lasted days, sometimes hours. There was no way she would try to learn their names. And the intern didn't seem to care that she hadn't referred to him by name since he shot out of the room as soon as Andrea got the command out of her mouth. Andrea jumped when the paper tray on the fax machine gave way under the weight of too many unattended faxes.

"Ms. Shaw, I am sorry for bothering you before your newscast, but you hadn't responded to my last phone call or the letter," Principal Pimpkins continued, snatching Andrea back from her surroundings.

The newsroom chaos didn't usually faze her, but suddenly she couldn't ignore it, buzzing, humming, unintelligible words spoken several decibels above normal, and then it all stopped. Suddenly all Andrea could hear was the sound of the brakes screeching in her head. *What phone call and letter?*

"You did receive my letter, ma'am? You were aware that a board was reviewing Amber's case and we've decided that a week suspension is our best option considering the violation."

Suspension? Violation?

How could she not know her child had been kicked out of school again? She could no longer hide her shock, and figured there was no point in doing so. The principal could already assess that she was completely in the dark. Still, she did not want to seem completely incompetent.

"I'm sorry Mr. Pimpkins, but this is the first I've heard about any of this."

Inadequacy swept over her at such speed that she felt a chill. She tugged at one side of her tasteful blue jacket, needing to do something with her hands. A child has to do something awful to be kicked out of school for a whole week, she told herself.

Amber had done plenty of bad things since her parents had gotten divorced, but Andrea had always been able to work something out. As she mentally flipped through the pages of her daughter's past transgressions, the overwhelming newsroom orchestration was replaced by one lone voice.

She glanced at one of the many newsroom monitors. The newscast had started. Dave was alone, reading from the teleprompter as he had done plenty of times in the past. Times when she was out sick or on vacation. But never when she was sitting at her desk being informed of her child's suspension from school.

"I should have known there had been a breakdown in communication. I'm sorry to have to get into this with you now, ma'am. The term of suspension starts this Monday, unless of course we find out more. All of this was explained in the letter and I went over it in a phone message," Mr. Pimpkins sighed, then stopped.

Andrea swallowed hard, hoping not to choke on the words. What could she say? He had called and left a message; a message that Amber had likely erased before she could listen to it. And who knows what happened to the letter. Typical teenager cover-up. There was nothing to do about it now. She couldn't help but wonder what her daughter had done to be kicked out of school for a week.

"Ms. Shaw, I assume you are not at all aware of the list," Mr. Pimpkins said as if reading her mind.

"What list?" she yelled, drawing a few glances from reporters lingering in the newsroom.

After the newscast had started, the noise level dropped to a deafening silence and instead of running around, most of the crew stood dazed in front of TV monitors that aired their competitors' broadcast. Their job at this point was not only to make sure they had covered their story accurately but also to make sure no other reporter got anything they had missed.

Principal Pimpkins continued his explanation. "I was afraid of this. We found a rather troubling list. Threats against specific members of the faculty, school board and a few students. We're still trying to determine who wrote the list, but the students involved are being suspended until we get to the bottom of this."

Andrea's pulse was racing so fast she thought her heart would stop.

"A list like…" she asked without completing the statement before the principal chimed in.

"Yes, ma'am, a kill list. I suppose you know from covering stories like this, we have to take it seriously. And

I'll assume, despite your professional position, we can count on you to help us keep this from getting blown out of proportion with the media."

Andrea's breath caught as she tried to wrap her mind around what she was hearing. A kill list. Media attention. She couldn't focus on either. Of her two children, Amber and Ray, Amber had been the most volatile since the divorce, but not to the point of violence. Amber couldn't be threatening people, Andrea told herself as her stomach began to sour.

There had to be an explanation for all this, she thought, as the principal continued. "Ma'am, I talked with your husband earlier this week when it happened. He said that you were out of town working on a story. I just assumed that by now, you were aware."

But she was not aware. And her *husband,* or bastard ex-husband to describe him more accurately, did not intend to give her a heads-up on any of this.

"Andrea? Is everything okay?" her news director, Ted Baxter, stood in the doorway of his office, clearly concerned about the stress he saw on her face.

Ted had been more of a mentor and friend to Andrea than a boss. As much as she wanted to rush to his side and tell him the frightful news, she merely forced a smile and stifled the tears brimming at the corners of her eyes. She waved Ted off only wishing she could use the same hand to slap her ex.

Ted turned and retreated into his office, but not before pointing to the seat in front of his desk. A simple signal that meant she would not get away free and clear with not telling him what terrible family emergency had prevented her from doing her job. Andrea quickly weighed all the cards on the table and decided for the sake of professionalism that she was better served by keeping her family emergency to herself. As much as she respected and adored Ted, she did not want to find out which side he would take if he knew about the potentially high-profile story brewing in Andrea's personal life.

"Mr. Pimpkins, you can't believe Amber would really hurt anyone. After the incident in Detroit, some schools have reported copycats, kids writing lists to get attention. If I had to guess, I'd bet that's the case with this one."

Andrea's speech was bordering on begging by the time she got the last word out. She knew how serious these kill lists were and why school officials had to take drastic action, but the suspect was her daughter this time. And she had to plead Amber's case.

"Ms. Shaw, I assure you, we will do everything possible to get to the bottom of this. But we would not be doing our jobs if we didn't treat this as top priority."

In the crazy mix of everything, Andrea remembered that Amber had already missed several days of school for earlier behavior problems and a bout with flu.

"Mr. Pimpkins, a week suspension is pretty harsh, especially since you're still gathering information. It's near the end of the school year. She may miss too much work to pass her finals," Andrea added, hoping to get some additional sign that the principal was leaning toward a strict warning and nothing more.

"Yes ma'am, you're right, and missing this week,

coupled with the time she's already missed means Amber may have to repeat the seventh grade."

After hearing that her daughter was connected to a kill list, Andrea didn't think the news could get any worse. But it had gotten worse. Much worse in fact. Even if she could prove that Amber couldn't possibly have anything to do with the list, which she was sure she didn't, her daughter could still fail her grade.

"Mr. Pimpkins, I thank you for getting hold of me, and I do apologize for everything that has happened."

Andrea jotted down a number where she could reach the principal if she had any other questions and then ended the conversation with pleasantries despite the fact that she was not in the mood for lighthearted banter. Still, she felt the need to keep up appearances. She couldn't go anywhere in the city without people recognizing her name or her face. Even on the brink of catastrophe, she had to remain professional…forever the TV personality.

No sooner than the phone handset hit the cradle, Ted was back at his door, his face a bright shade of red, sweat beads popping off his forehead. He looked the way Andrea felt.

"Andrea, we'll talk on Monday. I got a last-minute meeting upstairs," he said as he slammed his office door shut on the way out.

He stalked toward her desk as if he was off to the firing squad instead of a meeting. He stopped cold in front of her, the sweat forming a pool at the bottom of his double chin. A man as tall and rail thin as Ted should not have two chins hanging from his face. But there they were, flapping up and down, dipping close to his Adam's apple as he spoke.

"Family emergency...anyone sick or dead?" he asked.

"Not yet."

Ted forced a smile. Andrea didn't bother. Her calm demeanor was slipping despite her gut-wrenching effort to keep it intact.

"Then we'll talk on Monday. First thing?"

"I'll pencil you in," she chanted back at Ted as she watched him stalk down the hall.

Only the smell of his aftershave remained. Part of her wished he was still there, and that she could confide in him. Anyone for that matter. Anyone except the man who knew what was going on and who had chosen to keep her in the dark.

Ronald Grimes, Andrea's husband of twenty years, and the father of her two children. She could already see the look on his pudgy face and the gleam in his beady little eyes as he rubbed in the fact that she had been busy with a breaking news story and had no idea that her daughter had gotten into trouble and subsequently been suspended.

"And when was he going to tell me?" Andrea whispered to herself.

She knew the answer. He wasn't. He wanted it all to unfold just as it had. For Andrea to be left in the dark and then get the news late on Friday afternoon when there was no time to do anything to rectify the situation. And he had to know how explosive it could be if her colleagues or another station got wind of it.

Andrea recalled times in the past when Ronald had tried to prove that she could not be the "TV news star," as he called her, and mother to two teenagers. He had insisted that she needed him. And she had been determined to not need him. And for two years, she had managed just fine without him.

But the more she thought about it, the less sense it made. Even Ronald couldn't be selfish enough to put Amber's future at risk for the sake of making a point. At least she hoped he wouldn't stoop that low. But so far, all evidence was pointing to just that. Too afraid to think about what could happen to Amber if she did have anything to do with the list, Andrea chose to focus on her ex-husband's immaturity.

"This was just what he was waiting for," Andrea said aloud, just as Christy walked past her desk...the same reporter who had looked as if she wanted to hit Nancy with her videotape rather than hand it to her. She glanced at Andrea, wide-eyed and startled, but she didn't say a word about the station's lead anchor talking to herself instead of the thousands of viewers she should have been talking to.

"Dave wants to know if you're going to pitch your piece on set," said the plump news intern who had returned from his earlier assignment of informing Nancy that Andrea would not make it for the show open.

He stood still, staring at Andrea, waiting for a response. She couldn't answer him right away because anger had risen to her throat like a forceful hand determined to cut off her air supply. She hadn't had time to be on top of her daughter's discipline problems before, and again, she didn't have time to deal with it.

Duty calls, she thought as she sucked in air, releasing the pressure of her rage. She had a job to do, and considering everything, it was even more important that she didn't draw any extra attention to herself.

The intern sighed extraloud and threw his arms out to the sides as if waiting for an answer. Andrea wanted to slap him for being so insensitive when her life was unraveling. She couldn't blame an intern whose name she didn't even know. Still, she had to blame someone.

Andrea snatched at her news copy, knocking the teacup over, and its contents spread across the paper like wildfire. She watched the beverage soak the pages, wishing she could disappear from the roomful of eyes that were pretending not to stare at her. But she could not disappear.

"That bastard. If this is what he wants, well, he'll regret the day he started with me!" she yelled, her anger again aimed at her ex-husband.

She wanted to run out the back door, away from the questioning eyes of her coworkers. But there was no escape, and more eyes were waiting. The thousands of viewers who invited her into their homes each night with trust and confidence that she would keep them abreast of what was going on in the world. Viewers confident that Andrea Shaw would deliver the latest news and information, never suspecting that she might one day be the subject of one of those news stories.

The mere thought made Andrea's knees buckle, but she held her composure as she stood to leave the newsroom.

Despite the weight bearing on her shoulders and the churning in her belly, she tossed her head back and pranced out of the newsroom, down the corridor and into the studio, to play her starring role.

CHAPTER 2

With the troubling phone call behind her, Andrea made her way onto the news set. She had practically turned her brain on autopilot as she sat beside Dave and clipped on her microphone. The lights blaring into her eyes, three cameras pointing to various points on the news set. Walter, the floor director, motioning the cues from beside camera one. Everything except Andrea was business as usual.

"Back from commercial in thirty seconds," Walter announced.

Dave leaned toward her and whispered, "Be careful when you plug in your earpiece. Nancy's screaming about wanting this story in the first block."

The story Andrea had been working on all week could have been the lead story for the newscast, or at least second, but because of her troubling phone call, it had fallen to the second news block, right before weather. Not a good position for an exclusive report that she had scooped all their competitors on. But there was nothing she could do about that now, as she plugged in the earpiece and got an earful of just what Dave was talking about.

"What the hell was she doing?" a female voice shouted into her ear as Andrea adjusted the earpiece so that the wire ran behind her hair and down her back.

"She got a phone call right before airtime. What else matters?" she heard Nancy say, and then scream, "Ten seconds."

Walter's hand flew straight up in response to Nancy's words, and Andrea watched as each of his fingers dropped for the five-count. By the time he got to three seconds, she was ready. Somehow, despite everything, she was ready.

As soon as the red light on the camera popped on, Dave spoke, "As we mentioned earlier in the broadcast, Andrea Shaw has been investigating yet a second charge of money laundering against a top University official. She joins us now with the latest," he said, turning toward Andrea as a second camera light popped on, indicating that she and Dave were now on camera together.

"Sounds like this one was quite unexpected," Dave said as a segue into Andrea's lines.

"That's right, Dave, we've been following this story since the grand jury filed the first set of charges several weeks ago, and just this week, a surprising new set of charges with much further-reaching implications than anyone had imagined. According to University officials, this latest charge puts a whole new spin on things."

Andrea tilted her head toward the studio monitor as her prerecorded telling of the story played. When she turned back to the camera, the teleprompter operator was shoving ahead to the clever lines Nancy had written to wrap up the story. The two-minute taped recording seemed to last much too long as Andrea fidgeted, trying not to make eye contact with anyone.

"Stand by, Andrea, camera one," Walter shouted.

Nancy's voice shot into Andrea's ear just before it was time for her to speak. "Are you staying on set to finish the show, or wrapping after this piece?"

Andrea ran her hand across her neck in a slashing straight line.

"Gotcha," Nancy whispered, just as the red light popped on and Andrea spoke.

Still on autopilot, Andrea added some clever lines about staying on top of the story to keep the viewers informed, and then tossed the show back to Dave. She had signaled to Nancy that she was not finishing the show with Dave so there was no point in staying on the news set when she was done, but somehow her body wouldn't move.

For years she had been able to separate the two, home life from work life. Even after the divorce when she was playing mother and father and Ronald was off playing with his new girlfriend, she had been able to stay on top of things.

Dave glanced at her from time to time as she sat beside him, afraid to move as if the sheer act of getting up would make it all crumble in her hands. The delicate balance of career, family and a meager social life. Somehow, the three worlds had slammed together and she wasn't sure she could continue the juggling act.

During commercial breaks, she could hear the camera guys talking about which bar to hit after work. Andrea had never gone out Friday night drinking with her coworkers. It was primarily the singles and a few of the younger married types that hit the bars each Friday night as soon as the eleven o'clock show ended. Andrea was usually in bed before the party began. Tonight she would do the same, but unlike nights in the past, she was not her usual self.

Andrea and Dave's thirty-minute segment wrapped up the hour-and-a-half-long evening WVTR news broadcast and it was time to go. On a normal day, it was time to take a dinner break or make a few phone calls about story leads, but Andrea could do neither. Dave and the others rustled around preparing to head out of the studio. After the early-evening news, they had a good two hours before it was time to get ready for the eleven o'clock show, but Andrea felt glued to her seat.

"Anything you care to talk about?" Dave asked, his deep voice tantalizing her eardrums.

He was a real pleasure to look at and listen to with his lean tanned frame and Barry White-toned vocals. But despite his sex appeal, Dave was not a person known to keep things in confidence. His deep-set brown eyes held Andrea's and for a second she considered confiding in him.

After her divorce, it was rumored that the two of them were dating. And if she had suddenly lost all self-respect and had a few too many drinks, it could happen. Dave was gorgeous to look at and fun to hang out with.

At that moment, the look of him enveloped her to the point that she almost spilled her guts. Then a flashback hit her. Six months ago… Nancy rushing around the newsroom doing damage control after she had told Dave about her oldest daughter having a marijuana joint in her coat pocket. The incident was simple: Nancy had preached to a teenager under the influence of peer pressure about the dangers of drugs and the legal ramifications if her daughter had gotten caught.

Dave had gone on to add his own bobs and weaves to the story, spicing up the details with each telling. A story that ended up portraying Nancy's daughter as badly in need of drug rehab, and narrowly escaping jail time.

Fortunately Dave never approached telling his news stories in this fashion, but that incident made one thing clear: Dave's mouth was like a broken refrigerator. Couldn't keep a thing. That was all Andrea needed now with her daughter's name attached to a kill list.

"I just need a minute," Andrea said, pulling her eyes from Dave's.

"Good piece, by the way," he said as he tossed his wireless microphone onto the desk.

Andrea nodded and forced a smile. With that, he was gone, and she was still sitting there. For how long, she wasn't sure. Just before stomping into the newsroom, she had called Ronald's cell. Three rings and then nothing. She tried again, and immediately got the computerized blow off. She was even more pissed that he was deliberately avoiding her.

"Ms. Shaw, Ms. Shaw, you coming?" a voice said from the other side of the news studio.

She had thought the room was empty by now, but someone was calling to her. Was it her subconscious, riddled with guilt for doing such a wonderful job on the news story but botching up her personal life? No, it wasn't her subconscious. It was only Josh, the camera guy.

"I didn't wanna leave you sitting there in the dark," Josh added.

Still seated, she glanced into space and then over at Josh once more. He stared back as if threatening to toss the light switch. He could just leave the light on and go, she thought, as she motioned for him to go ahead and kill the lights. And no sooner than she got the words out of her mouth, she was engulfed in complete darkness. She could hear Josh's shoes shuffling across the tiled floor. A faint light pushed through as he opened the studio door and left. Then utter darkness once again.

The darkness gave fuel to the fire of her emotions. Anger at Ronald for not telling her what was going on, irritation at Josh's lack of consideration in leaving her in the dark even though she had told him to, and fear. Yes. She was very frightened. Not just about the terrible news about her daughter, but rather how she would get off the news set, down two steps and across the pitch-black room without tripping and injuring herself.

She could just sit there forever, she thought, and then deciding against permanently attaching herself to the news set, got up and started the journey. The first few steps were easy. The carpeted floor guided her to the edge of the set. Then the two-step decline off the news set and onto cold hard tile. Her feet were bare. One of her many newscast quirks. Bare feet, skirt or slacks unbuttoned and the tea prior to the newscast. The last few sips of tea had been interrupted by the phone call. There it was again. As much as she had wanted to divert her attention from the horror of how out of hand things were, it kept smacking her in the face.

She kept stepping; her hands flapped to each side, grasping for something, anything to guide her toward the small strip of light showing beneath the doorway. She felt something. TelePrompTer cart. She ran her hand along it and kept stepping until her pinky touched something prickly. Probably just a brush left behind from an earlier show, but she didn't want to chance it. She snatched her hand away and sprinted the remaining few feet toward the light.

She yanked the door open to the usual, empty hallway; threadbare carpet, dingy beige walls and the smell. The classic TV newsroom smell. A combination of hair spray, cigarette smoke, coffee breath, body odor and cologne to mask the body odor. The building was a nonsmoking environment, but there was forever a lingering residue of the chain-smoking that took place just out the back door, rain or shine. The other smells were just the nature of the beast.

Nancy rushed in behind her; arms full of tapes, her voice filling the air with a trail of Spanish swearwords. Several others kept a safe distance behind the angry producer. Although none of the others spoke Spanish, it was clear from Nancy's tone that she was not singing their praises. The scene was just a normal newscast wrap-up to everyone else, but to Andrea, something felt different.

For the first time ever, she was questioning whether she could be an award-winning journalist and a single parent to two teenagers. Andrea flopped at her desk and moved papers from one side to the other, hoping that her uncertainty wasn't visible. She contemplated another call to

Ronald. Perhaps this time she would call his house and speak directly to his new wife.

"Looks like trouble in paradise," Nancy announced, tossing a videotape of Andrea's investigative story onto her desk.

Oh God, Nancy could see it on her face, Andrea thought. No matter how troubled she was, she could not let it show. Not at work.

"To who's paradise are we referring?" Andrea asked, avoiding direct eye contact with her friend.

"Big meeting upstairs. Bunch of old white men in suits. That's never a good sign."

"Perhaps they're here to offer us all more money and praise us for our hard work," Andrea responded, still trying to hide her troubled demeanor.

Nancy tossed another tape. This time making certain to playfully hit Andrea's arm with it.

"Ouch, watch it, lady," Andrea said, forcing a smile.

"I won't bother asking what the call was about, because you won't tell me until you're ready."

"Nothing major, just something I had to take. Now, tell me what you know about the suits' meeting," Andrea said, not ready to divulge the nature of her daughter's trouble.

"Station's been struggling financially for some time now. We should have seen it coming," Nancy explained.

"Seen what coming?"

Andrea really didn't care to discuss this now. She wanted to get hold of Ronald and figure out what to do about Amber. There were already too many things on her plate to deal with what might simply be a late-day budget meeting. But this was her livelihood, and she figured it might be a good idea to know what signs she had supposedly missed there, since she hadn't known about the ones she had missed at home.

"All I know is, Ted was sweating bullets, and that can't be good for us."

With that partial explanation of pending doom, Nancy rushed off to throw tapes at other people. Andrea made her peace with the idea that Nancy didn't have a clue what was going on in the meeting and was being her usual paranoid self, so she picked up the phone trying to form the words to professionally, yet sternly, give Ronald a piece of her mind.

She knew he would have to answer eventually, and she would say things she might regret down the road, but after that, she wasn't sure what to do. She would have to do something to get her mind off the uncertainty of not knowing the full story and not really wanting to deal with it.

When things were bothering her, there were two choices. Work it off at the gym, or go home and sulk in her bedroom alone. Neither seemed appealing this time. The gym would require too much effort, and sulking would feel more like hiding. She twirled the phone cord around her hand, and then a voice booming from across the room startled her.

"Ms. Shaw, your ride is here," called the intern whose name she did not know. He was at the back newsroom door.

"My ride?" she said to no one.

She had driven herself to work. There wasn't supposed to be a ride waiting for her. Considering the way her day had gone, she wasn't certain that stepping out the back door to an unknown situation was the best idea.

"Who is it?" she yelled back, placing the phone handset back into the cradle.

"How should I know? No one ever picks me up in a limo," the intern announced, his voice dripping with sarcasm.

A limo.

Even when she hired a driver, they had never come in a limo. It had always been a luxury car, but never a limo. She slid from her seat and grabbed her things. A limo can't be a bad thing, she reasoned. It was an unspoken rule in the luxury automobile manual. Limos are good. How often does a limo mean something bad?

Except a funeral.

Andrea picked up the phone again and dialed Ronald's home number. She spoke to his machine as if it were the human she loathed.

"This is low even for you, Ronald. I received a call from Principal Pimpkins. How dare you keep something like this from me?" she screamed and slammed the phone hard onto the receiver.

Grabbing her things, she rushed to the back door. No sooner than she shoved it open, two hands grabbed her, wrapping something silky around her head. The only thing she heard was the car engine and giggling. Laughter she knew as well as her own.

The hands, both tugging her along like the helpless being that she was, since she couldn't see much, shoved her into what she presumed was a black superstretch limousine. The door slammed hard and the giggling continued. As her butt rested against the cool leather seats and the car jerked into motion, a sigh of contentment slipped from her lips.

A normal person would be concerned about a stranger accosting and shoving her into a vehicle, even a luxury vehicle. Especially with a family crisis brewing. But Andrea didn't fight the kidnapping. She didn't even bother to remove the blindfold. Not only did she recognize the giggling, she had picked up the signature fragrance of her sister, Charlotte's, perfume, and her sharp acrylic nails practically punctured Andrea's arm while she was shoving her into the car.

Her sister playfully handed her a glass of bubbly to help calm her nerves. The car swerved out of the station parking lot, tossing Andrea over into her sister's lap.

Perfect. She didn't bother to move, just leaned and sipped.

The cool liquid crept down her throat. And she let the tears roll, the blindfold serving as permanently affixed tissue. She had no idea where they were going or why, but she had been rescued, and even if only for a few hours…she didn't have to hold her head high and be the responsible mother, the sensible ex-wife, the bighearted friend, or the polished TV personality. She could just be a woman. Just a regular woman, with too many mounting problems, and no easy answers.

CHAPTER 3

While Andrea sipped champagne in a limo headed God only knows where, Ronald exited I-95 heading toward suburban Maryland.

"Serves her right," he whispered, as he ignored her number on his cell-phone screen.

He shot a look into the backseat at his daughter to make sure Amber hadn't heard him. Her eyes were glued to a tiny handheld video game, and there were earpieces sticking out the side of her head. Andrea had bought the earphones for the game so she wouldn't have to listen to the constant beeps and annoying music. Ronald didn't mind the sound. In fact, he had missed those sounds around the house since Andrea and the kids had moved out, even though it had been a couple of years. Sure, the constant noise and arguments between their daughter and son, Ray, had been bothersome when they were a happy family. But now that the three of them lived clear across town, he missed the fullness the noise added to the house.

It was his weekend with the kids, even though he had gotten them earlier in the week when Andrea had to rush out of town on assignment. His visitation rights were twice a month, sometimes more, sometimes less depending on what was going on. He looked forward to the visits and tried not to focus on what had been his ideal family. He certainly had not wanted to be a weekend father.

Ronald had once spoken scornfully about the men and women who tugged their children back and forth between two homes, dividing time, attention and love, in his opinion. But that's exactly what he had become. Still, he tried to convince himself that he was not like those other weekend dads who were not real parts of their children's lives and merely fulfilling an obligation.

Amber's eyes shot up from the game, locking instead on the rearview mirror. "Everything okay, Dad?"

"Tough day at work, baby, and this traffic doesn't help," Ronald said, diverting his eyes away from his daughter.

He hated to look directly at someone when he was lying. He always thought people could see the truth in a person's eyes. Traffic and work weren't the only things frustrating Ronald as he steered the car from one lane to another.

"You sure?" Amber insisted.

He nodded, still not looking into the rearview at her. It didn't take a brain surgeon to see that he was upset. And even a thirteen-year-old girl wouldn't believe his lie.

For all intents and purposes, he had a right to be upset. Amber had once again gotten into trouble and wasn't showing any sign of remorse for her actions. She had seemed sorrier she got caught, than sorry for what she had done. He didn't think she understood the seriousness of what had happened. And he had been too busy trying to put out the fire to explain everything to Amber.

That was the part of parenting that he felt least comfortable with. He could fix the problem just fine. That had been as simple as a couple of phone calls to get her into a private school. The part he couldn't handle was helping Amber understand the serious nature of what she had done. To not only help her see that making threats on human life is serious, but also help her understand why, since her parents' divorce, she had felt the need to act out to get attention.

Ronald wanted to embrace that side of dealing with his children, but Andrea had always been the nurturing one. He had made sure they had what they needed financially, and Andrea had taken care of the emotional stuff.

"Turn it up, Dad. That song is hot," Amber urged, still punching at the buttons on her game.

"You would be able to hear just fine if you took those plugs out of your ears."

She glanced up, smiled, and then went back to the game. Her eyes were his eyes, he thought; identical thin slits with huge black pupils. The rest of her face was Andrea, and for that, he was glad.

His receding hairline had made his already-ample forehead appear oversize as if it could accommodate another face. He was grateful that Amber hadn't gotten anything from him but his eyes. She looked up at him again, and he felt a tightening in his chest. He loved his children, even if he wasn't good at showing it.

Ronald hated the fact that Andrea played his lack of

emotional involvement with the kids against him. It wasn't as if he didn't try. But she had used his inadequacy to further alienate him from the kids. He couldn't deny that she was closer to them, but that didn't mean they didn't need him, too.

He bit his bottom lip and tried to concentrate on something else, but just like clockwork, his right index finger jabbed at the radio dial. As much as he loathed her attitude, he chose to keep tabs on his ex-wife. And it wasn't difficult since all of Baltimore had an eye on her every evening, and for those who couldn't be in front of a television, there was the one-hour-delayed radio version of the same show.

At seven o'clock on the dot there was a second of radio static, and then the newscast theme music filled the air. Ronald ignored a grumble from Amber when her hot song ended midnote.

The WVTR theme music halted and a male voice rambled about a high-profile investigation ending. Ronald glanced down at the radio dial when he didn't hear Andrea's voice. She and Dave had always introduced themselves at the beginning of their show. Ronald's eyes darted around at the other cars as he slowed to a stop at a traffic light. Where was she? Off on another assignment? Taking a day off to do God only knows what while he took care of their daughter's disciplinary problems? But the second part could not be true. In all likelihood, Andrea was not aware of Amber's problem. Not yet, anyway. A smile slipped across Ronald's face as the light turned green and he drove off.

"Mom didn't do the news. Wonder why," Amber said, but Ronald didn't respond.

He had made it a personal rule not to bad-mouth Andrea in front of the kids. His goal was not to make his former wife look bad or seem incompetent in front of the kids. No, in his opinion, she did that all by herself. He had tried to tell her that she would have to work twice as hard to be the most popular news anchor on the East Coast and raise two teenagers. But Andrea hadn't listened to Ronald when he tried to talk her out of going back to work, or when her workload had increased after she won that journalism award.

From the beginning, she had insisted that she needed a creative outlet. And he had let it go. But year after year, the station wanted more from her. And they paid her well, and praised her often, which had made her work harder. That job had been the ruin of it all, in Ronald's opinion. Day after day, it got worse, and consumed Andrea even more. And in the end, it had driven a wedge between them.

Amber leaned forward to converse with her father, "This new school is really far from the city, Dad," she said, interrupting Ronald's thoughts of how his perfect family had fallen apart.

"It is, kiddo, but it's the only one that will take you at this late date. Getting kicked out of school is a serious thing, Amber," Ronald said, taking advantage of the opportunity to be the caring and sensitive parent.

"The only reason I'm even doing this is because I don't want them to hold you back a year."

"I know, Dad. I'm sorry. For real. We were just messing

around. I didn't think anybody would even find out. And I really didn't think they would take it seriously."

"I know you didn't, honey. But you can't keep doing things like this. The school board is still asking questions. I don't know how far they'll want to go with this, Amber. I just hope they drop it once I let them know I've gotten you into another school."

Ronald felt as though he should push further to find out if there was more to Amber making that list, but he didn't. Partially because he was afraid of what the answer might be. What if his teenage daughter had made those threats? He blocked it from his mind and slid his hand over to the turn signal. He popped the handle down and tugged the car into the parking lot of the Lakewood School.

"Mom is gonna have a fit when she finds out she's got to drive all the way out here every day. She hates driving five blocks to work. Sometimes she calls a taxi, but I don't think it's really a taxi because the cars are nice. Black cars and the men wear suits. No, that's not a taxi, right, Dad?"

Ronald pulled into a parking space marked Visitors. He hadn't known about Andrea using a driving service, but it didn't surprise him. The station had somehow convinced her that she was some kind of movie star. No wonder she wasn't satisfied with just being a mother and wife.

Ronald didn't bother to answer Amber's concern about her mother having to drive so far. It really wouldn't be an issue at all considering what he had planned. He could predict exactly the way it would play out. Andrea would put up a fight about the school. Then Ronald would insist that Amber stay with him since his place was closer to the new school. Andrea would give it her best argument, and then eventually agree. She'd have to acknowledge that she would never get to work on time if she had to make the drive. Ronald would then finish her off with the fact that this was the only school he could find and that if he didn't do this, Amber would fail her grade. In the end, Andrea would give in and agree that this was the best situation. And Amber would be living with him at least for the remaining couple of weeks of school.

As much as Ronald wanted the kids back with him, even that wasn't his ultimate goal. Although he sometimes hated himself for it, his real plan was to slam another nail in Andrea's coffin of doubt. He wanted to make her see that he had been right, and to acknowledge all that she had lost by trying to be a high-powered executive and a mother. He had been working on her resolve ever since the weekend she had packed her things and moved herself and the kids into that ritzy apartment near the Baltimore harbor.

He could still feel the pang of helplessness that swept over him when he got home and found the house nearly bare. The furniture was still there, and she had even left the paintings on the wall. The houseplants were where they had always been. Blooming and well cared for. But somehow, the house still felt empty. As if its life had been sucked out.

"You don't think I plan to stand by and be a nice little mother while you sneak around with that woman," Andrea had yelled at him, right in front of the kids.

Ronald wasn't in love with or even interested in Charity

Bains back then. But Charity had been there emotionally. When the decline had come at work and he wasn't getting clients as he had in the past, Charity was a friend. She had seemed concerned and could see through Ronald's claim that he wasn't worried about his business even though a several-month slump would have shut him down. Charity had listened when he wanted to talk about it, and just been there when he didn't, and for months Andrea had not.

They had rarely eaten meals at the table anymore. The kids would grab their food and eat in front of the TV set. And when Ronald insisted they eat at the table, the silence was so miserable it gave him indigestion.

"You're so wrapped up in your own thing, you have no idea what's going on with me. I could lose the firm, Andrea. Did you know that?" Ronald had asked in the heat of an argument right before their marriage ended.

She hadn't known. Because he hadn't told her, and she'd been too distant to figure it out on her own. And even as he had torn down the wall and let her into his pain and fear, he had wondered if she really cared at all.

"Oh, I'm so sorry. Your business is failing. That's a perfect excuse to have an affair. All is forgiven, Ronald," Andrea had said sarcastically and then grabbed her bags to pack.

"I'm not having an affair. We talk, that's it. Nothing else. Sometimes I need someone to listen to me, to care about my life. And you don't seem to care anymore about anything that isn't connected to that TV station."

"So it's just talk. Then why was she at your hotel room when you were in Cleveland?"

"Dammit, Andrea, I needed that deal. And when it came through I called you, but you were on assignment, so, so...I called her and she flew out to celebrate with me. I didn't ask her to, but she knew how important it was to me."

"Celebrating, huh? Spare me the details of how that went, will you?"

In the end, Andrea had left. Separation and then divorce. And Charity had remained. Ronald had married Charity within weeks of his divorce and was excited about their life together, despite the fact that Charity thought he spent too much time trying to sabotage his ex-wife.

No matter how hard Ronald had worked against Andrea, her life had looked so perfect. She was doing everything she wanted to do. Great-paying job, nationwide respect in her field, and he could have sworn she looked ten years younger. But even with her ear-to-ear grin every evening on the news, Ronald suspected there were cracks in her perfect finish. And he had just found the first one.

Just as Ronald found a space in the school parking lot, Andrea's voice shot through to snatch his attention from the past. She was rambling about some indictment and he flipped the ignition off before she could finish. It was the story she had been out of town working on for the past four days. The reason he had been in place to deal with Amber's problems.

Ronald and Amber got out of the car and ducked through the front door of the school. Before they could get two steps down the hall, they met with a stern look from a resource officer. Despite the gun resting against the officer's hip, Ronald assumed the man was there more as a threat to outsiders than to directly deal with the students. At least he hoped that was the case.

Ronald gave the officer a name and, without a single utterance, the man pointed toward an office. As they walked down the hall, Amber spoke, "What kind of school is this, open so late in the evening. It's after seven?"

"It's a private school. They have other activities going on in the evening, like night school for adults, and a few other things. Plus, they knew I was coming."

Once inside the office, Ronald gave the receptionist his name and while she scurried out of the room to pull the file, he yanked out his checkbook to start the damage control.

"You have to pay for this school, Dad?"

"Like I said, Amber, this isn't a regular school, dear. It's a private school and yes, you have to pay."

"Mom is gonna freak," Amber whispered as she peered over Ronald's shoulder as he wrote the check.

Initially Ronald was going to hide the amount from Amber, and then decided against it. He wanted her to know the extent of what parents have to go through for their children. He wanted her to know he would do anything for her. He hoped that letting her see his actions would make up for what he could not put into words.

"That's a lot of money, Dad. Are you sure this is a good idea? My old school is free."

"Honey, this is my part of making sure things get back

on track," he said with a glare as he ripped the check from the others.

"And I need your word that you'll do your part. You have to give me your word that this behavior will stop."

Amber nodded her head and peered at something on the wall. Ronald handed the check to the receptionist when she returned. She assured him that she had the other paperwork and they were all set for Monday.

As he and Amber exited the school, he thought of the check, the hundreds of dollars he had just paid to keep his daughter out of trouble. At least partially out of trouble. If the school board decided to press the issue and wanted to take legal action, he wasn't sure he had anything in his bag of tricks for that. But then again, he'd cross that bridge when he came to it.

Back in the car, he sagged into the seat and rubbed his hand across his forehead, thinking how fortunate he was to have the income to set things back in order. His cell phone chirped as soon as he started the engine. Amber was back into her video game, so he punched the power button, ending the relentless beep. It was Andrea, again.

Since before that day, her number had rarely shown up on his cell-phone screen, Ronald assumed she was now aware of their daughter's troubles. Like a card game, the players were in place, the card dealing set to begin. Ronald couldn't help but breathe a sigh of relief. After two years, the deck was finally stacked in his favor.

CHAPTER 4

Just as the sun was starting to set, the limo rolled along toward Annapolis, Maryland. Andrea had yanked the blindfold off after the first glass and was nearing the bottom of a second, while filling her sister in on the call from the principal and Ronald avoiding her calls.

"I say he did it on purpose, to make you look bad," Charlotte quipped while refilling her glass.

Andrea extended her glass to Charlotte as her eyes ran down the length of her older sister's frame. Not a stitch out of place, every curve accentuated with lush fabrics and bright colors.

"Don't you think?" Charlotte asked when Andrea didn't speak.

Charlotte had always been into high fashion. For a fifty-year-old woman, her attire was always far more glamorous than the younger gals. And since she'd married one of the wealthiest entertainment attorneys in the state, Andrea had come to expect a virtual fashion show every time they got together.

The whole thing was really backward. Andrea was the one

on TV, who should have been wearing the gorgeous clothes. But instead, she had slipped into an ultraconservative mode that became more boring with each season. Watching her older sister now, Andrea committed to glam things up as much as the TV news focus groups would allow.

Charlotte was not only her sister, but her best friend in the world. Always had been. There were seven years' difference in their ages, but Charlotte made it seem like more. Even that day, she had carried herself like the more experienced and sophisticated one.

As a child she had been the one to introduce Andrea to everything from bribing their parents to how to deal with the opposite sex. So Charlotte felt right at home handing out information about how Andrea should handle her ex-husband.

"He's been doing little things ever since you got separated."

Andrea simply nodded and continued sipping.

"Like the time when the police caught that serial rapist and your station pulled you in to cover the story instead of Dave because of the nature of the crime. And you couldn't go with Amber on the class trip. He acted ugly then if you ask me, waiting until the last minute to agree to accompany his own daughter."

Andrea remembered the incident, but she couldn't remember feeling as torn or troubled as she did now. Back then, she had known that in the end Ronald would go with Amber. He had only held out to make Andrea look like the bad guy for choosing work over family.

"And then always asking about who you're dating. He

shouldn't be checking on your social life by asking the kids. And what should he care, anyway, since he married that woman."

Charlotte had worked herself up into a fit of anger all by herself. Andrea still hadn't voiced her thoughts, mainly because she wasn't sure what she felt about this new path her life was veering down.

"Then again, you were out of town when this thing happened. And don't say it, I know it was work. But it couldn't have slipped his mind, even though you know how men are when it comes to the kids."

Still Andrea didn't speak. Just wondered how Charlotte could possibly know how anyone was with kids since she'd never had her own crumb snatchers.

"So you see, that man has been out to get you from day one," Charlotte added, grabbing the near-empty bottle from Andrea. "Then again, Amber is manipulative and deviant behavior is a major part of the problem. Perhaps you should want to know what's going on at home to cause your daughter to want to kill people."

Andrea stopped sipping, but otherwise didn't flinch at the harsh comment. She was either numb from the alcohol or she really was too confused to care. She just kept quiet and stared at her sister. As much as she should have been scurrying around trying to figure out what to do and make sure a bad situation didn't get worse, she could only sip champagne. Charlotte had a calming effect on her, even when she was only offering up insults.

The most the two women had in common was gender and the fact that they had the same parents. Apart from that, they were as different as day and night. They both liked nice things, but Andrea's answer to getting what she had wanted out of life was hard work. Charlotte's answer had been meeting and marrying a millionaire. And both women had accomplished their goals. As honorable as Andrea felt inside about her strong work ethic and the rewards it had brought her, Charlotte could still make her feel as though she had been the smarter of the two.

"I'm not saying it's all your fault, but children go through any number of things when parents split, especially when the mother is away from home a lot," Charlotte added for clarity.

Andrea shifted in her seat and waited for more enlightenment, or to be further insulted.

"What I mean is, Amber's not a bad kid, and you're not a bad mother. It's just a bad situation, and you have to figure out how to make it work for everyone before the school decides to make an example out of Amber," Charlotte said as if trying to make this definition of absent mother and delinquent daughter sound appealing.

But if Andrea had wanted to speak, she would have had to admit that Charlotte was right. It was a bad situation and, to make matters worse, Andrea couldn't honestly say she had done everything in her power to make the best of things between her and Ronald.

"Oh goodness, I sound like one of those radio psychologists who try to solve major life issues in ten-minute sessions," Charlotte said to herself. "You could get counseling, for yourself and the kids. Maybe even Ronald, too," she added, directing her thoughts back to Andrea.

Charlotte's face was aglow, as if she had found the answer to all her sister's concerns. Andrea, however, was still silent, noticing the boats docking out the side window.

"Or you could just quit your job and be a stay-at-home mother. Then you wouldn't have to keep wearing awful blouses like that," she continued, pointing toward Andrea's blouse with her wineglass.

Andrea glanced briefly at her blouse, a silken mass of bright vibrant colors, which wasn't as conservative as her usual blouses, but rather her feeble attempt to jazz things up. A blouse, that until this moment she had worn with pride. It had gone nicely with the navy jacket and she thought the colors looked great on television.

Andrea tilted her head back toward the window to see a really large boat with several men yanking and tugging at what looked like fishing nets. She blinked her eyes, begging them to focus, and yes, they were near water and anglers.

The limo stopped, the door opened and Andrea followed Charlotte, still not sure what was going on. Going anyplace with her sister could be a challenging experience, since Charlotte believed in going to the extreme. Extreme shopping, extreme outfits and extreme marriage.

But since Andrea's life seemed to be a downward-spiraling mess, she decided it would be okay to take on one more risk. She felt a rush of breeze up her back as they stood on the pier, watching the men yanking at nets and ropes. The wind was picking up, making the early-summer temperatures feel rather pleasant.

"We're going fishing?" were Andrea's first words as the limo driver tugged bags from the trunk of the car.

She recognized the area of Annapolis and the waterfront was lined with all kinds of fishing and cruising vessels. Andrea had come to the area plenty of times for dinner, but never to board a vessel.

"Not that fishing boat, dear. That's us," Charlotte explained, pointing to a luxury yacht a few paces ahead.

A pearl-white three-tier mini cruise ship with smoky gray-tinted windows awaited them. *Princess Pride* was scrawled in large black letters on the side of the boat. Two men in uniforms waved to them from the edge of the pier. Andrea scanned the streets that flanked the waterfront. Restaurants and shops with all kinds of goodies. She could smell the succulent aroma wafting from one of the eateries preparing for the dinner crowd. Her mouth watered as she looked out over the horizon. A small piece of paradise less than an hour away from the crowded streets of Baltimore.

A grin, comparable to that of a kid at Christmastime, covered Andrea's face, only to be instantly replaced by panic and agony. Her left slingback-clad foot slid off the edge of the curb sending her crashing to the ground. The fall was not graceful by any means, and when she reached for Charlotte's hands, she felt the large overpowering hand that could not belong to a female.

Suspecting the limo driver, Andrea scooted herself to sitting, then felt herself being lifted to standing, coming face-to-face with an older gentleman who had a cane in his free hand. Before she could steady herself, her skirt went sliding down her thighs.

"Oh God," she moaned, as she yanked and tugged at the linen fabric, and fumbled for the zipper and button. "I didn't realize I was so close to the edge," she said, ignoring the fact that her skirt had slid down to her knees.

Pulling it up, she zipped the skirt, snapped the top button, and rubbed her hands over her apparently hideous blouse to make sure nothing else was out of place.

But what else could be out of place? She had flashed lacy panties and mocha thighs at God only knows how many people. When she looked back at Charlotte, she noted her sister's hand lifted toward her mouth, imitating someone drinking.

The entire group found Charlotte's jesting humorous. Group meaning not just the two of them, the limo driver and the old guy with the cane who had rescued her and seen her underwear up close and personal. Two more men and a woman had appeared out of nowhere and seemed to be with their party.

Andrea did her best to avoid eye contact with anyone specific in the group as they all made their way to the yacht. She had wanted to ask questions. Who are these people? Whose boat is this? Where are we going? But she kept quiet and focused instead on staying on two feet, and keeping her clothes on.

Andrea popped open her cell phone to make a quick call to the station. Nancy picked up on the first ring, which meant she had read Andrea's number on the caller ID.

"Where are you? I came up with a few ideas about your piece. I'm going to have them make up some nice graphics to add extra effect. And we'll lead with it again on the late show."

Nancy was rambling and not noticing the fact that Andrea had not spoken.

"You will make it back here before eleven, right?" Nancy asked as if suddenly reading the silence.

"Actually, I'm in Annapolis and I was calling to say I wouldn't be back tonight."

"This has something to do with the limo? I heard about that. What gives?" she asked.

"My sister. A yacht. And I have some heavy stuff going on at home right now, so I need this break. I'll call you this weekend with the details."

"You'd better. No holding out. A yacht, damn," Nancy said before hanging up without saying goodbye.

Andrea turned her attention back to the yacht where a crewmember met them at the edge of the pier, swept the bags from the limo driver's hands and hurried off. They were then ushered onto the yacht and into a room where another crewmember was serving champagne and hors d'oeuvres. Andrea refused the drink, made another quick call to Ronald's home answering machine, and opted to get some food into her stomach in order to not further embarrass herself.

The atmosphere was divine. Andrea had been on a number of cruise ships in her day, but this was the first yacht. She was awestruck by the fact that it was basically a smaller, more compact version of a luxury liner. The owner had not cut corners on one single amenity. The two sisters sat in a duo of plush suede chairs, their eyes scanning every inch of the room.

"Juan's coming later. Those folks are his clients," Charlotte said, pointing to the other people who had chosen to get ready for their meeting, instead of lounging.

"They're doing business, but I thought, since the firm's paying through the nose to charter this puppy, we might as well enjoy it, too," Charlotte added, wiggling around to get extra comfortable.

Andrea glanced at her as she reached for a glass of something. "Are you serious?" she asked. "We're crashing one of Juan's business meetings?"

"No. You worry too much. This thing accommodates at least fifty people. They won't even know we're here. Besides, it's just for a few hours," Charlotte said as she quickly emptied her glass and hurried toward the ladies' room.

Juan Cabrera, Charlotte's husband, was an entertainment attorney, which, as Andrea had come to learn, didn't really mean he worked with anyone in the entertainment field. Not famous people, anyway. In her assessment, the entertainment part of Juan's job title had more to do with what he did with all the cash he made from his chosen profession.

Juan was the gorgeous guy that most women wouldn't date because they thought he was either too cute or gay. His jet-black hair and emerald-green eyes were only part of his appeal. The chiseled body would be enough to send any woman over the edge, but Juan's best qualities seemed to be those of a nonphysical nature. He was sensitive, caring, and he swooned over Charlotte as if she were dipped in dark chocolate. Everyone close to Charlotte avoided conversations about Juan's age. The standing joke was that if Charlotte had kids, they could have been Juan's playmates.

When Charlotte first started dating Juan, Andrea had tried to get the inside scoop. Why was she falling madly in love with a wealthy, hot Latino man half her age? The mere mention of any negative comments about Juan's business dealings or his age would lead to Charlotte taking offense, which resulted in her making lewd comments with blatant sexual overtones.

In Andrea's opinion, whether they had married for love, sex or a little of both, for Charlotte and Juan, the binding force boiled down to one word. *Cash,* and lots of it. Yes, they loved each other, too. And, yes, she also believed that it never hurt to wrap that love in a wad of dead presidents.

Charlotte had plenty of her own money before she married Juan. Not because she worked especially hard or was frugal, but because she let other people spend money on her. Charlotte could go anyplace and do just about anything without ever dipping into her purse. She had the kind of personality that got people so swept up in the excitement of an experience that before they realized it, they were shelling out cash not only for themselves, but for Charlotte, too.

"So, what do you want to do now?" Charlotte asked, as she returned and made herself comfortable again.

Andrea sighed and slumped back into the seat hoping to switch gears from incompetent mom mode to relaxing sister mode.

"I'm not sure and I have no idea what the school board is up to. I'm going to call the principal back after I find out what alien creature captured Ronald's brain. Maybe you're right. Counseling might not be a bad idea either way."

"True. I suppose it couldn't hurt." Charlotte reclined back in the chair as one of the crew servers placed a tray of goodies on their table.

She then gave a sly little laugh. "Time for a subject change. Any signs of a love life on the horizon?"

"I have an impressionable teenage son and a daughter who, regardless of what happens, has some serious anger issues. No time for men lying around trying to get a free ride. Pun intended," Andrea added, closing her eyes to acknowledge the scrumptious tastes filling her mouth.

"Yes, you have a son and a daughter, and life isn't perfect...but you also have a body. Which, regardless of your denial, needs the company of the opposite sex every now and then, right?"

Andrea reached for the tray again and slid tastier morsels into her mouth, then shook her head from side to side as if her mouth was too full to comment. That really wasn't the case, but she would never give Charlotte the satisfaction of knowing she was right. And she also couldn't let her sister know that she was secretly attracted to one of the guys who worked at the driving service she used when she didn't feel like fighting downtown traffic.

It's not that Charlotte was snooty or anything, but Andrea wasn't even sure why she was drawn to the man. She had never spoken more than a few words to him. And they were mostly about the weather and where she was heading. He had never sparked conversation, either. Not like some of the cab drivers she'd met. Those guys would talk from the time they hit the fare button until she handed them the cash. As if it was their job to not only drive, but entertain.

But this driver was different. No words, just glances in the rearview mirror. Looks they exchanged that seemed to communicate volumes. At least in Andrea's mind. And for now, with everything going on, she reasoned that she was held to a mental relationship instead of an actual one.

"Did you bring extra clothes for me? I'd like to get comfortable and I don't have anything, since I didn't know," Andrea tossed at her with a hint of sarcasm, hoping to change the subject from both her family problems and her nonexistent love life.

"I brought clothes for you. Nice things, not those tacky anchorwoman suits. Something sexy. But I must insist that you keep your clothes on from this point forward."

A quick flash of her stripping incident zipped across her brain. She blinked it away by grabbing more food.

Charlotte stopped chewing and paused as if she was deep in thought.

"So, we know about Amber's problems, but what about Ray? He's a boy. I would expect him to be giving you hell, especially with the girls."

She was right, and Andrea had thought about that, too, while sitting on the news set not able to move after the newscast had ended. Ray was sixteen years old, with perfect grades, a so-so athlete and an accomplished saxophone player. He seemed too good to be true, except the little hot girls that were standing in line to be his one and only.

"Speaking of Ray, I have a box of condoms in the trunk of my car," Andrea announced.

"Speaking of Ray, those things should be for you," Charlotte exclaimed a little too loudly for Andrea's taste.

Juan's business clients were sitting at a table across from the sisters. Even though Andrea was certain they couldn't hear the conversation, she still felt a blush at the mention of needing condoms for herself.

She hadn't dated since the divorce, because she hadn't found anyone decent enough to make the physical advance. The months had turned into years and she wasn't sure how long good judgment would prevail.

"I can't decide whether or not to give them to him. Raising teenagers is so hard. I don't want to give him a license to do it, but I really don't want some girl showing up pregnant on my doorstep."

"Oh, girl, and you can't even pronounce some of the diseases out there now."

"Okay, you're not making this any better," Andrea shot back.

Charlotte mouthed "I'm sorry."

"So, what have you decided?"

"I asked if he was active. He said no, like any sixteen-year-old who likes living would do."

"You're his mother. What did you expect him to say?" Charlotte added. She deepened her voice to sound like a man, "Yeah, Mom, I'm hitting those hotties left and right.

"But you don't believe him? What about that girlfriend of his?" she asked while Andrea giggled at the really bad impression of Ray.

"I don't know. She's a good enough girl and Ray is a smart kid, but libido can be a powerful thing. Gets the best of even the smartest. Anyway, right now, Ray is the only sane one of the bunch. Grades, perfect. Part-time job, saving money. Even rubbed my feet one night when I got home late."

"Your sixteen-year-old son rubbed your feet, and you're not concerned," Charlotte joked.

Andrea giggled again, but somehow as the joke rested on her eardrums, it lost its humor. Was Ray really okay? Or had she missed something important with him, too?

CHAPTER 5

Ronald wasn't sure why he had called the driving service. But he had. As soon as he walked into the house, he waited until Amber was in her room before he looked up the number. Fortunately, Amber had remembered enough of the business name that Ronald found it in the book with no problem.

The man who identified himself as the owner had been polite and articulate. He answered all of Ronald's questions which ranged from what area of the cities they covered to their rates. The more he learned about the driving service the more he knew that Andrea would consider it a waste of money.

The rates were high and their coverage area was limited unless the passenger was willing to pay extra. The staff was minimal. Family owned and run by two brothers. Ronald wouldn't have patronized the business himself, unless he was trying to court them for future business dealings.

Perhaps that was Andrea's angle. She was working on a story angle and the service provided her with information. That had to be the catch. She wouldn't just shell out money for no reason.

By the time Amber was bored with her magazines and video games, Ronald was done with his background interrogation of the driving service Andrea had been sinking money into. Amber announced that she was hungry and before Ronald could grab the pile of carryout menus, Charity was coming through the door with bags of food. Jamaican from the smell. Amber's and Ronald's faces glowed like two high-beam headlights.

"And good evening to you, too," Charity sang at Ronald and Amber who were ignoring her, their full attention on the bags.

She tried to toss her keys onto the kitchen counter, but they hit the edge of the marble countertop and crashed onto the floor.

"Hello, Ms. Charity. Thank you for dinner," Amber said, throwing her arms around Charity and removing a bag as she stepped away.

"Hey, baby," Ronald added as he planted a kiss on his wife's cheek and removed the second bag from her arms.

She bent to retrieve her keys while Amber carried the food into the dining room to set the table and to give the adults time to talk. Ronald knew what she was doing. His daughter was hungry, but she also knew that her actions had tossed all of their lives into the air. Amber was smart enough to settle her losses and keep a low profile.

"Did you talk to her?" Charity asked as soon as Amber was out of the room.

"We talked. On the way to the new school."

"But did you really talk, Ronald? Amber is playing both you and Andrea. She knows what she's doing. Each offense gets the desired result, your attention. And when things get back to normal, she does something else. Don't you see that?"

"And what do you want me to do?"

"Something other than spy on your ex-wife," Charity said as she tossed her purse onto the kitchen counter and walked toward the dining-room door.

She peeked through to make sure that Amber was eating and not eavesdropping.

"I agree with you, Ronald. This is a perfect opportunity for you to spend more time with both kids, but you won't focus on that. You want to rub Andrea's face in this."

"And that bothers you?"

"I'm no fan of Andrea Shaw. Trust me. But I do think that this is getting too much of your attention. Is Ray joining us?" Charity asked, signaling that the conversation was over.

"He called to say that he was staying at home tonight for some reason and coming over tomorrow."

Although Ronald would much rather have joined Amber in the dining room to munch on Jamaican, he waited until Charity finished with her daily ranting. She had valid points, but after everything that had happened, Ronald was not in the mood.

"Is the school still asking about the list?"

Ronald shrugged. He had hoped she wouldn't ask about the list. He had wanted the principal to drop the issue of the threatening note since Ronald had assured him that Amber and the other kids were not capable of any of the acts mentioned in the note.

"What does that mean?" Charity pushed, not satisfied with Ronald's flippant answer.

"She's enrolled in the new school. A few days will pass and they'll realize this was all just a few kids playing pranks."

"Pranks? Do you realize how serious this could be? Apparently you don't. There was a case a few months ago, and the kid got jail time…and does Columbine ring a bell for you?"

"Gosh, Charity, are you serious? We're talking about Amber, not some hard-rock punk kid on drugs."

"And your little girl could not be capable of anything like those other kids," Charity said, her tone brutally sarcastic.

Ronald sighed so loudly it sounded more like a groan. "You keep twisting my words. And blowing this way out of proportion. Amber was an honor student. She's gotten a little off track. And I've made arrangements to correct that. The school officials will respect a proactive parent and drop this whole ludicrous mess."

Charity threw both hands in the air to signal surrender. She shoved at the door to the dining room, and without further discussion, they joined Amber in the dining room and tore into the steaming hot Jamaican food. After eating enough beans and oxtails to give an army a stomachache, Amber slumped off to bed, which really meant watching music videos until she fell asleep and Ronald went in and turned the television off.

While Ronald fumbled around in the garage, Charity set up the kitchen counter for the wine tasting she was hosting over the weekend. She moved through the kitchen setting the decanters into place, the glasses for both white and red, all in their proper place. She loved doing things in her home, making it a haven for not just her and Ronald, but their friends.

The wine tasting was part of one of the committee fund-raisers she put on each year for the literary council. Although Charity didn't work in the traditional sense, she did plenty of work for several notable organizations in the community. It was what her mother did, and her grand-mother before her. When Charity had graduated from college, instead of sending out masses of résumés into corporate America, she simply signed up for numerous committees and put her skills to work to raise money and awareness. And she knew just how to do both.

Prior to her taking the reins of the literary council, they had had trouble raising money for the programs they needed. But Charity had turned all that around with a few off-the-page ideas, like a wine tasting for one. Somehow just asking people to donate large sums of money went down easier with a glass of Pinot Grigio and good con-versation.

She was marveling over her clever idea when Ronald came back into the kitchen to help her finish the dinner dishes.

"I did get a snippet of information you might find interesting."

"Do tell," Ronald said, planting his hand on her behind and nibbling at her earlobe.

"It seems there's something going on at WVTR. Some kind of undercurrent. Talk of changes."

"Who told you that?"

Ronald spun her around so that they were face-to-face.

His interest was in both her tantalizing full lips and the juicy gossip about to spill from them.

"Does it really matter?"

"Of course it does. Was it a reliable source?" he asked as he kissed her lightly, trying not to distract her from the story.

"I'd say so, but she didn't know much."

"Who's 'she'?" Ronald had backed away from Charity, wondering if she really did have bad news about Andrea's job.

"You remember the woman who cleans my father's office buildings?"

Ronald nodded his head up and down, his eyes locked on a puddle of suds on the kitchen counter.

"Anyway, her daughter works there. Nancy something or other. And she called her mother, daddy's housekeeper, and insisted that there was trouble brewing. This Nancy chick is afraid for her job. What do you make of it?"

By the time Charity finished her story, Ronald was doubled over in laughter and swiping at the sudsy counter.

"What's so funny?" she asked, growing more concerned by his reaction.

Ronald slid the dish towel from her hand before he answered, "That Nancy. She's Andrea's producer. And she's a real pain in the rear. She's always afraid for her job. Crazy thing is, according to Andrea, she does a great job."

"So there's nothing to it, you think?" Charity asked, still puzzled by what had sounded so troubling when she heard it earlier.

Ronald wiped the counter down, and popped the light switch over the kitchen sink.

"Who knows? I wouldn't trust Nancy's telling of the story."

"She mentioned a high-power meeting late this afternoon. Bunch of department heads."

Ronald stopped, stared into space, and then continued straightening things in the kitchen. "Could mean trouble, but remember they love Andrea. She can do no wrong. They worship the ground she walks on."

Ronald stopped with that statement. It always happened. When he was trying to insult his ex-wife, it always came out as praise and admiration. At least to Charity it did. He had tried to assure his wife that there was no need to be the least bit anxious about his feelings for Andrea.

Charity had told him time and again that she thought he was still in love with his ex-wife. Although he hadn't been able to convince Charity that that wasn't the case, he knew for himself that love was not what was going on between him and Andrea. It was a battle of wills. Who would prove right depended on who could last the longest. For two years, she had put up a solid fight.

"There's extra in the refrigerator for Ray in case he decides to come here tonight instead. I'm going to get a hot bath and call it a night," Charity said, stepping toward Ronald for their routine goodnight kiss.

"You take great care of us, baby. The best."

But when he kissed her on the cheek, he could sense the distance. He just couldn't figure out how to bring things back together, so he didn't bother. He watched her push through the dining room door, a halfhearted smile making her look tense and worried.

Once Charity was alone in their bedroom, she slammed her eyes shut tight to ease the pain in her heart. From the outside, she and Ronald looked like the perfect couple. He, the successful architect, traveling from city to city making deals. And she, the hardworking yet supportive wife making a difference in so many arenas; the illiterate, the blind, and the list went on.

She ran her hand over the solid cherry oak armoire. Not a speck of dust in sight. The perfect home, finely decorated and not a thing out of place. But none of it made the pain in her heart go away. As hard as she tried, she had not yet joined the ranks that sang the praise of the honorable Andrea Shaw, and she feared her new husband's obsession was becoming her own.

Each day she had wanted more than ever to bring that woman to her knees and finally claim first place in Ronald's life. But even if she did that, there was the issue of the kids. She couldn't figure out how she had gotten herself into a marriage where she played second fiddle to an ex-wife and kids. And worst of all, she really did love Ronald.

During their brief courtship and few months of marriage, she had made him the center of her world. She just wasn't sure she would ever be the center of his. Perhaps children of their own, she thought. That just might be the thing to keep Ronald's attention at home.

CHAPTER 6

For an early Saturday afternoon the arcade at the mall was buzzing with activity. Ray Grimes had chosen that spot as the meeting place since it was normally less crowded when the mall first opened. No such luck this time.

The buzzing and zapping of the video games coupled with the yelling and laughing was more than he could take with such big problems on his mind. When he had arrived and found the place wall-to-wall kids, since it was too late to switch to another location, he had hoped the noise would help drown out his thoughts. But as it turned out, no amount of noise could quiet the turmoil swirling through him.

When his mom had called him the night before to say that she was spending the night with his aunt Charlotte on some boat, he was relieved. He had stayed at home alone, instead of going to his father's as he was supposed to. He had been at his dad's all week and really needed some time to clear his head and figure out what to do next. So, he had been happy to have the house to himself for a whole night. Not that it had helped him figure out very much.

He slid his wet hands from the video game. He hadn't

realized he was sweating. He shoved his hands into the deep pockets of his Hugo Boss jeans, the ones his mother, the infamous Andrea Shaw, had insisted were overpriced and had forbidden him to buy. But it was his money, so in the end, he had walked out of the store with the jeans, and not a dime left from his meager paycheck.

Ray liked the idea of having a famous mom. At least most of the time he did. It was times like this when the idea of being the center of attention was not such a good thing. He would have preferred just being a regular guy, with a mom who could walk into the grocery store and not have ten people stop her before she could get through the produce section. The attention would be the last thing any of them would want after they found out what he had gotten himself into.

Ray was deep in his thoughts and trying to wipe the perspiration off his hands when a girl's voice yelled into his ear, "I think you have to deposit a token."

He turned to her, not bothering to address the issue of pretending to be playing a video game. He could look into her deep hazel eyes and see the answer.

"Positive?" he asked anyway.

She tilted her head and planted her hands on her hips.

"Sorry, Ray, but I told you it probably was. Those things aren't usually wrong. And I used two."

It had been three days since Ray had gone to his girl-friend Tammy's house with the pregnancy test. And then rushed out to get another when the first one was positive. She hadn't been sure if she had done it right, so he had gotten another and then watched her do it the second time. She had done it right, but still, it couldn't be true. They had been so careful.

Even with the positive home test, Tammy's friend, Pam, had suggested she go to the free clinic and get a blood test to make absolutely certain that it was right. She had lied to her parents and was supposed to be getting breakfast and then hanging out at the mall with Ray. The mall part was true, but breakfast was actually a trip to the clinic that had confirmed their fears. But Ray still couldn't figure out how it had happened.

He wasn't stupid enough to have sex without a condom, so he couldn't figure out how she could be pregnant. He had almost mentioned the possibility of it not being his, but as his mother had often noted with frustration, Ray and Tammy spent all their free time together. He couldn't imagine her having time for anyone else. He certainly didn't. With school, band rehearsals, and his part-time job, he barely had time for a girlfriend. And Tammy's schedule was more crowded than his own.

Tammy ran her fingers over the top button of his shirt. "Silk, I like it. But you might sweat a lot when we start dancing at the party tonight."

Ray wanted to move her hand, but he didn't want to seem insensitive. He also wasn't in the mood for a party or small talk. He stepped away from Tammy and turned back toward the video game.

"The doctor gave me some vitamins to start taking and a bunch of pamphlets. And one for you."

Ray took the papers from her hand, but he couldn't focus on the words. There was no way this could be happening. Not to him. He had worked so hard to do things right. Straight As, and not because he was a genius. No, he wasn't like his sister, Amber. He had to study hard to get anything. Amber could just look over material and remember it as if it was already part of her. But he could spend all night with something and still only squeak out with a B. So, he had worked extra hard to get his As.

Especially when his parents split. And then when his dad had remarried, he had worked even harder. As much as his mother had tried to act as if his dad's marriage didn't bother her, Ray knew that it did. He could see things about his mother that she couldn't see herself. And he knew that her work and her children weren't enough. As much as she loved them, she wanted something more. He wasn't sure what, but he could tell she was missing something.

"Let's get out of here. It's too noisy," Tammy insisted as she pulled Ray's hands away from the video game.

They went to a table outside the Chick-fil-A restaurant. A couple with a baby in a stroller and another child holding his father's hand sashayed past as if they were the happiest people in the world. Their smiles made Ray's stomach flip. He knew that would not be him. No smiling and sashaying through the mall. There was no way he was ready to be a father.

"Tam, I was thinking…this is crazy. I used a condom every time. I mean every time," he said, adding emphasis.

Tammy fumbled with the rhinestone brooch closure of her cashmere cardigan. The one Ray had given her for her last birthday. Pale blue, his favorite color on her.

"I know what we did, Ray. Remember, I was there," she joked, still fumbling with the brooch.

He could tell that she was nervous despite her constant joking. Whenever they talked about what had happened, she had to do something with her hands. Now her hands had moved from her blouse to the container of napkins on the table.

"And I didn't buy the cheap ones. So, I really don't see how this could have happened," Ray said, his eyes glued to the napkin container.

He didn't want to make eye contact, but her hands drew his eyes to her head. She was now twirling a finger through her long spiral curls. She stopped abruptly as if she had caught on to what Ray as saying.

"I know you're not trying to say that this baby isn't yours," she said, tears brimming at the corner of her eyes.

He hadn't meant to upset her, but he wanted to know. Her reaction made him think that there really wasn't another guy. He had never thought she was like those other girls. That was part of the reason he had chosen her over the others, the prettier and more popular girls. Even his mother, who had admitted she wouldn't like any girl he brought home, had said that Tammy was from a good family.

When they first talked about having sex, they had made rules. They had said they wouldn't actually go all the way, just kissing and touching, but then they had gotten carried away and did it in her den that time while her mom was upstairs asleep. But even that time, he had used a condom. One of the ones his dad had given him when they had "the talk."

Ray had been fifteen when his dad took him bowling of all things and told him about waiting to have sex and never doing anything without protection. Ray had taken the box of condoms even though he felt silly having them. For months he had hidden them in his old saxophone case where he was sure his mom wouldn't find them.

But then when he had started dating Tammy he had taken one out of the box and put it into his wallet as his dad told him, just in case. Better safe than sorry. And when they had started having sex regularly, he had bought more, but was careful to get the same kind his dad had given him. Still thinking of "safe" and not "sorry." But safe hadn't worked for him. And now as Tammy sat in front of him fighting back the tears, he knew he couldn't take the coward's way out and just say it wasn't his baby.

"I'm sorry, Tam. That's not what I'm saying. I'm just scared. What are we going to do? How will I tell my parents and what are you going to tell yours?"

She didn't answer. She snatched a napkin from the silver bin on the table and dabbed her eyes. She had cleared the tears from her face just in time.

"The gruesome twosome," a voice said from behind Tammy's head.

Ray had seen Ralph approaching, but had hoped that by not making eye contact with his fellow jazz band member that he would take the hint and keep walking. Ralph either didn't get the hint, or didn't care.

"You going to the party tonight?" Ralph asked, as he laid his hand on Tammy's shoulder.

They had planned to go to the party. Everyone was

going to the big end-of-the-school-year party. Ray and Tammy had been part of the planning committee and were excited about kicking off the summer before their senior year in grand style. But that had been before the pregnancy test.

"Not sure yet, man," Ray mumbled with little enthusiasm, hoping to end the conversation quickly.

"Both of you look like you need a good party. And this one is supposed to be hot. Tam, you look like you've been crying," Ralph said, sliding to her side and kneeling on one knee.

If Ray had wanted him to leave, there would be no way to get him to go away now. Ralph had smelled trouble with Franklin High School's most popular couple. Ray would have to be twice as smart to get rid of him now.

"I'm cool. Coming down with a cold," Tammy said, as she sniffled and blew her nose into the napkin.

Ray was impressed with her quick thinking as he watched Ralph stand and back off as if trying to avoid the cold germs.

"Well, you keep that to yourself. I got a party tonight. A few people expect me to be there."

Ray knew that the expectations were all in Ralph's mind, but he wasn't in the mood to match wits with his classmate. Ralph didn't wait for further conversation; he simply scampered away as quickly as he had approached. It seemed like the perfect opening for Ray. He didn't want to chance running into anyone else from school.

"I gotta go, Tam. I need some time to think. I'm supposed to be staying at my dad's this weekend, but I really want to go back home."

"But I just got here and we were supposed to do something tonight. If not the party, then what about a movie?"

"Listen, you know my mom's been out of town all week. And she stayed out last night with my aunt, so I was thinking I could probably help her get settled."

Tammy threw her hands up in surrender. "Ray, you act like you're the parent and she's the child. Your mother will be fine. I'll bet if you call, she'll tell you the same thing."

Ray didn't want to call. And he didn't want to be with Tammy right now. She was acting as if she was okay with being pregnant. Ray couldn't understand it. Didn't she realize how it would change everything? He had a great chance of getting a music scholarship if he could keep everything together during his senior year. But how could he do that with a child? Even though the baby would be with Tammy, he would still have to do something. His mother would make him use the money from his part-time job to help. And she might not want him to move across country for college if he had a kid in Baltimore.

"I gotta go. You can ride with Pam, right?"

"I can, but I thought you wanted to hang out. Even if we don't go anywhere, we still need to talk about what we're going to do."

"What we're going to do? What can we do, now?" Ray's words punched across the table.

Tam lifted a finger to her lips to get him to lower his voice.

"Ray, I know you don't want this baby. And I'm scared, too. The doctor gave me one more pamphlet."

She handed the paper to Ray and the only word he saw was *abortion*. There were lots of other words, and he looked over the paper as if he was reading it, but his eyes were locked on that one word.

"It's not just about abortion, but adoption and other alternatives. The doctor said there was someone there at the office that would be willing to talk with us."

Ray couldn't speak. He hated himself for the fact that it had crossed his mind. And he hated himself more for wanting to keep the pamphlet and read every word of it.

There had to be a way out. A way to make things right again. And perhaps there was something on the pages of the pamphlet that he and Tammy could do and not feel bad about afterward. And not wreck their families. His family had been through enough.

"Take it," she said as she sauntered off to meet her friend Pam.

He watched the sway of her hips in the lowrider blue jeans until she disappeared around the corner. The same hips he had thought he couldn't get enough of. Now, he wasn't sure he'd ever be able to touch her in that way again.

But why him? he wanted to ask. All of his friends were doing it. Most of them had several girls and weren't half as careful about protection as he was. So why had this happened to him? And why now?

Ray folded the papers and stuffed them into his pocket. He rushed out of the mall, but the last place he wanted to be was his father's house. His mother would see trouble in his eyes, so he couldn't risk going home and running into her.

He had told his dad he'd be gone most of the day and back home by midnight, which meant he had lots of time. He boarded the subway and decided to ride and read. He hoped the long hours to himself would give him time to figure out how to save his life, and not feel guilty for wanting to end another.

CHAPTER 7

Saturday night knock-off time hadn't come soon enough for Maxwell Leonard. During the three years since he'd been working at his brother's chauffeur service, he'd never had a day as tough as this. He should have known things wouldn't go well when he had the flat on the way to work. But still he had been optimistic.

"Professional Auto, this is Wayne, how may I direct your call?" Maxwell heard his brother say.

Wayne had insisted that he might be a small family-owned business, but he didn't have to look like it or sound like it. The downtown storefront office had only three small rooms, but listening to Wayne on the phone, you'd think he was running Grand Central.

The lobby, or Wayne's throne as the drivers called it, was the most uniquely laid out twelve-by-twelve space Maxwell had ever seen. The walls were painted a deep cherry red, with tinted moldings and window trim the color of baby's breath. On one side of the room was Wayne's workspace…a long antique white desk atop two file cabinets, connected to a corner CPU cabinet with one drawer. The polished and stained hardwoods were partially covered by a cherry red-and-gold Oriental rug.

The other side of the room was decorated nicer than Maxwell's living room at home. A single club-style java-colored leather sofa with a glass and espresso-stained hardwood coffee table completed the ensemble.

"Let me see if he's still around. He may be gone for the evening," Wayne said, winking at his older brother.

Before the call came in, Wayne had been pecking away at the laptop, while Maxwell sat on the soft leather sofa dreading the drive home.

"Damn right I'm gone. You can take that one yourself. Or hire someone else to run some of these departments," Maxwell whispered, and then laughed.

As tough as the day had been, there wasn't much he wouldn't do for his brother. Six years ago when Wayne had the car accident that left him in the wheelchair, Maxwell had vowed to help his brother keep the business running. At that time, he had thought his help would be more of the financial nature, not actually driving the cars. But oh how things had changed in a matter of years.

"Could I put you on hold, ma'am? Thank you, one minute, please."

Wayne wheeled himself across the room, which was a rare occurrence. He was pretty much able to handle all aspects of his business and the three drivers that worked for him from his little corner of the room. Even when clients would visit the office, Wayne had purposely designed the room so that he was never in an uncomfortable situation. As soon as someone walked through the door, Wayne would introduce himself and offer the person a seat on the sofa.

"Get them on my level," Wayne had told Maxwell repeatedly.

Maxwell couldn't help but be proud of how professionally his brother had handled his handicap. A customer may come into Professional Auto, and be taken aback by seeing the owner in a wheelchair, but before long, with their butts cushioned in enough leather and their brain numbed with comedic banter from Wayne, handicap virtually disappeared.

"It's her. And this time, she asked for you specifically," Wayne whispered, although he had put the call on hold, and there was no way the caller could hear them.

Without another word, Maxwell knew exactly who his brother was talking about. The psychic bond between the two was amazing, not once had they talked about her, but without a name, he knew his brother was referring to Andrea Shaw.

She hadn't used the service often, but whenever she did, it had worked out that Maxwell had been the only driver available. He assumed it was because he was always stuck in the office, juggling responsibilities that would physically challenge Wayne.

"You want it? Or should I tell her that we don't have anyone available? It is Saturday night. Even a large firm might be all tied up on a Saturday night," Wayne said as he rolled back across the room, his hand extended toward the phone.

"Hang on. Where is she?" Maxwell asked, shoving

himself from the comforts that had molded around his large muscular body.

"TV station. Says she's going home."

"That doesn't make sense. It's Saturday. She doesn't work on weekends, besides she only lives a few blocks from the station."

Maxwell ran his hand over the soft folds of his bald head. A second later, he wished he hadn't, once he realized his palms were damp.

"Maybe she had a tough day, is too exhausted and doesn't want to drive. I don't care, she pays on time and I assume she tips well since you wear better suits than anyone else in this outfit," Wayne added, only half joking.

Maxwell did wear the better suits, but not because of tips. They were leftovers from a life long gone. His only reminders of a short-lived tour of the upper rungs of the corporate ladder.

"Tell her I'm on my way," Maxwell said, turning quickly to head out the door before his brother could toss him any questions.

It didn't matter that he had dodged his brother's queries. While he drove, he asked himself all the same ones Wayne would have asked. What about his car? The auto shop down the street had repaired the flat and Maxwell was supposed to pick it up before the shop closed at eight-thirty.

But now he was going to be too late, and would have to take the subway home and hope the shop opened on Sunday so he could retrieve his car then. The subway. How he hated public transportation. Especially after hours. It was a major inconvenience, but regardless, he was still on his way to the TV station.

The more they drove, the less sense it made. Why was he putting himself out for her?

He didn't need the money. He wasn't likely going to ask her out. So, why bother? He was tired and in need of a bath and a good night's rest.

Still he drove. The station wasn't far, fortunately. In fact, none of it was far. The station, her apartment. Again, he wondered why she needed a driver. He wondered even more when he drove into the station parking lot and spotted her car.

The silver Porsche stood out like a sore thumb. Not because it was a high-dollar sports car, but because it was really old, and it looked like a big bullet parked beside a calm brown sedan. He pulled the car up to the back door where he'd picked her up at least a couple of times before and waited.

"Piece of junk probably won't start," he said to himself, still staring at the Porsche.

He hadn't seen her come out the door and when he did notice her, he had wished he had more time to get himself together. She was not dressed in her usual dark suits and white or multicolored blouses. Her loose-fitting skirt had blown against her thighs just enough to cling and give him far too much to think about. He swallowed hard and tried to get out of the car to help her get into the backseat.

"Good evening," was all he managed before realizing that his voice was breaking up.

"Thank you for coming. I know it's a busy night for you

guys. I would have called earlier, but I hadn't realized I would be out tonight and need a ride," she rambled as she slid into the center of the backseat.

She always sat midway. At first he hated that because it gave her perfect line of sight to his rearview mirror. In most cases, he was able to check out his passengers without them knowing that he was checking them out. But not with her. She was staring right back at him. And still, many times, he hadn't been able to keep his eyes on the road.

"Car problems?" Maxwell finally managed, as they pulled out of the station parking lot.

"Oh, no. That car works as well as it did the day it rolled off the assembly line. Actually, my sister kidnapped me last night. We had an adventurous day and some champagne this evening and I didn't think I should drive."

Maxwell wanted to run his hand over his head again. It's what he did either when in deep thought, or in an uncomfortable situation. Tonight was a case of both. His thoughts were all over the place, and he hadn't been comfortable since he realized whom Wayne was talking to on the phone.

"You two celebrating?" he asked.

This would usually be the point where he would clam up and not utter another word until it was time to settle the fare. But for whatever reason, he wanted to keep her talking tonight.

"Celebrating, no, not really. That's just my sister. She doesn't need a reason."

"Sounds like fun," Maxwell said, and then glimpsed into the mirror where their eyes met.

He felt her gaze in the pit of his stomach. Was she

flirting? He could never really tell. He assumed she was just being nice. That's possible in a city like Baltimore. A woman being nice just because. No ulterior motive.

"I'm glad you were still on duty. I must admit, I get a little uneasy getting a ride." Andrea felt the need to explain. "I guess I'm comfortable with you now. Thanks for coming."

She hated that she needed to play childlike games. Why couldn't she just be bold and admit she asked for him because she wanted to see him? She glanced at the mirror again. He was staring back. She could feel the heat rising under the silk of her skirt. She rubbed her hand over the fabric and the texture made her feel sexy. She was glad to be wearing Charlotte's clothes rather than her own. It was her only choice since Charlotte had talked her into spending the night with her and Juan on the yacht.

A night she wouldn't soon forget. Once Juan had arrived, Charlotte was off making nice with his guests, so Andrea had decided to duck into one of the staterooms to change. The room had been small, more compact than she would have imagined, but even in such a tiny space, there had been great attention paid to detail.

The layout had been logical, with a bed and a side table with ample storage for anything that might need storing while yachting. In the corner opposite the bed, there was a shower stall and pedestal sink with a very small closed-in area beside it. She had assumed that to be the toilet and hadn't bothered to check it out. *If you've seen one…*

The bold fabrics on the bedding and window treatments had melded with the rich tones of the wall coloring and artwork. The crown molding had run around the room with intricate details from the hands of a skilled craftsman. All she could think about was getting whoever had done this place to spend a few hours in her bland condo.

For years Andrea had completely trusted Charlotte's judgment in clothes and hadn't been able to wait to see what she would spend the evening milling about the yacht wearing. There were four outfits in the bag, so she had plenty to choose from.

She had gone with a more sleek and elegant dress for yesterday evening and saved her favorite for today. The heather-toned Andrew Marc corset top with a beige Ralph Lauren silk skirt. Just before the boat docked in Annapolis, Andrea had slid the delicate fabrics over her body. She had watched as her frame filled the thin full-length mirror that lined the wall near the tiny toilet room. There was no way to get around it. Charlotte was right about the news anchor garb. Sexy and daring were the words that had raced through Andrea's mind as she had opted for bare feet. Before she had stepped out of the room, the word *slut* had seeped up from some place deep in her brain. She had then slid her feet into a pair of sandals. That had only been a couple of hours ago, and now she was with him in his car and feeling sexier than she had while on the yacht.

"I keep staring because you look familiar," she said, although she was really staring because he was handsome and staring back at her.

Maxwell didn't respond, just glanced in the mirror before bringing his eyes back to the road. He didn't want her to get a good look into his eyes although that was all she could see and had seen for the past few months since he had been driving her around.

"It all starts to run together after a while," she said. "I interview people for stories and then I can't remember names and places. Did I ever interview you?" she asked.

Fortunately, she had asked the question the right way. He wouldn't have to lie.

"No, sorry. I've never had the pleasure," he answered, adding the pleasure part at the last second, and then regretting it.

"Maybe I've just seen you around the city, then?"

"Maybe," he responded, and didn't bother to look back at her.

The eyes. His mother had always told him that people would know his eyes anywhere. Piercing dark eyes that looked black as night. His mother had said that he could have his entire face restructured and people would still be able to pick him out in a crowd by his eyes. He didn't want to find out if dear mother was right.

"We're here," he announced as he pulled up to her apartment building.

But she wasn't ready to get out. She had wanted to chat, spend time with him, anything. But it was over. She no longer had an excuse to stay in his car. Anything longer would have been strange. She didn't want to seem weird, which is exactly the way she felt still sitting in the backseat of the car.

"Everything okay?" he asked, still looking into the mirror, meter still running.

"Sure. If you don't count raising teenagers and a stressful career. Oh, and ex-husband," she added, making sure he didn't think she was still attached since she had mentioned kids.

He didn't speak, just smiled and stared. The car was stopped and he could have turned around and looked at her straight on, but he didn't.

"You have kids?" she asked.

"A son. Fifteen."

"Divorced?" she continued, hoping it didn't feel as much like prying to him as it did to her.

"Five years. And you?"

Good, she thought. He was going along with the interrogation.

"Two years divorced. Two kids, son, Ray, sixteen, and a daughter, Amber, thirteen."

She stopped. Now that the facts were out there, she wasn't sure where to go next. Perhaps inside her apartment and to bed would be a good start.

"I hope I'm not keeping you from something. I start rambling and lose all track of time. And the champagne didn't help," she added, reaching for her purse.

"You're fine."

She pulled cash from her wallet, did a five-count and reached for the door.

"You don't have to rush. I can run the meter as long as you like," he said, and then turned to look at her face-to-face.

His smile softened the words so that she might have considered paying him to sit there and peer at her through his rearview mirror for several hours yet. But that wouldn't have made sense. She had already made herself out to seem desperate and having no life apart from two kids, an ex and lots of drama.

Having stared at him from behind, she had come to love his bald head, but seeing him face-to-face made her heart flutter. He had deep-set brown eyes, dark chocolate skin and full lips, no facial hair. All she could think about was drowning in chocolate. Willy Wonka had nothing on this man.

"Good night, and thanks again for coming," she said to keep herself from licking her lips.

She handed him two twenties, which was more than what was required for the five-block drive. But she had felt bad for sitting in his car yapping as if he had all night. He didn't look at the bills, simply slipped them into his coat pocket and got out to open her door.

As she stepped out and rounded the backside of the car to her building, he didn't bother to look at her. Not right away. That wasn't his style. He knew that women hated that. A man gawking at her behind as she strolled away. As much as he wanted to stare, he gazed down the street instead, until she was a good distance away from his car. Then, when he was sure she had turned away from him, he glanced in her direction. And it was all over. He could not take his eyes off her. The swaying silk was by far the most beautiful thing he had seen in some time.

Once she was at the door, talking to the door attendant, he got back into the car...but he didn't drive off right away. He watched her go inside, telling himself that there was no harm in window-shopping, but knowing full well he'd never have the courage to make the purchase.

CHAPTER 8

Ray had spent most of the day riding the subway, getting off at points of interest, but mostly reading the pamphlet from Tammy over and over. By nightfall, he had ridden from one end of the city to the other and then back again. He needed to go home, but still there were so many questions. The thing he wanted most was an adult to talk to. An adult who wouldn't blast him out for what he had done wrong.

His mind went back to everything he had done in the past six months to get ready for his senior year. The SAT prep course and his first shot at the SAT. A twelve hundred wasn't bad at all, and he still had another chance to do better. And the music scholarship. He had the paperwork and plenty of things going on during the summer to add fuel to his fire of possibilities. Everyone was on his side, teachers, guidance counselors and his parents. Would that all change when they found out about what he had done?

The train had cleared out going toward his father's house. Most of the folks were heading downtown to parties and nightclubs, so the train to the suburbs was nearly empty. Ray had felt better surrounded by all those strangers. Now, with himself and one other passenger, he felt out on a limb with his situation.

He had read the pamphlet Tammy gave him at the mall three times, not skipping one word. Still he didn't know the answer. He let his head fall into his hands; an almost silent sigh slipped from his lips.

"Everything okay, young man?" a voice rang out from behind him.

He didn't bother to turn. He had seen the gentleman board the train and watched him for a few seconds to make sure he didn't look weird or creepy. There are some strange people in the city and his parents had taught him to stay alert when he rode the subway.

"I'm okay," he said, hoping that would end the conversation.

But no such luck. The man had moved to the seat across from him. His dark suit looked like the kind funeral directors wore. He wondered if the man was returning home late from a meeting, or if he really did funerals for a living.

"I'm waiting for my dad. He's supposed to join me at the next stop," Ray said, feeling threatened by the man moving so close to him.

He had heard of a few down-low brothers going after young guys. And this guy would be too big for him to fight if it came to that. Ray looked around for a quick exit at the next stop.

"You don't have to be afraid, son. It's nothing like what you're thinking," the man added, but Ray didn't look at him.

"Maxwell Leonard," the man said, extending his hand toward Ray.

Ray didn't reach for it. If the rule was not to talk to strangers, which he had already broken, he was certainly not going to go as far as touching one.

Maxwell continued. "I have a son about your age and I haven't seen him in a while. His mother and I split and he doesn't really care to see me."

Ray glanced at Maxwell. He was an older guy, about his dad's age, maybe older. He didn't seem harmful and if he was, the next stop was coming up soon. Still Ray wouldn't let his guard down.

"You look troubled about something, so I just stepped up like I wish I could do with my son."

Ray looked at him straight on. It was late, he was tired and confused. He figured he had nothing to lose by a few words with a stranger.

"You know anything about abortion?"

Maxwell looked at the pamphlet, then back up at Ray.

"Not much," he said, and then blew out a sigh.

From the time Maxwell had stepped onto the train, he had been relieved that the only other passenger was a teenage boy. Somewhat clean-cut and respectably dressed instead of baggy pants and white T-shirts like the young boys he usually encountered when he rode the subway.

The boy had looked distressed, and although it was not Maxwell's usual nature to get involved, he was drawn to Ray. Instead of turning his head toward the window and staring into the darkened tunnel they were punching through, he had chosen conversation. Now, he was starting to regret it.

"So, you got yourself into a little trouble?"

"Nothing little about this."

"Your folks know?"

"They're split. I'm with my dad this weekend. And no, they can't know."

Maxwell drew in a deep breath, and then said, "What if they're able to help? Could be worth letting them in on it."

"They can't even help themselves. Besides, my sister is acting up. Got kicked out of school and everything. The last thing they need is me dropping this kind of bomb on them."

"Maybe you don't give them enough credit...."

"And maybe I give them too much credit. Maybe they should know how screwed up our lives are now. They can't get along, so they just go their separate ways. Well, what about us?"

Maxwell wasn't sure what to say. He tried to imagine what he'd say to his own son in a similar situation, but there was nothing to draw upon. His son was only eleven the last time they talked, so teenage issues were not his area of expertise.

"Dad has a new wife now and I'm sure before long they'll start having babies and forget all about me and Amber."

The name Amber struck Maxwell. He had just heard it, when Andrea was in his car earlier. Even before Andrea had told him about her family, he was already aware of their existence. Everyone in Baltimore was. You could hardly go anywhere in town and not hear her name. The conversations ran from how beautiful and smart she was to speculation about why her husband had left her. Maxwell assumed the name was a coincidence, but he had to make sure.

"I didn't catch your name," Maxwell interrupted before Ray could continue.

The question caught Ray off guard. He didn't feel completely secure with talking to a stranger and he really didn't want the man to know who he was, especially after what he had just shared with him.

"Ray Grimes," he said, telling himself that it was harmless, and that he'd probably never see this guy again.

Maxwell was now certain of the connection. It was also common knowledge in Baltimore that Andrea Shaw never used her married name on television and that she had been married to an architect named Ronald Grimes.

Maxwell felt sick after coming to the conclusion that he was talking to Andrea's son about abortion and bad parents of all things. He wanted to end the conversation and rush off, but he knew that would make the boy suspicious and he really did seem to need someone to talk to.

"So, you're an adult with a teenage son, what would you tell him to do?" Ray asked, taking Maxwell by surprise.

Maxwell stuttered a second before answering, realizing his hope of ending the conversation was fading. "I would get all the facts before making a decision. And if you were my son, I'd want to help with something like this."

"Oh, you would? But you said you don't even talk to your own son. So, how the hell would you help him? You don't even know what he's dealing with!" Ray yelled.

Ray hadn't meant to take his anger out on this Maxwell person, but there was no other adult he could do this with.

"Okay, so this is all your parents' fault. You did nothing wrong," Maxwell put in.

As much as he didn't want to get into something so personal with Andrea's son, it was too late.

Maxwell's statement gave Ray pause. He knew Maxwell was using psychology on him, trying to turn it back into his issue, putting none of the blame on his parents.

"I'm not a bad person, Mister Maxwell. I made a mistake. I really didn't even want to have sex…I mean, I did. How can you not want to? But I wasn't sure, and there wasn't anybody to talk to. I wanted to talk to my dad, but whenever I was at his house, his wife was glued to his side. What was I gonna do, ask my mother what to do? She can't even be honest about her own sex life."

Maxwell put up a hand to try to stop Ray, but there was no stopping where this was leading.

"She pretends she doesn't need a man, that she's not jealous of Dad's new wife 'cause she's young and pretty and can really cook. Mom goes out on dates and pretends she's going out of town to work. She would never bring a man home overnight, like we don't know what's up. I'm not stupid, and neither is Amber."

"Listen, Ray, parents aren't perfect. I'll be the first to tell you that. But I think that in most cases they mean well. Their intentions are right most of the time, and when they aren't it might help for you to say something."

Ray was exhausted. He felt as though he had run a mile barefoot on hot asphalt. He had wanted to talk about all the feelings he kept pent up inside. Now that he had, he felt stupid.

He wanted to get off the train. But they had passed the stop and the next station was his dad's house. Both he and

Maxwell went silent. They didn't look at each other or utter another word until the stop.

Maxwell stood first and let Ray go out ahead of him.

"Good luck, son," he said as the two went in opposite directions.

CHAPTER 9

By Sunday morning Andrea had talked to Principal Pimpkins again and gotten more details of the incident. She had calmed down enough and was ready for the task at hand: dealing with her troubled daughter and worrisome ex-husband. Ronald had called her on Saturday after she'd gotten off the yacht, but then she'd decided not to answer. Two can play that game, she had thought.

Plus, she wanted to ream him out in person, as well as snatch Amber by her collar to find out what her daughter had been thinking lately.

Andrea skipped her morning workout since she didn't have transportation. She opted for a bagel and coffee at the corner deli instead. Even if she'd had her car, the gym on Sunday would probably be elbow to elbow with people. Everyone who missed their workouts during the week, and all the women who read the latest magazine describing the gym as the perfect place to meet Mr. Right, would be clogging up the stair machines and free weights.

After coffee, she trudged the four blocks to the TV station, punched in the parking lot code and retrieved old faithful, the silver Porsche that had been her father's and now her own. She wasn't big on sports cars, and should have junked the old car and bought something more reliable, but it was her truest connection to her father.

She had heard the story a million times about how he had hunted that particular model of Porsche and ended up having it shipped from Italy, where the previous owners had let it sit in the garage. Andrea could remember her father's eyes lighting up as he told the Porsche story. And when she drove it, and sent it in too often for very expensive repairs, she had been transported to a time when her father's words had helped shape her future...the conversation they had when Andrea told him she was giving up her newspaper reporting job to be a stay-at-home mom.

"Andrea, this isn't about Ronald, is it? You're sure this is what you want?"

Andrea had been nursing Ray when her father paid a surprise visit to see his new grandson. But she wasn't surprised when the conversation drifted to her latest career move.

"It's just easier this way, Dad. Besides, Ronald travels so much. One of us needs to be in place to raise our son. And we plan to have at least one more child, maybe two. I'll go back to work once the kids are in school."

"I'm not saying you're wrong, honey. I just know how much you love journalism. And being a working mother doesn't mean you can't still love your children and give them your best."

"That from a man whose wife never worked a day in her life."

Andrea had watched as the smile slid across her father's face, making his mustache stretch into a straight line. She handed Ray to him as he let out a chuckle and an explanation. "That's your mother, Andrea. And that suits her just fine. You just need to make sure this suits you."

Ray squirmed in her father's arm until the two of them found a position that was comfortable for them both. She loved watching her father with Ray, the same way she could sit for hours and watch Ronald holding his son. The pride on each man's face, the awkward way they moved as if the child were fine china and might break under too much pressure.

"I don't know, Daddy. I've been out of work for two months so far and I miss it. But I really think this is what I need to do for now."

"Then you have my support. But please keep yourself sharp, Andrea. Take a class every now and then or something. Your mother or Charlotte can help watch baby Ray. Even though you're out of work, you need to keep your skills up. I can just see you doing big things one day. Maybe even TV."

"Daddy, TV? Look at me. I'm twenty pounds overweight, my skin is splotchy and my hair hasn't held a curl since the day I took the pregnancy test. Only a father could see this on TV," she said, pointing to her still-protruding belly.

Her father had passed away before she ever made her first step into television. But despite all her dreams and aspirations, it was his words that day that had sparked her first notion to take her journalism skills from print to broadcast.

The day she had driven to the WVTR studio to interview for the producer job, she had sat in the Porsche for a full thirty minutes rubbing the dashboard and praying for the surge of conviction from her father's words. And during the years to follow, despite the often numerous and pricey repairs, she had held on to the Porsche, feeling his presence each time she sat behind the wheel.

When she arrived at the single-family brick house that had become the love nest of Ronald and Charity, there were no cars in the driveway.

"Great, no one home."

She parked anyway, and jumped out of the car, a woman on a mission. A mission that would have to wait until whatever fun activity the kids were doing with their father was over.

She decided to knock anyway, all the while praying that Charity was not at home baking cookies or running a hot bath for Ronald. That is what she imagined the woman did all day. Catered to Ronald's every whim. At least that was what Charity had done while he was still married to Andrea.

Charity's family was old-money Baltimore and the woman had never worked a real job to Andrea's knowledge. When Ronald came along like a lost puppy in need of more attention from his wife, Charity had been ready to fill the full-time position. A position Andrea would have gladly handed over to her, had she known Ronald was out taking applications to replace her.

Before Andrea's hand hit the door, Ray yanked it open. "Saw you drive up, Mom."

"Oh, good, it's you. Your sister around?"

"Nope. Gone with Dad. Something about a new school," he said as he closed the door behind his mother.

"A new school?"

"I don't know, Mom. And I really don't want to get caught in the middle of it."

"Well, someone should give me the courtesy of a little information. I got a call from your principal Friday. Until then, I knew nothing."

Ray shrugged his shoulders as if he was sworn to silence.

"If it makes you feel any better, I think Dad was able to get her into another school. She might not fail her grade now. I don't know anything else."

"Great. That makes me feel just peachy."

Ray sighed and rushed off down the hall. That left Andrea with a few seconds to scan the house. Immaculate, just as a house where Ronald lived always was. Everything in its place, and if it wasn't, he would promptly throw it out. The only difference this time was the lemony fragrance. That had to be the remnants of Charity.

And it was probably not the fake lemon fragrance air fresheners that most women purchased at the local Giant supermarket. No, Charity had probably driven miles away and picked the lemons herself, then hurried home to slave over a hot stove making her own air freshener. The mere thought of it made Andrea vow to never buy lemon fragrance for her apartment.

Andrea went farther, looking for Ray. He had disappeared. She couldn't blame him. The middle of his sister's mess was not the place he deserved to be. But that didn't stop Andrea from meandering through the hallway to find him, and pick his brain for any valuable information about what Ronald was up to.

"Raymond," Andrea called out.

Not because she was in such a hurry to find Ray, but rather she didn't want to appear to be doing exactly what she was doing...snooping.

The door was slightly open, so when she leaned her body into it and it opened fully, it really wasn't her fault. The room with a huge king-size four-poster bed had to be the master bedroom. Andrea put her hand to her eyes to block the blinding yellow walls, and then wanted to scream when her eyes fell onto the bright red-and-yellow flowered bedspread.

Andrea could only think of Tweety Bird on crack. It was clear that Charity was going through a yellow phase. Andrea shut the door before her vision was permanently damaged.

"Ray," she called out again.

She finally heard his voice from another doorway down the hall. She rushed toward it and once inside the room, she wished she had just stayed in her car until Ronald and Amber returned.

"What the hell?" Andrea shrieked.

"I know. She likes yellow. Amber's room is just like this, but with a queen-size bed. I think this room is going to be the nursery," Ray announced and shot down the hall toward what was probably more yellow rooms.

Andrea blocked the nursery comment out of her mind

for two seconds. Then, she thought what the heck and decided to be pissed. What woman wouldn't be? There's a rule in the ex handbook that says you must hate everything about the new wife.

It would have been bad enough if Ronald had simply dated a younger, more attractive woman. He could have done the normal male thing and slept with her, got her all strung out emotionally, then dumped her. But no. He had to go and make an honest woman out of her.

"My God. Even Tweety couldn't take all this," Andrea said when she walked into the den where Ray was playing video games.

"What?" he asked as his mother stared at him.

"Nothing. I was just thinking out loud," Andrea answered as she scanned the room, taking in the vibrant red couches, and what else but yellow throw pillows and heavy mustard-yellow drapes.

Before she could be further disgusted, Ronald and Amber shoved through the door. Andrea glared at the two of them. They both glared back as if they were caught with their hands in the cookie jar.

"Just thought I'd check on things. Any major developments the mother of this child should know about?" she asked, teeth clenched as she directed her words to Ronald, and rolled her eyes at Amber.

Amber ignored her and walked past, heading toward the couch where her brother was playing games.

"Excuse me, young lady?"

"Listen, Andrea, we need to talk about this," Ronald interrupted. "Adults only. Let her go."

Amber kept walking as if he was the authority and Andrea was a mere sibling.

"So can we talk now? What about when this happened?"

Ronald motioned for the door. Andrea followed him into the kitchen. It was the room she had come through when Ray let her into the house—thankfully there wasn't a speck of yellow.

"You were on assignment. It all happened so fast...."

"So fast that you couldn't call my cell. Or even leave an emergency message at the station. Nancy always knows how to get hold of me."

"I'm sure she does."

"What's that supposed to mean?"

"You're a mother, Andrea. Or have you forgotten that? Your producer is not the only person that needs access to you."

That was an uncalled-for blow. The kids had her cell number and the strict instruction that in an emergency they could get hold of her.

"Well, I'm back in town now. What's the excuse?"

Ronald walked to the window over the kitchen sink, flipped the curtain back and peeked out before answering, "Principal Pimpkins said he had called and sent a letter to the house."

"And you don't think that little troublemaker would counteract those things to keep me from finding out what was going on?"

"I suppose so, but it's all in the past now. It happened, and something had to be done."

"So, Daddy has come in and saved the day," she added, the sarcasm thick enough to cut.

"And what's wrong with that? She is my daughter. Why wouldn't I take responsibility for her problems?"

"So this is just another problem? That's all. A problem, and you'll come up with a solution and everything will be better. Until she decides to blow something up or shoot someone."

"Andrea, watch your tone. This isn't healthy for Amber. This constant bickering back and forth."

Andrea knew that he was right, although she would never give him the satisfaction. Since their separation, the two of them hadn't gotten along for more than two minutes. Andrea had wanted to, and even caught herself trying on several occasions, but it never seemed to work out. He would always do something to get under her skin. She had read plenty of books about the effect of divorce on children. According to the experts, fighting between the parents is not a good thing. It only makes a bad situation worse.

"So what's the answer, Ronald?"

He handed her a folder full of papers.

"She's registered for an alternative school. Lakewood. She starts Monday. As long as she keeps her nose clean and does her work for three more weeks, she should be able to make her grade."

"This school is all the way out here. I'll never be able to get out here on time with the traffic in the city. It would take two hours. On a good day."

"Not if she stayed here." Ronald spoke as if he had said something as simple as "have a nice day."

"Stay here. That is not the agreement. You get them two weekends per month and most of the summer."

"It's three weeks, Andrea, not the rest of her life for God's sake."

He was right. She hadn't thought about the amount of time. In fact, Andrea wasn't sure where the emotion was coming from. The terms of custody were lenient enough that the judge had left it up to the two of them to divide the time as it best suited their situation.

And it was only three weeks until the end of the school year, so why was she freaking out? She knew why. She had been feeling the pressure ever since she got the phone call. Was she really not living up to her job as a parent? Amber seemed to prefer her father, and although it wasn't a competition, Andrea didn't like it.

"Is she okay with this?" Andrea asked referring to Charity, when she didn't know which direction to go with her anger.

"My wife—Charity is her name—she's fine with it. If it's all right with you, I'll come by this afternoon and get the rest of Amber's things."

"She shouldn't need that many things. It's only three weeks."

"And then summer break. We always take our vacation first week of summer break."

So there was nothing left to discuss. He had it all figured out. Andrea left Ray and Amber with their father. With the understanding that on Sunday afternoon only Ray would be coming home. For three weeks…no four weeks. Counting vacation, she would be the parent of only one live-in teenager.

She wanted to cry. What had she done wrong? When she had walked out on Ronald demanding that she could handle the demands of career and parenting, she was doing it with great success. Both Ray and Amber had been honor students, and she had snagged the prestigious Peabody award for journalism. So when had things gotten out of hand? And why hadn't she seen it coming? And was Ronald right?

It couldn't be. She refused to believe that her career had caused all this, despite the fact that it was the point Ronald had clung to all along. When they were married and he played that card, Andrea had insisted that he was being selfish, and was only satisfied as long as she was keeping his house clean, shirts ironed and a hot meal on the table.

It's the way he was raised, she thought. His mother never worked outside her home a day in her life. Therefore, it made sense that Ronald would be against her working. Even though she had insisted that she would work once the children were in school.

Her heart nearly broke from having to admit that somehow she had dropped the ball. It was obvious. No matter how many ways she tried to look around it. There was no way she could deny the evidence before her, not even with her most compelling argument.

Her daughter had been kicked out of school for threatening to hurt people, and now she was living with her father. Not forever, but long enough for Andrea to feel like the visiting parent. She was never supposed to be that parent. Never a mother who shucked off the responsibility of her children. That had never been part of her plan.

But it had happened. One child was gone, and Andrea felt like someone had slapped her on the wrist for improper behavior. Only it wasn't her wrist that was hurting.

CHAPTER 10

It was Sunday afternoon and before Maxwell could stop himself, he had driven the hour and a half to her house, walked up the flight of stairs to her apartment and rung the doorbell. When his ex-wife, Deborah, opened the door, the words flew from his mind as if a strong wind had blown through.

"Maxwell, you are the last person I expected to find," she said, stepping back to allow him entrance.

She was Deborah Clark before she had married Maxwell. And he had heard that she had gone back to her maiden name. He wasn't sure about that, but one thing was for sure…she had lost weight. He shouldn't be surprised by that, either, since he knew how much everything that had happened with him had put additional stress on her. And he knew all too well the results of days on end filled with regret. You either eat too much or too little.

"I should have called first, but I was afraid I'd talk myself out of it again," Maxwell said to fill the uneasy gap of silence.

She nodded as if she understood. He didn't know how

she could. She had gotten the house, custody of their son, the car and a huge chunk of his weekly pay. All he could tell was that she wasn't spending the money on food.

After a year of mistreatment by the neighbors, Deborah had moved with their son, Tim, away from the small, close-knit Montgomery County community to southern Maryland. Another small town, surrounded by corn, tobacco and other crops. But most importantly, not surrounded by the people who had turned their backs on his family because of his wrongdoing.

"Is Tim around? I got tickets to an Orioles game," Maxwell said, ignoring how strange it felt for his son's name to be in his mouth.

He hoped his voice wasn't shaking as bad as his insides. If it was, Deborah didn't seem to notice. She went on as if his presence was normal. She waved him into the apartment and pointed toward a couch. Maxwell didn't sit.

It had taken all his nerve to pay a visit. He felt as if sitting might break his momentum and leave him with no place to go with the emotions swarming inside him.

"He's at the park playing ball, but it's almost six so he should be bursting through that door any minute for food. He still doesn't miss a meal."

Maxwell smiled at the notion of familiarity. It had been years since he thought about Tim's eating habits. Or anything else about his son. He had forced himself to block those thoughts from his mind just so he could make it through the day.

Now the conversation hit a lull. Maxwell didn't know what to say next. He had hoped that Tim would be here and he'd have a chance to apologize, beg his forgiveness and start again. He could picture his son shooting the ball into the hoop just as he had so many Saturdays before everything happened. But that had all ended five years ago, and Maxwell had no idea what his son might look like after all that time. He may be dunking the basketball for all he knew.

"Have a seat and wait for him," Deborah suggested, and Maxwell sat since he had no idea what else to do.

The chitchat wasn't working between the two of them. Too much bad blood had passed. He wasn't going to fool himself by expecting that he could be chummy with Deborah at this point. He could just imagine what she thought when she looked at him. He had thought those same things when he looked into the mirror.

Maxwell thought of Andrea and the way she was so different from Deborah. Or perhaps they were a lot alike, but he was merely judging from the outside. Where Andrea was refined and articulate, conservatively dressed and always in control, Deborah was a plain Jane. A simple woman who didn't want lots of things. Deborah wasn't into fancy houses and cars. No, material things weren't her game. It was evident in her look: no makeup, hair pulled back into a ponytail. Her attire that day was a flowered skirt and white blouse, probably bargains she'd grabbed as an afterthought instead of an elaborate shopping spree with her girlfriends.

"I know things didn't go well the last time I tried, but I thought he might have had enough time to let things settle in," Maxwell said, since Deborah was still standing over him.

He had called Tim a few times in the last three years, but none of their conversations ever resulted in a friendly word. Tim was taunted because of what his father had done and he was dealing with it in the best way he knew how. Maxwell couldn't blame him for that. And Maxwell had always held out hope that time and distance would help them all put the past back where it belonged.

"I think it might just be a perfect time. He asked about you the other day," Deborah offered as she joined Maxwell, taking a seat in a wingback chair across from him.

Maxwell thought about his conversation from the night before on the train with Ray Grimes. Ray had been angry, but from his telling, he had never voiced that to his parents. Maxwell had experienced just the opposite. Every negative feeling his son Tim had, he had heard it.

"Are you still working with Wayne?" Deborah asked, bringing him back to the tiny apartment.

"Yep, still there. And he's still trying to be big-time."

The two of them laughed, but the sounds fell too loud onto the hardwood floor. The tension was still in the air even though so much time and so many years had passed. He knew she was still angry, but trying to be adult about it. She had every right to be upset with him for as long as she needed.

"You're still at the hospital?" he asked, hoping the conversation would pick up, carry itself for a while, and not feel like such a strain.

She nodded, but didn't even bother with words or questions. She got up from her seat as if the words had been too much. She walked toward what he assumed was the kitchen, then yelled back that she had dinner on the stove and asked Maxwell if he'd like anything to drink. He refused, although his mouth felt dry and barren. He could use a glass of water.

While Deborah was gone, he looked around the room, but didn't bother moving. The apartment couldn't be any more than two bedrooms. He hoped it was at least two. When Deborah had moved she had downsized because of the higher cost of living. Ah, the price we pay for peace.

The decor in the apartment was much like Deborah's clothes, simple. The sofa and chairs were likely discount furniture store purchases, and the window treatments hand sewn. Maxwell knew that not because they looked homemade, but because he knew Deborah. If she could make it with her own hands and save a few dollars, that's exactly what she'd do. That quality had to work in her favor now, since money was tight.

Deborah walked back into the room with a glass of water. She had ignored his insistence that he didn't need anything. She still knew him too well. When she was gone again, he gulped it down and got the courage to stand and look around.

His first stop, the pictures along the mantel. There were none of him, but of course he hadn't expected any. There were none showing their lives together. Hadn't expected that, either. There were pictures of Deborah's family and a few earlier shots of Tim, but nothing that would give him any idea of what his son looked like now. Maxwell thought back to Ray Grimes and how tall he was. He wondered if Tim had inherited his height.

"We're having sandwiches and Tim still likes those nasty noodle soups. You're welcome to join us," Deborah said, standing in the doorway between the living room and kitchen.

Maxwell refused as was to be expected and she ducked back into the kitchen to finish the wonderful-smelling soup and sandwiches. If he stayed long enough, she would feed him. He knew that much. That was her way.

She loved being at home, taking care of her family, making things pleasant and safe for them. That's why she had such a problem when five years ago he nearly threw it all away. And for nothing more than a crooked business deal.

Maxwell had been a rising star with one of the top manufacturing companies in the city. He had worked his way up from the bottom and commanded the respect and admiration of upper management, but not enough so that they let him in on their dirty dealings. Not at first, anyway.

It wasn't until after Maxwell had discovered a malfunctioning circuit board in some of the models of their pool heater division. He had his people run additional tests to verify that there was a problem, and then reported his finding to upper management to have the line shut down until they could sort out the problem.

"When the circuit malfunctions, the heaters fail to ignite, and then the gas builds up. Wouldn't be a problem unless that gas accumulated for a long period of time," were the exact words Maxwell had delivered in his boss's private office suite.

He had also made an explosion sound at the end of his explanation. Not because the issue was humorous, but he had worked hard to have a friendly relationship with the men in control in hopes of one day being one of them.

"Maxwell, you could be right. But it's minor. No point in shutting down a whole line just for what-if," had been the reply.

Those initial words made Maxwell feel sick to his stomach, but he had ignored it and laughed it off over a midday sherry and homemade cookies. Only to find that several more units had been tested and showed the same problem. The more Maxwell looked into it, the more he was sure that the problem was serious enough to shut down the line. He went back to the head cheese.

"Maxwell, because I like you and because I hope to continue to steer this company with your help for years to come...I'll share something with you."

Those had been the words that changed his life forever. Maxwell learned that his company was buying inadequately wired circuit boards from another company at a much cheaper price, thus shaving a huge chunk off the cost to manufacture the heaters. He was assured that the change was only temporary to help the company get through a slump and then told how companies do it all the time, and not to worry.

Maxwell didn't worry. He went home, celebrated his new promotion and rolled around in the cash that was

merely hush money in the form of a salary increase. He
didn't care. At least not until the explosion.

Maxwell nearly stumbled backward when the front
door flew open and a tall boy rushed through, barely
glancing at him as he made his way toward the kitchen.
The boy paused just around the corner and stepped back
to look eye-to-eye with Maxwell.

"Dad...you're shorter and bald," Tim blurted out.

The two of them laughed. Maxwell wasn't sure why
Tim was laughing, but he couldn't get over the fact that
his son's voice had deepened.

Almost as deep as his own.

"Yes, I decided to shave my head for a new look, but
my height is still the same. I think you've done some
growing, son," Maxwell added as Deborah walked back
into the room.

Tim stood at least six foot one, a few inches over his
father. His broad shoulders spilled over onto bulging
biceps, long arms and hands at least as large as Maxwell's.
He was Maxwell as a teenager. Tall and bulky for his age,
and forever with a basketball in his hands.

The last time he had seen his son, all he could see in his
eyes was the fallout that had come after the heater explosion that killed Tim's best friend, Paul Baker. Paul had
played baseball, basketball and tennis with Tim. Their
families had picnicked together, celebrated sporting vic-
tories and soothed their sons' wounds during the defeats.
And then Paul was gone.

At first everyone was certain that the explosion was just

a freak accident, but the moment Maxwell saw the nearly melted-out serial number on the heater, he knew better. Still, he didn't say a word.

It was only after one of the manufacturing company line workers made an anonymous call to the TV station. None other than Andrea Shaw had started an all-out investigation that forced the local police to get involved.

Fortunately, when heads started to roll, Maxwell was far enough out of the loop that he never faced charges, but he did lose his job. But that had been the lesser of his losses. He also lost the respect of his peers in the business and any chance of jumping back into another company in the area. His hands were already dirty. He was a labeled man. But most of all, it had cost him his family, friends and the faith of his son.

While the company was under investigation, there were TV people all over the place making a public spectacle of everyone involved. Tim had been teased to the point of fights and was kicked out of school twice before he released the brunt of his hurt onto his father.

"You knew about it, Dad. And you didn't say anything," Tim had yelled at him.

There wasn't a word of comfort Maxwell could offer his then ten-year-old son. He tried to hold him and wipe the tears, but Tim wanted no part of it.

"It's like you killed him, Dad. Because you didn't do anything. It's your fault, too."

The words had hurt Maxwell, but not as bad as Deborah's had, that same night, long after Tim had gone to bed.

"That could have been your own son, Maxwell. I thought you were a better man than that. Sandy and Jimmy's boy is dead and you could have prevented it. I don't know you, Maxwell," she had said as she tossed item after item into a suitcase.

The most Deborah had wanted out of life was peace of mind and the comforts of her friends and family. And Maxwell had taken that away from her. Before morning, he had convinced her to stay and he had moved out. By the time Tim had woken that morning, his father was gone. Which in hindsight only made matters worse. His son then had two huge things to hate his father for... killing his best friend and running out on them.

"Did you win?" Deborah asked, her eyes locked on Tim.

Maxwell knew that she was trying to gauge Tim's expression at seeing his father after such a long time.

Tim nodded his head in response to his mom, but didn't take his eyes off his father. Maxwell was glad that he had ditched the business suit and staunch dress clothes that he found himself wearing even as casual attire. He had instead chosen jeans, a red polo shirt and tennis shoes.

He watched Tim's eyes scan the length of his body. Maxwell hadn't wanted to come across as the corporate jerk his son had known from the past, but rather a regular guy who deserved a second chance. He couldn't help but wonder what Tim was thinking as he sized up his fallen father.

As he stood in front of his son, Maxwell pictured Andrea Shaw's face the night in his car when she mentioned the fact that he looked familiar. She had been one of the main newspeople investigating the story, but her focus had been on his bosses, and less-seasoned reporters had focused on him.

She hadn't been close enough to his part of the story to tie his face to what had happened all those years ago. But he knew that in the right situation, she would. And he hadn't come to the place yet where he could face that. One thing at a time.

"What brings you by?" Tim finally asked his dad.

"I was thinking we might check out a game this season. I can get Orioles tickets pretty easily. I have some for this week, but if you're busy, then maybe another time," Maxwell rambled.

His own fifteen-year-old son had made him more nervous than he had been in some time. He felt completely at the teenager's mercy. But he would do whatever it took to gain his son's respect and trust again. He tried not to stutter or run his hand over his head. Those were clear signs of nervousness. Instead he ran his thumb and index finger along his clean-shaven face. He anxiously waited for a reply.

"That sounds good. I'm going to go wash up for dinner," Tim said, heading toward the kitchen.

He stopped before entering, turned and said, "What time's the game?"

"Tomorrow at eight o'clock, but we'll need to get there early. I can pick you up at six and we'll get something to eat."

Tim nodded and continued into the kitchen. Maxwell thought that had gone well and was pleased with the way things were turning out. He had actually expected worse, and even prepared his heart for a tongue-lashing like the one he had heard from Ray Grimes on the subway the night before.

Instead, he had a pending baseball night with his son. Things were looking up, until Deborah spoke.

"He hates baseball," she whispered, stepping close to Maxwell so that her voice wouldn't carry to the next room.

Maxwell opened his mouth to speak, but she raised her hand to stop him. She stepped closer again, and lowered her voice even more.

"So if he's going, then that means he must really want to hang out with you."

Maxwell couldn't hide the smile that beamed inside his heart. It spilled out onto his face, drawing an equally bright one from Deborah. He could tell that she had wanted this to work out, too. Even after the betrayal she had felt from him, she had wanted him to have a relationship with his son. And as much as he didn't deserve it, that was the best news he had heard in more than five years.

CHAPTER 11

The conversation and turn of events with Ronald had Andrea so shaken up that she didn't realize the front door of her condominium was slightly open until she had shoved it and stepped inside her home. The obscenities that had been building, ready to spring from her lips froze in her throat. Her first thought was to back out and rush down the hall toward the elevator, but whoever was inside was likely already aware of her presence.

"Think, think," she said under her breath, as the heat rose from under her blouse.

"What has you all riled up this morning?" the voice said from around the corner, near her living room.

Andrea was poised to hit the unscrupulous man with her purse until it dawned on her that the voice was female and very familiar. Her mother, Chloe Shaw, was the burglar in question.

"Mama, you could have called or something. You should be glad I didn't have a gun. I know how to use one, you know. How did you get in?"

Chloe stepped around the corner, and waved a key as

she grabbed Andrea into a bear hug before her daughter could issue further threats on her life. The two women rocked and hugged, despite the fact that it would take Andrea's pulse a few minutes to slow down.

"You've had that key for years and you just decide to use it? To what do I owe this visit?" she asked, giving her mother a once-over.

An almost mirror replica of Charlotte, her mother wore nothing but the top designers. And even though Chloe was twenty years older than Charlotte, she could have passed for an older sister rather than a parent.

Chloe's white flowing dress was sheer and sexy. And if Andrea had been wearing it, people would have kept asking her if she was feeling well, or needed to go back to bed. For Chloe, the sexy-nightgown look worked as everyday attire. Andrea noticed that what had appeared to be shoes on her feet were merely stringy jeweled adornments between her toes.

"No, you first. I asked about who or what you were swearing at when you came in," Chloe insisted, talking back toward Andrea as she sashayed into the kitchen.

"Mama, I haven't seen you in almost six months. Do we have to discuss the drama of my life, right now?"

Andrea followed her mother, wishing she didn't have the drama, yet feeling a little relieved for the additional emotional support.

"Yes, we do. I made coffee, but it's awful. You really should have beans shipped directly from that place in Costa Rica. You still have the number I gave you?" Chloe asked, leaning her delicate frame against the counter where Andrea spotted the remnants of her freshly brewed coffee going down the drain.

"I rarely drink coffee. No point in paying through the nose to have it shipped to me. The supermarket brand is just fine."

Chloe shrieked as if Andrea had slapped her.

"Didn't I teach you anything? You stock fine liquor and good coffee and tea for your guests, honey. You never get a second chance…"

"I know…to make a first impression," Andrea interrupted. "This isn't our first time meeting, so suck it up. We'll go to a coffee shop if you like."

"Some place local, not one of those chains. I hate chain coffee. Almost as much as I hate supermarket brands," Chloe said as she stepped out of the kitchen and toward the door where she stood waiting for Andrea to open it for her.

Her mother the queen, or so she thought. Andrea's father had treated her mother as if she was something special, from monthly spa treatments to never owning a car old enough to even need minor repairs. Chloe was certainly queen around their home growing up. And since their father died fifteen years ago, Chloe was still searching for ways to get people to wait on her hand and foot.

"I'm sorry but you're going to have to cover yourself if you're going out with me."

Chloe's mouth dropped open as if she had been insulted.

"Mother I can almost see your breasts in that get-up."

"What is it about Americans that makes you so ashamed of your bodies?"

"It's not shame, it's fear of breaking the law, Mother. I should turn you in myself for indecent exposure. Here, take this," Andrea said, pulling a wrap from the hall closet.

Chloe draped the cloth around her shoulders as Andrea stepped forward and tied it into place, covering her mother's nearly visible nipples.

"There, we won't get arrested, and you still look devilishly sexy. After you, madam," Andrea said as she opened the door and stepped aside for Chloe to pass through.

And just like clockwork, she did.

Andrea didn't mind the regal attitude of her mother. In fact, she was glad to see it. It certainly beat the way things were the few weeks after their father had died. Chloe had gone inward. Depression and not eating. Nothing Andrea or Charlotte could say would bring her out of the funk.

When Charlotte informed their mother of her meager financial state, it was as if something went off in Chloe's brain. Within days, instead of sulking around in her wool, granny-style nightgown, queen Chloe re-emerged. The woman that their father had doted on for so many years was back. She had dressed and sauntered out the door to God knows where. In a few more days, the old Chloe had completely returned with a house full of people, laughing and joking, drinking and making merry.

Charlotte was convinced that their mother had lost her mind, but Andrea remained silent on the issue. Andrea knew that grief affected people in different ways and hoped that the low point her mother had faced was over and she truly was as happy and free as she seemed.

Months passed and the traveling started, then Chloe sold the house and now she lived wherever she wanted to, for however long she wanted to.

Where did the money come from? No one knew. All Andrea hoped was that it was legal and she didn't end up visiting her mother in prison in some foreign country, where bare chests are the norm and stringed jewels between the toes can pass for shoes.

As the two women walked to a coffee shop in the harbor, a few heads turned. Andrea was accustomed to the looks. A television personality in a city the size of Baltimore can barely go anywhere without being noticed. But Andrea knew that the onlookers were not staring at her, but rather at Chloe.

One woman they met on the street stopped and stared at Chloe for a full three-count then said, "Work it, sister." After which Chloe continued her stride with more confidence than before. Andrea loved most of Chloe's eccentricities. The clothes, the free-floating lifestyle and quest for the finer things in life made Andrea's face light up, and Charlotte's stomach churn.

"Have you seen Charlotte? I don't imagine you'd break into her place?"

"She's married and as much as I'd like to see that Juan in his birthday suit, I think Charlotte would permanently disown me."

"You should call her while you're in town this time."

"Oh, Andrea, forever the peacemaker. Your sister is not interested in hearing from me."

"That's true, but what amazes me is that you let her get

away with it. You'd never let me act ugly like that and not ever have a kind word for you."

"Your acceptance of me has nothing to do with me, dear. And Charlotte's issue with how much she and I are alike is also not about me. So, she'll come around in her own time. And life will be just dandy. Is this the place, dear?"

Fortunately the coffee shop was not far from Andrea's apartment and it was not a chain store—Andrea had no intention of combing the city for a place that would appease her mother.

After ordering drinks and bringing dear mom up to speed on the recent turn of events with Amber and everything else that had happened in the last twenty-four hours, including the strange moments with the driver she was stalking, Chloe assured her that there was nothing to worry about with Amber.

Time with her father was good for her, Chloe had insisted, then had the nerve to focus in on work. Andrea's job at WVTR. The most normal thing in her life at the time, and her mother was casting doubt on that.

The waitress set two steaming cups of tea onto the table, and without a word or eye contact with either lady, she scampered off.

"At least we don't have to worry about a tip," Andrea said, watching the girl go back behind the counter and stick a cordless phone to her ear.

Chloe didn't seem to even notice the rude waitress as she jumped onto the topic of Andrea's job. "Well, you said yourself that Nancy thinks something is going on," Chloe said as she sipped tea with her pinkie pointed upward as if she was dining with royalty.

And Andrea was sure that at some point during her travels, her mother had in fact sat across from some king, queen or noble person.

"I did, but Nancy is always one foot on the edge of disaster. She and her husband work at the station. Uncertainty is doubly bad for them. And with four kids, she can't afford to miss a beat. Plus Nancy just enjoys worrying about something…anything."

"And your boss. Sweating profusely just before a last-minute meeting. You have to add it all up, Andrea."

Chloe sipped again, closed her eyes and moaned, "Simply orgasmic."

Her mother was like Charlotte in more than just looks and attire. Andrea chose to ignore the innuendo, although the notion of whether Chloe dated had struck Andrea once or twice. Andrea had never mentioned this to Charlotte since her sister had worshipped their father and would be really pissed off if their mother were having sex or even entertaining the opposite sex. Rather childish, Andrea thought, but that was their relationship.

The more she thought about it Andrea was sure Chloe was seeing someone. Considering how much her mother talked about sex, it was either that, or Chloe was just a very rich, dirty old woman.

"Sorry, but I've been a little preoccupied. I can't imagine what could be wrong at work. Certainly nothing that will affect me directly. I've been at the top of my game. And I have a lead on a great piece that should pop early next week."

Chloe didn't say anything. The silence was speaking volumes. Andrea knew that Chloe thought she was good at her job, but that a person should never be too confident, lest they tumble from the good graces that lifted them to the pedestal they currently occupy.

"What do you think is going on?" Andrea asked her mother, as if Chloe Shaw had the inside track on the TV station.

"I have no idea, honey. I just think you should stay on your toes. You're not getting any younger, and you know how TV people like to trade up for a younger model."

"Mother!" Andrea retorted, drawing a glare from the impolite waitress.

Andrea didn't care that she was being loud. The waitress should have had the common decency to put more time and effort into serving customers instead of yapping into a telephone.

"Well, it's true. You said so time and again yourself."

"But I have experience. You can't trade that in for a pretty face and perky breasts."

"Depends on who's doing the trading," Chloe added, ducking her head down and gazing at her daughter to communicate that she was not still talking about her job, but rather something worse.

Andrea's marriage to Ronald. The hit stung Andrea. No one had ever implied aloud that a trade-in was the case with Ronald and her, although Andrea was sure it had crossed several minds.

Charity, Ronald's ten-years-younger wife could have been Andrea fifteen years ago. It was as if he had cloned his ex and chiseled a younger model, the homemaker version of Andrea.

"You take things so personal, honey. I am on your side. I know you have everything it takes to continue doing a wonderful job, but it never hurt anyone to stay one up on the executives."

Chloe was a smart woman. Andrea knew that for sure. Not because her mother could step into her daughter's business at will, poke her nose around and end up being right about her far-out suspicions. But because Chloe had somehow turned her depression and loneliness into a life that bordered on hysterical excitement. Not at all Andrea's preference, but she loved the way freedom looked on her mother.

Although Chloe had worked odd jobs over the years, it was never anything that could sustain her lifestyle preference. So, Andrea assumed her mother had to be smart to be able to live in the lap of luxury and not have anything that resembled a real job.

"The young man from the driving service, are you going to see him again?"

From one hot topic to another. Chloe had made Andrea feel insecure about her job, now it was time to jump into her social life.

"He's a driver. I can see him whenever I need a ride."

Chloe's lips tilted into a smile. "I'll let that one slide. I know how you hate my brand of sexual innuendo." She paused, and then continued. "But you could have coffee with him. This place is nice. Quaint and the tea is great."

"I fear I might have come across as being a little desperate. What if he's only after sex?"

"Of course he's after sex. They all are. But so are we."

"Mother, I will not have this discussion. No sex talk, none. Not innuendo or real sex."

"Have it your way, but I think you should call him. Right after you poke around and find out if some young perky thing with great breasts is after your job."

"There is nothing wrong with my breasts," Andrea whispered, aiming the statement at both items of discussion, professional and social.

The waitress, who had been hovering nearby, eavesdropping, found that statement interesting enough to put the phone down altogether. They had her undivided attention. And that would have been perfect if only they hadn't finished their drinks and been prepared to leave.

CHAPTER 12

By the time Maxwell got to work Monday morning, his brother had handed out all the assignments and could give him his undivided interrogation.

"So, what did she want?" Wayne asked, rolling one side of his chair back and forth.

"Who?" Maxwell asked, although he knew where the conversation was heading.

And he knew he wouldn't be able to avoid it forever.

"The news lady. You picked her up Saturday night. And I tried to get up with you this weekend to ask about it, but you weren't home. You didn't get lucky, did you?"

Maxwell had gotten lucky, but not in the way his brother would expect. He had a near miracle with his son, and even gained the courage to ask Andrea out. He had only planned to ask her out for coffee, but it was a start.

Maxwell had moved from the front lobby to the back office where he could adjust his coat and tie. But that didn't stop Wayne from following.

"And who is Ronald Grimes?" Wayne added, getting Maxwell's full attention.

He stopped fiddling with the tie before asking, "How do you know Ronald Grimes?"

"I don't. But he called Friday after you left. Didn't identify himself. Like I can't read caller ID."

Maxwell didn't speak. He couldn't imagine why Andrea's ex-husband had called his place of employ.

"Did he need a ride?" Maxwell asked.

"Nah, he played that just-checking-out-services-in-the-area role."

"How do you know he wasn't?"

"Just tell me who he is. You aren't in any trouble are you?"

"Listen, Wayne, you did not just talk to some stranger about your business and then tie him to me and trouble."

Maxwell went back to the front lobby and flopped down on the sofa. Wayne rolled over to where he was sitting. He hoisted himself out of the chair and onto the couch.

"No, I didn't. Honestly, I thought he might be competition. You know, a new service sizing me up. I don't play that."

Maxwell stood and walked to Wayne's desk. He looked over the paperwork to see what the other drivers were doing. He didn't really care. He had to do something until he figured out why Ronald Grimes had called.

"After I hung up, I checked him out on Google."

"You what?" Maxwell yelled as if Wayne had just informed him that he had shot and killed Andrea's ex-husband.

"Looked him up on the Internet, man. You really need to join us in the twentieth century."

Maxwell noticed that one of the drivers was headed to the

television station with the eighteen-passenger limo. What was that about, he wondered as he held the work order?

"He's an architect in the city. Pretty heavy dude."

"So, if you need any work done, you know who to call," Maxwell said as he made his way to the door.

He had planned to gas up the remaining cars, but not without a trip past the TV station to see why they had needed such a large vehicle.

"And he's her ex-husband," Wayne added. "So, it got me to thinking that maybe you got more going on with this woman than you let on. You were missing in action all weekend."

"I don't know why Grimes called. There's nothing going on with me and Andrea, except I plan to ask her out for coffee this weekend."

"Coffee? That's a wimp's first date. At least spring for dinner."

"I'm trying to feel my way with this. Nothing too fast."

"She does know, right?"

Know meaning she was aware that Maxwell was the same unscrupulous man that the media had slammed five years ago for his part in the death of an innocent ten-year-old boy, he thought. He didn't bother to answer as he continued out the door.

"So many secrets, big brother." Wayne had rolled onto the front sidewalk beside him.

"I saw Tim and Deborah this weekend," Maxwell said.

"Damn. Busy man. How did it go?"

"Not bad. He's going to an Orioles game with me tonight."

"But Tim hates baseball."

Maxwell sighed, "Does everyone know that except his father?"

"I'm proud of you, man. Making tracks. And making moves on the TV lady."

"She doesn't know."

Wayne sighed extra loud and continued rolling back and forth along the sidewalk.

"Then tell her," Wayne insisted.

Telling her was a major hurdle that Maxwell had planned to jump, until he remembered what Andrea's son had shared with him. He assumed she still didn't know about the pregnancy. She wouldn't be happy if she knew her son was dealing with something so heavy.

As Maxwell got into the car and watched Wayne roll back into the building, he reasoned that he had gotten himself in over his head. Not only had he hidden his secret, but her son's, as well.

"I'll just tell her about me, and leave it to her son to handle his own business," Maxwell said, his words echoing in the empty car.

Then again, it was all too much speculation. Who was to say he'd get that far with her? He may not even get past coffee. He had to keep the horse in front of the cart and not get out ahead of himself. But she excited him as nothing had before.

He could feel her energy seeping from the backseat each time she got into his car. He needed that energy. Personally and professionally. He wasn't a bad person, personally or professionally. Just got caught in a bad situation.

He wanted to believe that she was what he needed. A fresh start, a new opportunity to get it right. A woman with her passion could give him the spark he needed. But there he was again. Getting out ahead of himself.

CHAPTER 13

When Monday afternoon rolled around, Andrea was ready to get to work. She had spent too much time bending her brain with the fact that Amber had moved in with her father, and started at another school. A school that Andrea had not even visited or approved.

She walked into the station to find Nancy in usual form, rushing about as if on the brink of disaster. She would have normally gone to Nancy to find out what was going on, but with the sleepless night she had had, she chose to go straight to the horse's mouth. She poked her head into Ted's office where he was just hanging up the phone.

"Andrea, dear God, there you are."

"You've been looking for me?" she asked, not bothering to take a seat or seem casual.

"Not me, the man upstairs. I've been calling your numbers all morning. Is everything okay?"

"You tell me. I assume when you say 'man upstairs' you're not talking about God, but why would anyone upstairs be looking for me?"

"Have a seat, Andrea."

"No thanks, Ted. I'd rather stand. What is this about?"

Ted pointed toward the seat across from his desk. She did not sit. Chloe's words had had time to stir around in her head for twenty-four hours and she was like a rocket ship on launchpad.

"I had a rough weekend. Sleepless night last night, so I turned all my phones off this morning. Why was someone upstairs trying to reach me? Was there a problem with my story last Friday?"

"Listen, I'll tell you as much as I know, but have a seat first. I hate it when people stand over me like that."

Andrea sat, still pouting as if she expected Ted to confirm her mother's words. She had always felt secure in their relationship, but that was when things were normal. She could count on Ted in a pinch. But could she trust him with knowledge that her daughter was involved in a kill list?

"The late meeting on Friday was about a station buyout. There's a huge corporation looking to snatch us up to expand their TV empire."

Stations faced buyouts all the time. Andrea decided not to be a pessimist about the news, but still she felt uneasy at the fact that someone from upstairs had been looking for her all morning. That could be good news or bad, or just news, information about the prospects. She chose to focus on first things first. She had been rude to Ted, and he of all people did not deserve her attitude. She went in a lighter direction.

"Anyone good?" she asked, smiling for the first time since her mother had left her house yesterday.

"I don't have any of the details, but I assume that's what they were looking for you to talk about."

"Should I start clearing out my desk?" Andrea said jokingly, but there was nothing funny about what they were discussing.

He didn't answer quickly enough. He could have formed the words, "No, you're on firm footing," in only a few seconds, but he had paused for at least five seconds. Too long to mean anything good.

"Oh God."

"No, Andrea, don't get ready for a fit. You should be fine. You're pulling your weight. Knocking out clean hits every week. Your show ratings are through the roof. No one in their right mind would get rid of you."

Andrea still couldn't breathe. He needed to say more.

"It's usually the management types who have to worry with things like this. If anyone should be cleaning out, it should be me."

She hadn't thought of that. She had been rather insensitive thinking of her own hide. Ted had been the one who gave her a chance so many years ago. A lowly producer wanting to get in front of the camera. Cute faces with no skill, bucking for the spotlight were a dime a dozen and to everyone else, that's all she was. But Ted had seen more. He had said she had that something that makes good news talent.

She had started late in life, but he wanted to give her a chance. And things had gone well for both of them. She had moved up the ladder, and his pockets and prestige had gotten fatter where he sat.

"Do you really think they'd get rid of anyone?"

"It's all too early to speculate now. They're just looking. And you know from doing stories like this on other corporations, these things can take months, sometimes years. We'll both be too old to care by the time anything permanent happens."

With that admission, Andrea was really afraid. He had needed to say more, but he had said too much. He had gone overboard with trying to make everything seem okay. Clever trick, diverting her attention from her own pending doom by saying that they might get rid of him. Good tactic, but it didn't work. It was just as her mother had said, and she hated the fact that Chloe was always right.

"I'm off. Got a hot one popping. You'll be around later," she said, suddenly eager to get to Nancy and find out what was really going on before she ventured upstairs to meet with her real fate.

"Always am," Ted answered, and at that moment, Andrea felt it all change.

He had always been there, and so had she. But was something about to change? Was some new suit coming in and ripping out the old crew, replacing them with a bunch of youngsters right out of reporter kindergarten? Probably not. But they might replace them with seasoned veterans looking for a good market jump.

Ted walked Andrea to her desk where Nancy announced that the hot story she had been working on had fallen through. The lead had clammed up and no amount of prying would get him to talk. The authorities had their eyes on him, and he was not about to lose out for the sake of a solid news story for anyone, even Andrea Shaw.

Ted patted Andrea on the shoulder and kept walking. She wanted to read more into the sentiment than was there. But Nancy would not let it be so.

"I tried to call you, like, a hundred times this morning."

"I know. Bad night, I turned off everything. What's this about? Ted doesn't seem to know much."

"What'd he say?" her unsettled producer asked.

"We were talking about personal things. You know, my family emergency on Friday," Andrea lied.

"Oh, that. How did it go?"

"Why were you calling me this morning? And why are you working the early shift?" Andrea asked with fire in her eyes.

"Desiree broke her ankle this weekend. I had to produce the noon show. Paula, from upstairs called down and asked me to gather all the news anchors for an emergency meeting in the conference room at nine."

"Was everyone here?"

"Except you."

"Are they still meeting? What are they talking about?"

"I haven't talked to anyone yet. But one of the cleaning crew told me that some guys she'd never seen before, loaded the whole bunch of them, Dave and all, into a huge limo and left just before lunch. She said they were laughing and talking like it was some kind of celebration."

"And they're not back yet?"

"Not yet."

Andrea let out the breath that had been pent up inside

her chest. They wouldn't be in a limo and celebrating if they had all just been fired. So, perhaps she shouldn't worry just yet.

"What happened to you on Friday? What was the family emergency?"

"Amber got caught being a bad girl and was suspended. She started in an alternative school and her father is parent god, while I'm the evil inadequate one."

"Oh, good, so things are pretty much normal at home," Nancy said, and walked away to answer a page from the front lobby.

Andrea was glad to have a few moments alone to think about all that had happened since she walked through the door. There hadn't been any bad news, but still she felt uneasy. She decided that it might be best to check in with someone upstairs and was just about to leave her desk when Carla yelled to her from across the room, her voice drowning out the powerful squeal of the police scanner.

"Ms. Shaw, line one."

Andrea didn't waste a second and snatched the phone before the first beep ended. "Andrea Shaw, how may I help you," she answered, fingers crossed that this was not a call about Amber being kicked out of the new alternative school, or actually following through on that kill list, or Paula from upstairs telling her she was fired.

"Is this a bad time?"

It was Maxwell from the driving service. He had called. And not just any call, but a call at work.

Was that a good thing or bad? Andrea couldn't decide.

It had been so long since she had any kind of call from a man that didn't have to do with work or the kids.

"No actually, my story just fell through, so I have a minute."

"Sorry to hear that, but I'm sure you have something much better in your back pocket."

He paused, but not long enough for Andrea to think about the fact that she really didn't have anything else. And a new company was taking over when her life was falling apart.

"Listen, I was wondering if you'd like to grab a cup of coffee sometime?" Maxwell asked, and Andrea thought of Chloe.

It was as if her mother was some kind of dainty little angel sitting on her shoulder, pointing the right way, and yanking her from the wrong. She could already see the two of them sitting in the coffee shop.

"Perhaps this coming weekend. That is, if you don't have plans," he continued.

"My calendar seems to be empty. Why don't you give me a call later this week and we'll nail down something more specific," she said, trying not to sound like a quivering teenager.

"Sounds good. By the way, your producer, Nancy, has something for you. From me."

Before Andrea could ask any questions, Nancy bounded around the corner. No smile, no pleasantries. Just a cup of hot tea in one hand. She set it on Andrea's desk and then placed both hands on her hips.

"Tell your boyfriend that I am not a damn waitress."

The tea was not the only thing steaming, as a very pissed Nancy stomped away.

"Tea, how did you know?" Andrea said into the phone, but still watching Nancy throw her tantrum from across the newsroom.

"You mentioned it once when you were in the car. I know its midmorning and not twenty minutes before your show, but I don't know what I'll be doing by this afternoon when you like to have your tea. I'm sure you're shocked that I remembered. It's crazy the things that stick with you. I hope it doesn't seem creepy," he said, and Andrea wished he hadn't remembered.

Hadn't remembered, and been so great, and wonderful, and handsome. She was sure she was going to ruin this. And for the first time, she really didn't want to mess this up.

The call ended with the two of them agreeing to talk again later in the week, and within seconds, Nancy was right back at Andrea's desk.

"I have too much work to do, but I have to know what that was about. He was really handsome," Nancy said, interrupting Andrea's fantasy.

She sipped the tea and smiled. Orange Pekoe. Andrea didn't speak.

"You witch. I have one teen, a preteen and two toddlers. My husband and I work opposite shifts, so we're never in bed at the same time. Give me something here," Nancy yelled.

"Okay, sit," Andrea said as Nancy plopped her butt on the corner of her desk.

"He works at this driving service that I use sometimes.

When my sister picked me up in the limo the other day...well, you know, we went to Annapolis where her husband was meeting clients on this yacht."

"Hold on a second. I don't think I want to hear this. I officially hate you. You get picked up in a limo and taken to a yacht? Was it an anniversary...a birthday? Did someone survive a bout with cancer?"

"It was a business meeting and my sister and I were just tagging along," Andrea explained, took a quick sip, and continued. "Anyway, we had a blast and then the next day Charlotte got seasick and threw up the entire time, and I came back here and was kind of tipsy and upset about what was going on with Amber and Ronald, so I called him. The driver, not Ronald. And he drove me home and we talked and he is so gorgeous, the most sensual-looking lips you could imagine. And did you see that bald head?" Andrea stopped and blew out a breath before continuing. "Okay, that's all."

"That cannot be all. Did you kiss? Any tongue? No wait. Hot, steamy sex...in the car, right in the station parking lot?"

"Nancy?"

"What's he like other than great lips and a bald head? Does he own the service? One of many?"

"He's probably Charlotte's age, early fifties. His brother owns the business, and I don't know anything else. Except he's very handsome. Nice body for his age, and he wears these gorgeous dark suits, you know the type."

Nancy stood, stared at Andrea and turned to leave. She stopped, and turned back around.

"He wasn't wearing a suit when he dropped the tea off. I don't think I'd like the suits."

"Well, he wears them when he drives. Great suits that fit every curve of his body. You know."

"Yeah, I know. It's called chauffeur," Nancy added and rolled her eyes.

She turned to leave again, but then threw in, "I'm officially not jealous anymore. He's old, drives people around for a living and is fashionably stuck on Wall Street. You know how to pick 'em, kid. At least you've been on a yacht."

Nancy rushed off, leaving Andrea alone to giggle about her comedic assessment of Maxwell. Driving for a living had sounded like an insult when Nancy had said it. Andrea had wanted to be defensive, even get mad at Nancy for being so insensitive. But the thought of seeing Maxwell on the weekend had lifted her spirits and she was sure nothing could bring her down. It had been a very long time since she felt on the verge of a date with possibilities.

As her lips pressed against the cup, she imagined his lips, his hands. Suddenly she wished he had chosen a cold beverage.

No sooner than Andrea had downed the tea, the chaos started. First the rumors whispered in corners of the room, then an announcement over the station intercom system.

Ted had mentioned the meeting might occur months, perhaps even years, down the road. The one where the new company came in and took over the station, tossing management types out the back door before the ink dried on the deal.

Within an hour of getting a cup of tea from Maxwell,

Andrea and every other employee at the station were crammed into the cafeteria to learn of their fate. There were rumors spreading throughout the room that they had already canned the general manager and some of the accounting folks.

"That's the way it happens, get control of the money first," she heard someone say, as they all filed into the conference room.

"Andrea Shaw," someone called from down the hall.

Andrea looked at the man, but could not place his face. The more she looked, she was certain she had never seen him before.

"I'm Daniel Tate, Public Relations Director from Claxton Enterprises. I'm sorry we missed you this morning."

He had given her a name and a title, but still Andrea wasn't sure who or what she was dealing with. She shook his outstretched hand and fought her clouded brain for the right comeback for Mr. Tate's introduction. She wouldn't get an opportunity to come up with anything.

"We wanted to meet with all our on-air people before this overall staff meeting, but I suppose you were otherwise obligated. Perhaps we can get together after this meeting to go over our preliminary plans," Mr. Tate said and then walked away as if he wasn't interested in hearing whether Andrea would be available after the meeting or not.

Just as she was about to follow the others into the conference room, Dave walked around the corner. She grabbed his shirtsleeve in a desperate attempt to find out what she was supposed to already know.

"Dave, quick, ten-second version of the meeting."

"Andrea, where were you?"

"Never mind that. What did they say?"

"Not a lot. Honestly, I don't know any more than I did before the meeting. I nodded my head and smiled a lot."

"Did they say the word *replacements* even once?"

"Not once. They did mention focus groups and transition period, which in my opinion is just as bad."

Andrea followed Dave and then Nancy into the room and they took their seats. Seconds later Ted walked in and joined them. Andrea could tell from the look on his face that Ted was as much on the outside of this decision as she was.

"So, it happened a little quicker than I thought. Who knew they had been doing the groundwork for months. I just found out on Friday," Ted whispered toward Andrea.

He was sweating again. If he wasn't careful, he would perspire through his shirt and lose one of those chins.

"Do you know anything? Is the General Manager out?" she asked.

"I didn't want to ask for fear that they'd send us packing in the same box," Ted joked, but neither of them laughed.

Folks were still filing in spreading tidbits of information that were in all likelihood only partly true. Andrea's cell phone began to chirp. She read Ronald's number on the screen and clipped the phone back onto her hip.

"Ronald…I really don't need this right now," she said into the air.

Ted glanced around the room at the frightened expressions, then back at Andrea.

"What happened Friday by the way?" he asked as the phone continued chirping.

Andrea thought of what had gone down with Amber and the new school and living arrangements and decided she had better answer Ronald's call.

"I'll tell you later."

"There may not be a later," Ted said, turning away from Andrea to chat with Nancy and Dave.

Andrea only heard a few of the many words Ronald threw at her; she knew the rock and hard place was slamming in on her. More men in dark suits were coming into the cafeteria. She assumed they were the rest of the Claxton team.

Ronald was yapping in her ear about the school board filing charges against Amber because of the list. He had said that the cops were at the Lakewood school to take Amber to the police station. *Arrested* was the word he used, but Andrea had to block it out of her mind so she could figure out what to do next.

The Lakewood School principal had called Ronald first, since he was the one who had enrolled her. And he was already there trying to calm a frightened Amber. Andrea could just see the horrible scene playing out. Her daughter had done a few minor things, but being hauled off by the cops was too much for a thirteen-year-old who until a few months back had been a good girl.

"I gotta go. I'll call you later to find out what happened," Andrea whispered to Nancy, as the blood drained from both Ted's and Dave's faces.

"You can't leave now. This is big, Andrea. Not the time to be out of place," Ted whispered.

"Do any of you know anything you aren't telling me?" Andrea insisted.

"I told you all I know," Dave said before Ted added his two cents' worth.

"I don't know anything for sure, Andrea, just rumor, and you know how I feel about rumors."

"Spill it, Ted. I have cops at my daughter's school about to arrest her. If I'm going to lose my job then I need to know so I won't bother rushing back over here for the damn newscast."

"Someone's arresting Amber?" Nancy asked.

Andrea didn't have time, patience or desire to answer. She just wanted to be with Amber.

"Let's just say, my daughter needs me right now and if I have to choose then I'll let my absence display my choice."

"But Andrea you were already out of place this morning," Dave whispered, drawing attention from those around them.

Ted wouldn't let her off the hook, either. "Andrea, this new company doesn't have a good track record with minorities, but you've never let that stand in your way. And if you continue doing what you're doing, you should be…"

Andrea didn't wait for Ted to finish. She was out the door, in her car, heading toward the outskirts of town, where Amber was dealing with some very adult issues.

Although Andrea wanted to be there for Amber, to help her deal with whatever her feelings were about the cops taking her downtown, part of her knew she was responding because of Ronald. Even in crisis, her pettiness was rearing its ugly head.

She hated herself for being so childish, but the last thing she needed was to be absent again, and have him throw it in her face. Not to mention the principal who probably also thought less of her for being so clueless when he had called.

She hadn't been focusing on the right priorities, but this trouble had been fuel enough to get her rear in gear. Even though she had no idea what her leaving would do for her career. She drove away from the station, letting that problem fade into the distance. For now.

"One fire at a time," she said, as she pressed the accelerator and flew past Professional Auto driving service where Maxwell worked.

Damn.

CHAPTER 14

After the conversation went so well with Andrea, Maxwell got the bright idea to make the baseball outing with Tim as wonderful as it could be. He took the rest of the day off from the driving service, called Deborah to get permission to pick Tim up early from school and made his way to La Plata, several hours earlier than he had planned.

When he arrived at the school, he realized that Deborah had already called ahead to alert them that he was picking Tim up early. He flashed his identification and within minutes Tim was coming toward him in the hallway.

"Dad, I didn't expect you this early."

Maxwell noted that Tim seemed genuinely excited at seeing him. Wayne had given him a few tips on dealing with a teenager. Maxwell had been prepared for a brush-off when his son was with his friends, but Tim's eyes were bright with surprise and joy.

"Your mother said it would be okay if we got an early start."

"But I thought the game was tonight," Tim asked as they walked down the school hallway toward the front exit.

"It is, but I have some other things planned."

"Hey, Tim, where you headed?" a boy asked as he passed the two of them going out the door.

"Orioles game with my pops."

Maxwell felt a swell of pride just hearing the words. They got into the car with Tim behaving a little reluctantly. Maxwell was confused by the change. His son had seemed pleased with the early trip, but as he sat next to him in the car, there was a frown on his face.

"I didn't get lunch. So could we grab something?" Tim finally asked.

Maxwell let out a sigh of relief. Hunger was the culprit.

"Can you hold on a few more minutes?"

Tim said yes, but Maxwell knew he must be hungry because he didn't seem too happy about it. When they got to the ballpark, there were only a few other cars and Maxwell could hear Tim sighing as if this was the last thing he wanted to do. He started to wonder if he should have just stuck to the game and left well enough alone.

"A friend lined this up for me. We're going to have lunch with the team, and then we're going to tour the place. By the time we're done, it should be game time," Maxwell said, hoping the information didn't throw Tim deeper into the somber mood.

"For real. We get to eat with the team?" Tim asked, sitting up in his seat for the first time since they left his school.

Maxwell and Tim met a team representative at the front gate and were ushered into a room full of men and a few other teenagers and younger kids. They feasted on a spread of sandwiches, chips, cookies and soft drinks.

Tim met a few of the players, got an autographed baseball and then left for the tour.

The tour of the stadium took them from the dugout to the press box and then to the exclusive players' suite. From there they went to the famous inner harbor and got a quick lesson in Babe Ruth. No real Orioles fan could do without that. And then it was off to the park where cars were lined up for miles filing into the stadium.

"This was awesome, Dad."

"It wasn't too much, was it? I know you aren't crazy about baseball."

"I'm just not good at it, so I stick with what I can play, basketball and football. But this was cool."

While they waited, they grabbed a souvenir hat for Deborah. Tim mentioned that she loved pulling her hair back and slapping on a baseball cap to run out to the store. He told Maxwell this as if his father hadn't spent more than twelve years living with the woman.

By the time the game started, Tim was sitting on the edge of his seat. Maxwell had been to quite a few Orioles games since the divorce, but this one was by far the most exciting. He hated that he'd missed so much of his son's life, but for now he chose to concentrate on the future and leave the past where it was. There was nothing he could do about what was behind them.

By the time they got back home, Tim had fallen asleep. Maxwell was tired, but no amount of fatigue could dampen the feeling of spending an evening with his son. He shook Tim as they pulled into the parking space at the apartment complex.

"Wake up sleepyhead. We're here."

Tim sat up and looked around for a few seconds as if he hadn't remembered where he was. Maxwell thought of how much of a change it had to be for him to be spending a whole day with a man he hadn't seen in five years. But he felt that both he and his son had handled themselves just fine.

"Sorry I dozed on you. Long day."

"Well, you should rest well tonight. We packed plenty into one day."

"Look, Mom's waiting up," Tim said, pointing toward the silhouette at the upstairs window.

"Surprise, surprise," Maxwell said then reached to the backseat to grab the box. "Before you go, I wanted to give you this," he said, handing the box to Tim.

Tim slid the ribbon off and popped the top open. Again, Maxwell was nervous. He wanted to do so much for his son to make up for the lost time. But he didn't want to overdo it. He hoped that Tim wouldn't think it was too much.

"I noticed that you didn't have a watch. So, I picked it up while you were hanging out with the team. Always helps to keep up with the time," Maxwell said, not wanting to be so sentimental.

"This is nice. Thanks. Mom will like it. She was gonna get me one, but she said she didn't have the extra money."

Maxwell looked up at the window again. She was gone.

"Listen, son, I want to apologize for what happened."

"Dad, I don't want to talk about it. I don't want to think about what happened to Paul. I'm okay now."

"I know you are, but I'm not just talking about what

happened with Paul. I'm talking about what happened between us. I'm sorry for leaving you."

"But Mom didn't want to be married to you anymore."

"No, she didn't. But that didn't mean I couldn't still try to be there for you. I'm sorry."

"I'm sorry, too. About the way I acted. I just didn't understand everything. I was sad and mad, and everybody was treating me so bad, like I did it. And I missed Paul. I still do."

"You had every right to feel all those things. But I should have been there with you. I was wrong, son. On all counts. And there's nothing I can do to change any of it. Trust me, if I could..."

"Hey, it's been a long night. I had a good time. I just want to keep going like this. There's nothing I can do about any of that stuff now, either. So, I guess we just move on, right?" Tim asked, strapping the watch around his wrist.

Maxwell couldn't speak. It had been years since tears filled his eyes. He had carried so much guilt and regret that he hadn't been able to cry. And now, sitting in front of Tim, nearly a man himself, he was about to break down.

Maxwell walked Tim to the door where Deborah was waiting.

"I had a good time, Dad," Tim said, and tossed his arms around Maxwell's neck for a quick hug.

Maxwell still couldn't find words. It didn't matter because Tim rushed off as soon as the hug was done. Deborah stared at Maxwell for a few seconds before saying good-night and shutting the door. By the time

Maxwell got back into the car, he glanced down at his own watch. One just like the one he had purchased for Tim, and the tears came. It was a good ten minutes before he was able to drive off. It felt good to know he was doing something right again.

CHAPTER 15

Andrea never made it back in time for the newscast on Monday evening. She had called Nancy and explained the situation. And Nancy had taken charge and made the show move seamlessly as she always did. Andrea didn't bother finding out what had come of the meeting with the new owners. She assumed that if her absence had sealed her fate, then there was nothing she could do about it anyway.

Her day had gone from the beginning of the intense meeting at the station, to the school, to the police station, a quick trip home and then to Ronald's house. Amber was spending the night in a juvenile detention center and her first appearance in court was in two days. The school board had taken the kill list very seriously, especially when they found out it was Amber who had penned it.

Once Andrea saw the note and the list that went along with it, she, too, wondered what her daughter had been thinking of, to do something so potentially devastating. The police officers and a court-appointed psychologist had asked Andrea a bunch of questions, most of which had simple cut-and-dried answers. No, she did not own a gun. No, she had no knowledge of anywhere Amber could get access to any kind of weapon.

As much as Andrea and Ronald pleaded, the board had chosen to use their daughter as an example for all the other juvenile delinquents who might be considering taking their minor infractions to the next level. Taking into account the incidents of school shootings and violence in recent years, there was nothing they could say to get her off the hook.

At some point during the chaos, two officers had escorted Andrea to her apartment where they went through items in Amber's room and scanned the hard drive of her daughter's computer. The men were neat in their search and careful to put things back the way they found them, but Andrea knew it would take some time for things to really be back where they belonged. If ever.

In the end, Andrea had left Amber at the juvenile center, fear still lingering in the young girl's eyes. As much as she wanted Amber with her at such a crucial time, her daughter had broken the law and would have to suffer the consequences.

When Andrea finally got home, she stopped in the hall entryway and kicked off as much as she could. She had set up a convenient space-saving unit that combined a coatrack, locker cubby and bench all in one. By the time she walked into the living room, all she had on were the slacks and blouse that she had worn to work.

Ray and Tammy were perched on the sofa in the throes of what appeared to be a heated conversation that ended as soon as they saw her. Andrea could not take one more thing happening, and she hoped that the two of them were not to be the bearers of bad news, as well. She didn't bother to ask, just walked past them toward the dining room.

"Everything okay, Mom? You weren't on the news tonight."

"Your sister is in juve," Andrea stopped to answer, as bluntly as it felt.

"What the hell?"

"Raymond Grimes, I will not have you using that kind of language in my house."

"This is crazy, Mom. Everyone with a brain knows Amber was just trying to get attention," Ray said, pacing the length of the living room floor.

He picked up a magazine off the coffee table, and then tossed it back down. Andrea continued into the dining room. He and Tammy followed.

"But she made a list of people to kill, Ray. And even went so far as to toss in how she planned to kill each of them," Andrea said as she ducked past the mahogany-stained dining table.

Her hip caught the corner of the table, anyway. She slammed her eyes shut from the pain, already able to see the bruise forming on her thigh. No matter, no one was looking at her thighs these days anyway.

"And do you really think Amber is capable of killing anyone?"

"I get your point, but this is serious, Ray. I had to stand there and watch them put her in that place. It was kind of like a college dorm room. Actually better than some college dorm rooms, but still...."

Andrea stood in front of the Graham buffet, opened one of the paneled doors, and removed a wineglass.

"What did Dad say?"

"He was yelling and screaming until Charity dragged him out of the place," Andrea answered, popping the cork on a bottle of red wine.

She poured the contents into a decanter and then a half glass for herself. She really did not want to talk about Ronald. And she hated feeling that she had to work with him and his new wife to help get her daughter back on track. But that was exactly what it was shaping up to be. Charity had arrived at the school as quickly as Andrea, which would have made her angrier if she hadn't been distracted by watching the cops toss her daughter into a police car.

Andrea took a big gulp and continued. "Listen, there's nothing I can do about this now, so I'm going to get a hot bath and go to bed. I would suggest you get to bed soon, too," Andrea said sneaking a peak at Tammy, who had been standing quietly in the corner.

"Mom, sit down, I have some news that might make you feel better."

Ray pulled out a chair and motioned for Andrea to sit.

"And it can't wait until I get a hot bath," she said, walking past the chair, still gulping wine.

"No, it can't," he said, waving a piece of paper in her face. His expression had run from anger to excitement.

Ray was buzzing around Andrea like a bee that had an overdose of honey. She smiled at him sneakily and made her way to the kitchen where she had designated the wall near the phone as a communication center.

She had learned that with teenagers and an active career, things ran more smoothly with everything accounted for. She glanced at the board still wondering why the system hadn't worked with Amber's recent trouble.

She sipped more wine, still ignoring Ray and the paper he was waving. She reached into the compartment for incoming mail. It was a clear rule in the house. Someone would check the mail every day, and promptly place it into the wall pocket, not on the kitchen table or counters where it might go weeks unnoticed. That system had worked.

Andrea finished her wine, set the glass into the sink and flopped at the kitchen table. There she continued thumbing through the mail, purposely setting Ray into a fit.

"Mom, please, put those things away. This is the important piece," he said holding a letter in front of Andrea's face.

Her heart almost sank when she noticed Tammy still following them around, saying nothing. The girl looked troubled and she and Ray had been at the point of arguing when Andrea walked through the door. Was there something wrong with Tammy? Then Andrea remembered she was talking to her son, not her wayward daughter, and he had said great news. And she really did need some great news.

"All right, all right…what is it, or are you going to make me read your mind?"

"The competition. The one in Myrtle Beach," he added, practically squealing.

"Yes, the band competition," Andrea filled in.

"I got it. I won lead jazz sax. That means we're going

to Myrtle Beach. Pack your bags, lady, we're heading for some sun and fun."

The beach. In the middle of everything else that was going on. Andrea forced a smile.

"Congratulations, baby," she said, tossing her arms around his neck.

She had noticed that Tammy did not seem as excited about the news. Andrea assumed she was angry because Ray would not be able to spend every second of his life with her.

Andrea had to admit, this was not the time to be off hanging out at the beach, competition or not. She wanted to be happy for Ray and support him one hundred percent. But being away from home was not a good thing right now. Although she was hopeful that Amber would get a stern slap on the wrist and this would be over soon, she didn't want to be away so soon after dealing with an arrest and appearance before a judge.

Amber would need her undivided attention, especially now. In a normal situation, she would be able to call on Ronald. But she wouldn't do that since she couldn't trust him any further than she could throw him.

Then the whole mess with work, whatever that meant. No hot story brewing to make herself look good in the face of new owners. No, a trip was not the answer.

"So, when do we leave?" Andrea asked, instead of voicing her true concerns.

"Not until July, but I am so pumped. You know how much I wanted this. And to spend four days and three luxurious nights at the beach absolutely free."

"Oh, four days?"

"Yes, and I did say free. For me that is. I think you have to pay your own way. And you know Amber will want to go. And maybe even Dad."

"I'm sure your dad will be too busy. Don't be disappointed if he's not able to take off."

"He's the boss. Of course, he can take off. Oh and Auntie Charlotte. And I told Grandma about it when she was here the other day, and she said she'd come back if I got it."

He was so excited and Andrea's smile was so fake. She felt ashamed for all the things that were running through her mind while he was trying to figure out if all the people he loved and cared about would be there to support him.

His mother was meanwhile trying to plan a way to get out of it. She tried to convince herself that he would be okay if she opted out of the trip. Besides, Ray had been nothing but a perfect angel through everything.

Even when she and Ronald had first announced that they were separating. It was as if Ray had become the man of the house, doing things for her that his father used to do.

Andrea remembered the first time she pulled up to a gas station and he jumped out to take care of things. He was secure and adjusting well to all of it. It shouldn't bother him too much if she had to lag behind. Especially if he had all those other people there, as well. Besides, her job could depend on it. And she had to have a job in order to support them. There. It all made sense.

"Mom, this is going to be so much fun. And you really need a vacation. I want you to relax and enjoy yourself this time. No worrying over me and Amber, but do something for yourself," he added.

Andrea hated herself for being so selfish. Again, Ronald's words slammed in her ears. She was not a good mother, and she was too concerned about her career to be there for her children.

"Of course I could use a vacation, but it sounds like you're just trying to get rid of me. So you can spend all your free time with that one," Andrea said pointing to Tammy.

"She's not going to be able to go, Ma."

Andrea assumed that was the cause of Tammy's long face and was probably the subject of the battle she had walked in on. Andrea threw her arm around her son. He was tall, lean and handsome. She could understand why the girl was so into him. But she still wished Ray would not take this dating thing so seriously.

"What will you be doing, Ms. Tammy?"

"I got a summer job," the girl said, still no smile.

"Good for you," Andrea responded and left the room.

There was no mistaking the fact that she did not care for her son's girlfriend. But it was nothing personal, really. She would have hated any girl that captured her son's attention the way Tammy had.

Andrea left the teenagers to say good-night and went into her bathroom where she swabbed off her makeup, wrapped a silk scarf around her head and stripped out of the rest of her clothes, opting for only panties.

She walked into the bedroom and eyed the heavy oak sleigh bed all decked out in white and baby blue. She continued past the bed and chose instead the white leather recliner in the corner. She collapsed into the cool folds and continued thumbing through the mail.

She was committed to the trip. And she'd have to figure something out for work and Amber's legal trouble. She knew this was a test for her. One that she had to pass. She would not let Ray down.

With one child on the fritz, there was no point in losing another, she concluded, as she pulled a terry-cloth throw over her near-naked body and closed her eyes, wishing she would wake up to find that this had all been a bad dream. But life isn't a soap opera, with crafty writers to make everything come out just right. When she awoke the next day, there would be more of the same, and she would have to start the juggling act all over again.

CHAPTER 16

Ray peeked into Andrea's room to make sure she was sound asleep. He could hear the snores coming from her corner recliner, so he joined Tammy in the kitchen to finish laying down the plan.

While Ray was spending a week at the beach, Tammy would stay in Baltimore, and have an abortion. Ray had given her the money and the address of an office where she could go to have the procedure done.

"But what about my parents?" Tammy was crying again when he came back into the kitchen.

She had been doubled over in tears before Andrea came home, and had only stopped crying long enough to get mad and scream at Ray before his mother had walked into the room. Tammy had been a fit of emotions since she and Ray decided to get rid of the baby without telling either of their parents.

"You'll tell them you're staying with Pam. Her grandmother is so old and senile, she won't even know you're not there."

Tammy wouldn't be at Pam's house. Instead she would

be at a hotel near the clinic, where she would stay for the remainder of the week, recuperating. By the time Ray returned from South Carolina, everything would be back to normal. At least that was what he had told himself. Although he knew that after this, nothing would ever be the same for him or Tammy.

"I don't know, Ray…."

"Dammit, Tam, how many times do we have to go over this?"

Ray was still holding the letter about the band competition. He tossed it from one hand to the other, only wishing he could focus his attention on the good that could come out of an opportunity like this. But he didn't want to seem insensitive to Tammy.

He felt as if he couldn't make a clear-cut decision unless he was being harsh and unfeeling. Whenever he tried to put himself in her shoes and think of the fact that she was carrying a child, his child…his chest felt tight and a knot would form in his throat.

"It's not that I don't understand. I know what I'm supposed to do and where I'm supposed to go, but I just don't know if this is really what I want to do."

Ray was furious. No matter how frightened and unsure he felt, he could not continue to waver. He wanted to make a decision and stick with it. Tammy had gone back and forth on the issue one time too many.

One day she was sure she wanted to get rid of the baby and that it was the best thing. She had hopes of getting into an A&T State University in North Carolina. She and Pam were going to be roommates. Tammy's mother had gone to school there, and the two of them had talked about her going to her mother's alma mater since Tammy was a little girl. So Ray couldn't figure out why Tammy couldn't stick with the plan to ensure her chances of going to college without any hindrances. He was tired of the back-and-forth.

Ray grabbed Tammy's arm and tugged her from the kitchen to the living room, and ultimately the front door, and said, "It's getting late. We can talk about this again tomorrow. I just can't do this tonight."

He opened the door and stood there waiting for Tammy to leave. She didn't. He closed the door and sighed.

"What now?"

"You're right. I'll do it, just the way you said," she sighed and stepped toward the door. "This is the only way. Besides, look at all the trouble your sister is getting herself into. Your family doesn't need this right now."

Just like that, she had changed her mind again. Ray didn't bother to speak. There was no point in voicing his opinion. He would just wait until he saw her the next day, and deal with whichever direction she was swinging then.

He didn't have the patience to go over the plan, the problem or the solution. And the last thing he wanted to risk was having his mother overhear what they were talking about. He wanted to protect her from any more trouble. Amber had done a pretty good job of throwing their lives into chaos. He still couldn't believe his sister was spending the night in jail. He hoped it would teach her a lesson, but Amber was stubborn and confused about how their life had changed since the divorce.

Amber had been the one who insisted that their parents were getting back together even after their father started dating Charity. It wasn't until after their dad's wedding that Amber had given up that fight. And now she had taken to acting crazy to bring the family together.

After Tammy finally left, Ray locked the door, and turned out the lights. He grabbed a glass from the buffet and poured himself a glass of wine, and fell into one of the dining room chairs. Andrea had forbidden him to drink, but considering everything else that was going on, he considered wine the least of his offenses.

It was all so ridiculous it almost made him laugh. His thirteen-year-old sister in jail, and him on his way to being a teenage father. He had no idea how his once-normal family had gotten so screwed up, so quickly.

CHAPTER 17

On the day of Amber's first appearance, Andrea was on pins and needles as she, Ronald, Charity and Charlotte arrived a full thirty minutes before the procedure was scheduled to start. The previous twenty-four hours since Amber had been released into her custody had been a whirlwind of activity. Before they had allowed her to pick Amber up, she had gone through a second round of questions. This time in reference to her divorce and the potential impact it might have had on her daughter.

After leaving the detention center and filling out a pile of paperwork, Andrea and Amber had rushed around trying to find something for Amber to wear to appear before the judge. Their attorney had suggested something she'd wear to church, but since Andrea couldn't remember the last time she or the kids had gone to church, shopping was inevitable. They poured through store after store, a whirlwind of mother and daughter in a desperate search for the right outfit. Their movement had been quick, words few and Andrea knew that if she didn't keep moving, she'd have too much time to think about how badly things were spinning out of control.

Finally, at the courthouse on that morning, Andrea had dropped Amber off a few hours early to meet with the attorney and for another round of questions with the psychologist. Andrea had gone back home to dress and pray. To pray extra hard for a break in the nightmare. When she got to the courthouse and saw her ex-husband with his wife hanging supportively on his arm, she wondered if she should have added one more thing to her prayer. But she didn't think God would really answer a prayer to break up someone's marriage.

She turned to Charlotte, nudged her head toward Charity and whispered, "I suppose he had to bring her."

"Probably won't hurt to have her here, too."

"Meaning?"

"Meaning, you are all trying to raise this child. She is his wife and Amber spends half her time with the two of them. I think the judge will find her presence favorable."

"Is that what Juan said?" Andrea asked.

"Yeah. You know I didn't come up with anything that clever. Relax, you don't want Amber to see fear in your eyes."

Charlotte rushed off to chat with Juan before he left to meet one of his own clients, which put Andrea in the middle of a conversation between Ronald and Principal Pimpkins. She assumed Charity had gone to powder her nose or something equally menial. The principal appeared somewhat nervous, yet eager to explain to them why the school had chosen to treat their daughter like a common criminal.

"Mr. Pimpkins, I had really hoped we could have avoided this. I assured you that I was taking care of things," Ronald whispered, as if Andrea was not now standing a mere few feet away.

"What exactly were you taking care of?" Andrea said to Ronald.

He ignored her, and continued staring at the principal, who said, "Mr. Grimes, I realize we had gone over this, but it's more complex than what we initially expected. Let me explain."

"Yes, why don't you do that, sir?" Ronald stepped closer to the man and his calm look had gone more toward the fierce expression he had the day Amber was arrested.

Andrea reached over and placed her hand on his forearm. She didn't want what was shaping up to be a bad scene to get worse.

"The board decided to press criminal charges after talking to a few of the kids who were in on creating the list."

"Oh, the list. A kill list. You can't tell me you believe those girls were going to kill anyone. They're kids, twelve and thirteen years old."

"And many of them were perhaps playing a game, but according to our investigation, your daughter wrote the note and created the list, adding names that the other girls requested."

"What the hell? It was a silly prank, kids do it everyday," Ronald insisted.

Mr. Pimpkins was now stepping closer to Ronald.

"And that is the problem, Mr. Grimes. This happens far too often for us to not take it seriously. How do we know which list is a prank and which will end like Columbine or any of the others?"

Andrea watched as if she were an outsider as the two tried to come to terms with where this was heading. She finally stepped forward before either of the men said something he would regret.

"What do you think will happen in there?" she asked the principal.

"This judge is pretty good. He should go light on her and all the kids, in fact. But he's not going to brush over this like nothing happened."

"She won't have to go back to the detention center, and continue to miss school?"

"Ms. Shaw, if you both and Amber cooperate with this judge, he will more than likely come up with a plan that will be in your daughter's best interest. What most folks call a slap on the wrist...."

"But so far she hasn't gotten a slap on the wrist. She got kicked out of school, and had I not called in a favor from a friend, she wouldn't have gotten into another school, and had the chance to make her grade," Ronald said, his voice no longer conversational.

He was yelling and drawing the attention of the others filing into the courtroom.

Andrea grabbed at his forearm again before interjecting, "So don't you see? She did something bad, they tried to punish her, but you came back in and made it all better. In the end, she would get off as if she never did a thing and go back to school next year. Her peers would see that nothing really happened to her. That is the problem, Ronald."

Ignoring Andrea, Ronald addressed Mr. Pimpkins, "Because we as parents care enough to help make the situation better, now the board has decided to take it to the next level?"

"Mr. Grimes, we would really like to concentrate on the issue at hand. If you'd really like to help your daughter, it may be best to stay focused on where we are right now. This may not be as bad as you think."

"How the hell can you say yanking my daughter off to jail isn't bad? Have you ever had a kid tossed into jail, Mr. Pimpkins, sir?" Ronald asked, stepping closer to the red-faced man.

"No, sir, I have not. But I've seen plenty of good kids lose their way. And I've seen them pay the price for their indiscretions and learn a hard lesson. And I've seen many get back on track as a result."

"So you're saying…"

"So, I'm saying that Amber needs to know the true impact of her actions. And I hope that it helps her get past this stage."

"Well, I don't agree," Ronald added and stomped down the long hall leading to the courtroom.

Once inside the courtroom, Andrea and Charlotte took seats next to Ronald and Charity. Andrea was careful to place her sister between herself and the dynamic duo. She couldn't argue against Ronald involving his wife, but she didn't have to pretend to be buddies with her.

Andrea had done the courtroom scene plenty of times covering news stories. The setup was the same as it had always been; tables facing an elevated podium area for the judge. One table for the ones pressing charges against her baby, and another for Amber and the other two girls involved in the list.

Although Andrea knew most of Amber's friends, she had not heard the names Beth and Michelle until this incident. She wanted to assume that they were the bad seeds. The two troublemakers who had led her daughter down this slippery slope.

But then the three teens filed into the courtroom dressed in clothes they would have likely worn only to church when they were eight. Amber was not wearing the tasteful outfit they had spent several hours picking out.

"What's with those little-girl dresses?" Andrea asked Charlotte.

"Probably the attorney thought it would make them look more like innocent little girls. I don't think this is the time to make a fashion statement."

Andrea couldn't believe any of them were capable of the crime they were being charged with committing. After a quick glimpse of Beth and Michelle, Andrea's eyes were glued to Amber's. She could have cut the fear with a knife. It lurked around the girls like a foul odor.

No sooner than the three girls were seated, the judge started his statement.

"After reading over the preliminary psychological reports and the evidence obtained by the officers conducting the investigation, I have a better command of the nature of the threats and the young ladies who made them. And I feel that regardless of how troubled we all are about incidents like this, the punishment must fit the crime."

Andrea hadn't realized she wasn't breathing until Charlotte squeezed her hand. She took two quick puffs and went back to holding her breath wondering what punishment this man felt would fit her daughter's crime.

"It doesn't appear that these young ladies had any means of carrying out any of the crimes described in their note. Not that they couldn't obtain the things they needed, but we see no signs of any of them trying to do so."

Two more breaths.

"Unfortunately we have a few precedents for cases like this and there are usually several other factors present when these types of threats are made. This case does not show any of those factors so that leaves this court with the belief that the true nature of this crime is less threatening in reality than it presents itself on paper. My ruling is for an additional psychological visit for Beth Brown and Michelle Warren along with one hundred hours of community service."

He hadn't mentioned Amber. For the two seconds that he paused to give the other girls a stern look, Andrea felt queasy. Was Amber going to take the rap for the list?

"In the case of Amber Grimes, I order six months of psychological evaluation with a full report issued to this court as well as one hundred fifty hours of community service."

The judge asked if any of the girls had anything they wanted to say. Andrea's eyes drifted to the other two girls and then back to Amber. Would she say anything?

Of course she would, Andrea thought as Amber's hand flew up. The attorney nodded toward her and she stood, looking briefly around the room as if to make sure what she was doing was okay with everyone else.

"It was a dumb thing to do. The list, I mean." Amber's voice was low and cracked like a teenage boy in the throws of puberty. But she continued anyway, raising her head and voice. "I really am sorry for causing so much trouble at school and for my family. Thank you," she said and took her seat as if she was playing a game of musical chairs and the song had just ended.

The judge thanked her for her statement, and then added a few stern comments of his own about handling anger and the consequences of certain actions. In Andrea's opinion, the entire court proceeding was more of a stern lecture and as Principal Pimpkins had said, a slap on the wrist.

Andrea could not resume normal breathing quick enough. She squeezed Charlotte's hand to fight back the tears. They had dodged a bullet with this one. She knew that Amber could have gotten into a lot more trouble than she did even though she had never been serious about anything on the list.

As they exited the courtroom, Andrea threw her arms around Amber for an overdue embrace. Charlotte followed suit and then they made room for Ronald and Charity. Amber was just about to speak when Andrea noticed the camera crew from WVTR lurking behind them.

"This can't be happening," she murmured, and slumped against Charlotte.

Until that point Andrea had felt a wide range of emotions: fear, guilt, and then relief. She hadn't been ranting and raving like Ronald. But she knew that at some point in time she would feel the anger as the ugly truth of what had almost happened slap her in the face. The gloating stare of her colleague, Christy Tyler, stalking toward her was that slap. Christy had only been at WVTR for a few months and in that time managed to alienate most everyone in the newsroom. With the exception of the photographer she was rumored to be sleeping with. That same photographer was pointing his camera lens at Andrea, and then whirling around for crowd reaction.

Charlotte tugged Andrea's arm as they tried to duck around the eager reporter. But Andrea knew retreat would only make her look worse. Christy was in a position of power. A position Andrea had been in more times than she could number. But Christy wasn't just looking for a story, she was after blood. Her approach was brutal, unrelenting and dangerously close to harassment. But Andrea knew the power of editing and that none of Christy's tactics would make their way onto the newscast, only Andrea's own fumbled words. To speak or run away were her only options. Neither of them were appealing. Anger was rising to near boiling point in Andrea as Christy threw out her first question.

"According to police reports, your daughter is the ringleader of a group involved in a kill list at an area middle school. Is it true that you and your ex-husband tried to cover up this charge by moving your daughter to a ritzy private school outside the city?"

CHAPTER 18

"Shit, Andrea, I swear I did not send them," Nancy yelled as she ran toward Andrea at the TV station back door.

It was an admission Andrea was glad to hear, but she was no less pissed that she had to confront one of her own at the courthouse. Despite the fact that she had refused the interview, Christy had not let up with her barrage of questions.

"It's reported that your daughter actually wrote the list. Was your name on it? Or your ex-husband's? There are also claims that due to your status, news outlets are covering this up, with no regard for the public threat. Is there a cover-up?"

All Andrea had said was "no comment," and then kept her attention on getting the rest of her family out of the courthouse without attacking the reporter with an ax to grind. But the sick bastards hadn't given up even as she drove away. Again, they hounded her until Charlotte threw up her middle finger and let go of a string of curses. Fortunately the car window was rolled up. Her sister's words were not audible, but there was no mistaking the sentiment that accompanied the finger. And that scene would probably lead off the evening newscast.

"Andrea, say something," Nancy pleaded. "Whatever footage they have will not be in our newscast. I swear it will not."

"Hang on, Nancy," Ted said, stepping from his office door. "We have to say something about this. It is news."

"But, Ted, you know Christy. She goes for the jugular, and Andrea is one of our own."

"I'll look at what she puts together and make sure it's tastefully done," Ted added and then rushed off to grab his ringing phone.

"Why were they there and how did they find out?" Andrea wanted to know.

She had been so careful to keep everyone except Ted and Nancy out of her personal affairs.

"Anonymous phone call. Christy is a bitch, but a pretty well-connected one. Apparently photographers aren't the only ones she's willing to sleep with to get information. I tried to stop her, but you know eager reporters."

Andrea knew eager reporters all too well. She had been one. Hell, she still was one. But this time, the camera was in her face. Everything changed when it was her face blushing under the lights and scrutiny.

"What did the judge say?" Nancy asked.

"Community service and counseling."

Nancy brushed her hand across her brow.

"Tell me about it. I don't want to deal with it right now. Are you sure we have to mention it in the show?"

"Were there any other stations there?"

"I didn't see anyone."

"This means the others probably aren't aware. We'll mention it, just a reader, and no video."

"Sounds like a plan. My life is in and out of the toilet—anything exciting going on around here?"

"The cockroaches would know before we got wind of anything."

"Kid update," Andrea asked as she took a list of phone messages from Nancy's hand.

She wanted to talk about anything, even Nancy's wild bunch, to keep her mind off what had happened at the courthouse. She craved Nancy's humor to brighten her mood.

"Same crazy stuff, different day. What's there to tell? They are kids, there are four of them, and my life is chaos."

"Is that why you love this job so much? No chaos," Andrea joked.

She wanted to crack jokes and laugh. With the kind of day she'd had, she needed a stand-up comic to plant himself beside her desk for the rest of the afternoon.

"I was born for chaos, that's why I'm perfect for this job. And if anyone from the new company asks you about that, please put in a good word."

"You're still worried about that? No news is good news, right?"

"Yeah, right. I'm not you, Andrea. Beautiful, articulate, and multifunctional. You can fit most anywhere in this operation, even management."

Andrea threw up a hand of protest. "Not interested. And you really should drop the pity party. Nothing big has changed. Ted's still sitting at the desk as he has been for the past twenty-five years. And we're all still doing what we do."

"But what about Tom?"

The station general manager, Tom Brown, had been the only Claxton casualty so far. The word from Claxton was that Tom had been looking into a better opportunity and saw this as the perfect time to jump on that. Unless that opportunity was retirement and long days on the golf course, it appeared that the truth of the matter became that Tom was fired.

"He didn't seem to mind. And he was the top guy—even you said that was to be expected. Always happens. They have to get their own captain to steer the ship," Andrea explained.

"And the rest of the crew?"

"The rest of the crew is functioning as a well-oiled machine and they see no reason to shake things up. They especially don't want the viewers to notice any changes on air."

"Which makes your spot secure, missy," Nancy added as a slim dark-haired young lady cruised into the newsroom.

Every male head turned to watch her strut. And the strut was something to be seen. Perfect body and just the right sway to give you plenty of time to take in every inch.

"Who is she?" Nancy murmured.

"She doesn't look like an intern," Andrea said, talking to Nancy while her eyes were still glued on the woman.

"Go ask her. She's obviously waiting for Ted. He's on the phone, so you have a minute to be nosy."

"Not me, that's your job."

Before either of them could get the nerve to find out who the mystery woman was, Ted came out of his office and shook hands with her. He escorted her into his office and handed her a folder, said a few more words then brought her back out into the newsroom where he introduced her.

"Attention, everyone. Carla, turn that scanner down a little. Thank you."

Nancy stood as if not sure what to do with herself. She looked as though Ted was going to shove her out the back door and introduce this woman as her replacement right here in front of everyone. Andrea wanted to reach up and calm her but she never got the chance.

"This is Leslie Shore. She's from Claxton's Milwaukee station. She'll be here in Baltimore as part of some of the new things the company is doing to train personnel. She's a news anchor. Leslie, this is everyone, and that's your desk," he said, pointing to the desk beside Andrea's.

In two seconds Ted had scared the daylights out of Andrea. Her security was snatched from under her like a tattered and torn rug. The new woman was a news anchor, with a desk right beside hers, and she was already a Claxton girl. And she was white. Fit right into the claim that had been circulating that the company was not very minority friendly.

Andrea, who had missed two Claxton meetings so far because of family emergencies, couldn't help but wonder if they had booted her without trying to set up a third. She had called to schedule an appointment with the new owner, but none of them had been available to take her call. Probably busy hiring her replacement, she thought.

"Hey, Andrea, got Bruce on the phone. Doesn't sound good. Looks like the deal isn't going to go down this week after all. Want me to handle it?" Nancy asked.

Another hot story lead gone cold.

"Sure, I need to go for a smoke."

Nancy crinkled her brow and said, "But you don't smoke."

"Oh, yeah. Well, I just need to go," Andrea stammered and tried to get out of the room before Ted brought Anchor Barbie to her desk.

Andrea stood in front of the woman, trying to summon courage from all her years of climbing the ladder and breaking through glass ceiling after glass ceiling. But no courage came. In fact, she slipped further as Ted properly introduced the two of them.

"Leslie, this is the notorious Andrea Shaw you've heard so much about."

She has heard about me, Andrea said to herself.

"It's such a pleasure to meet you," Leslie said, extending a perfectly manicured, delicate hand.

A hand that had probably never picked up a video camera or helped a camera crew do anything on a remote shoot. That attitude wouldn't work in Baltimore. They were a family. No big I's and little U's, but then again that was before Claxton took over.

"Leslie, is this your first time in Baltimore?" Andrea asked.

"No, I have family here. Spent most of my summers here. I was so happy when they told me I'd be coming to Baltimore."

But no one had told Andrea that Leslie was coming to Baltimore. Then again, why would they? Bosses don't usually consult with the person they are firing about the person that will replace them.

"Ted, do you have a minute?" Andrea asked.

"Sure. Leslie, would you like to get settled at your desk? I'll be with you in a moment."

Inside Ted's office Andrea fought for the words, but didn't find them.

"What is this?"

"What is what?"

"That," she said, pointing toward the back of Leslie, now seated comfortably at her desk.

"I just told you."

"Point number one, you just told me…no warning that she was coming, nothing. And point number two, why has another female anchor been hired? I didn't realize we were one short."

"We aren't."

"This brings us back to question number one. What is this?"

"Honestly, Andrea, I wish I knew half the things that were going on around here. I'm really concerned."

He paused and looked around as if someone might be watching.

It was a TV newsroom, someone was always watching.

"Go on," she urged.

"They're keeping me out of the loop on so many things. I think they may be getting rid of me. Early retirement like Tom."

"What makes you say that?"

"Everything. I didn't know Leslie was coming until an hour ago. And I don't even know what she's supposed to be doing except trailing you."

"And that doesn't tell you anything? She's trailing me. Probably plans to gun me down in a dark alley and step over my cold dead body just in time to do the evening news, with a lead story about me and my daughter's kill list."

"Oh, Andrea, they would be crazy to get rid of you and go with her. I've never seen her work, but from first appearance she seems green."

Whether she was green or not didn't matter to Andrea. She was white, with flawless physical beauty. Her look screamed "replacement."

"What should I do?"

"I don't know. Let her trail you. You're an ace reporter. Pick her brain for information. And if I find out anything else, I'll let you know."

"They'd be crazy to get rid of you, too, Ted."

"No, they wouldn't. I should have retired long ago. I just love what I do. Hard to give it up. There are plenty of young guys out there with fresh ideas and driving vision that could do so much more with this team."

"You sound like you want to go."

"I'm just setting my heart toward the inevitable. Anyway, enough about me. How did it go with Amber?"

"Not bad. She'll be spending her summer working at a nursing home and getting some much-needed counseling. I'd appreciate some help with Christy."

"Did you give her anything?"

"I no-commented my way to my car, but then my sister flipped her the bird."

"Good for her. I'll look at what Christy has before it goes on air."

Ted flipped his wrist as if it was nothing. That's the way it had been for the two of them. She wondered how things would change if they did replace Ted. A new chief probably would have run a series of stories about her wayward daughter and done an exposé on school violence just to add insult to injury. She had lucked out with this one.

Andrea wasn't sure how to broach the next topic with Ted. She found it tough at times to talk to a white person about racism. Most of the ones she knew didn't seem to think it existed anymore.

"Ted, Claxton is known for not being very favorable toward minorities. You said so yourself."

"And, your point?"

"My point? I'm a double dose. Woman, African-American. What should I do?"

"Andrea, you've never let that stand in your way before. I didn't think things like that bothered you."

"Why would you think that? Of course it bothers me. My gender and race are things I can't change, yet they determine so much. I don't see how you could draw the conclusion that it wouldn't bother me."

"Because you always seem to know where you're going and you work hard until everyone around you figures it out. Nothing you do is based on you being a woman or being black. It's all based on ability, intelligence and heart."

"So you're telling me not to be concerned about the glass ceiling?"

"Why would you? Besides, when has a ceiling ever kept you down? One thing I know for sure, you can't break through it by focusing your attention on it. Focus past it, like you usually do."

It was wise counsel and had life been anything close to normal for Andrea, she would have taken it to heart and done it. Focus past the problems. Seemed like a reasonable plan. But with all the turmoil at home, most of the time she couldn't see straight, let alone focus on one thing.

CHAPTER 19

Since the day of Amber's first appearance, Andrea had only played phone tag with Charlotte. So many things had happened in the twenty-four hours that followed the judge's decision that Andrea had to meet with her sister face-to-face. Or side to side, as it were, on the cardio machines at the local gym.

"I swear, I don't know how I let you talk me into these things," Charlotte complained as she climbed onto the stair machine.

"A little sweat is not going to kill you. You should get your heart rate up doing something other than sex," Andrea barked back at her.

"I can't do much since we will need to be able to gossip—I mean chat about world issues."

"You've never chatted about world issues in your life. And bump that thing up a few more notches," Andrea said, referring to the treadmill Charlotte was walking on.

Getting her sister to meet her at the gym was a task, but Andrea had promised information about a new man and a date. There wasn't anything going on, yet. But Andrea hadn't let on to that when she had called Charlotte. She instead used the opportunity to lull her sister into a workout, and a little quality girl time.

Charlotte had only been walking for a minute and she was already huffing. Not because she was out of shape, but because when she wanted to gossip, she wanted to give it her undivided attention.

"There's a rule about having a heart attack and dying on one of these things. They don't like it. Bad for business," Andrea teased.

"Kiss my really old, better-shape-than-yours rear end! And then tell me what's going on in your life. Juicy stuff first."

"I think Amber is going to be better off after all this. Kind of like a blessing in disguise."

"Not juicy. Next."

"So insensitive of you. She's an impressionable teenager who's having some real problems, and you want to know about a date."

"You had a date with him? You didn't mention a date."

"Oh, and Ray won that competition, so we're going to Myrtle Beach in a couple of weeks. No excuses, he expects you to be there."

"Oh, the beach. Count me in."

"And…"

"And the damn date," Charlotte said, pushing the stop button on the treadmill.

Andrea knew her sister was not going to start back walking until she started talking. She didn't want her to leave and she really did want her opinion about Maxwell.

Charlotte had her quirky ways, but she was a good sounding board.

The one thing Andrea didn't have to worry about from her was getting some sideline answer. Charlotte always came straight out with it and left nothing to the imagination.

"No date, yet. We're going out this weekend. Just coffee, but that's fine since I don't know much about him. That way, if he's a jerk, then I won't feel bad for bailing out early. How long can coffee last anyway?"

"You dirty rotten liar."

Andrea had told Charlotte that Maxwell was a driver and that they had exchanged seductive glances through the rearview mirror. But Charlotte assumed Andrea was lying because what woman in her right mind only wants to have coffee with an extremely sexy man.

"Seriously, Charlotte, I don't handle my love life quite like you," Andrea explained, "and regardless of how sexy he is, I don't want to be in any kind of situation that I'm not comfortable with."

"And getting hot for him in the backseat of his car is enough for you?"

"We'll have coffee, and then if all goes well, I'll suggest something later that night."

"Like a nice roll in the hay?"

One of the ladies that had climbed on the machine on the other side of Charlotte overheard the comment. Andrea ignored the woman since she figured Charlotte would say at least three more embarrassing things before they left. No point in making eye contact with anyone yet.

"Maybe dancing, but I haven't been dancing in years. I'm not sure where to go anymore."

"Nowhere. Go back to his place. Or since Ronald has the kids, your place would be better. Keep it on your turf, so you retain control. And have yourself some much-needed fun."

Andrea had to glance at the woman this time. Charlotte had gotten louder as she resumed her walking and had to try to maintain conversation in a deep, breathy tone, which only bounced around the room and echoed into the ears of the other gym rats.

"I'll think of something. And the station…"

"I don't recall asking about the station," Charlotte interrupted.

"But you should care. A new company just bought us. Fired the general manager, and yesterday, some new anchorwoman just sauntered in. I have no idea what that's about," Andrea whispered.

Charlotte didn't bother to lean over to hear her. By this time, she had clocked another five minutes on the machine and staying on her feet was a major accomplishment. The conversation was officially over until they got showered, dressed and had a decent meal under their belts.

Later, at the deli, Charlotte's interrogation continued. "So you like Maxwell, right?"

"Are you preparing to spout off relationship advice?"

"I might. And you should be so lucky."

"What if I'd like to get into a little relationship advice myself? About you and Mother."

"Dear God. This food is good and you're going to ruin it talking about that woman."

"She was in town recently."

"Sorry I missed her. Now, about your new man…"

"No, ma'am. This first. She's going to be at Ray's concert. You should give her a call before so the two of you can chat."

"Chat? I haven't spoken to this woman in…years, and you expect us to chat? About what, Andrea? Oh, perhaps about the fact that she traipses around the world, near-naked, doing heaven knows what, with no regard for the fact that she has a family here in Baltimore."

Andrea glanced at Charlotte's ample cleavage spilling forward from her blouse. Her sister was tastefully dressed, but still very sexy. Then again, Charlotte could look sexy in sweats and a T-shirt. And so could her mother.

"Why are you staring at my breasts, Andrea?"

"Because I'm sitting here listening to the pot call the kettle black."

"She's old, Andrea. Dad would roll over in his grave if he saw the way your mother dresses. And God only knows what or who she's doing when she goes off on her excursions."

"She's gorgeous, and exciting. Almost as interesting as you."

"She's had work done. I'll bet money on it."

"You've seen her, haven't you?"

Charlotte didn't say anything right away. Andrea guessed she had revealed more than she had planned.

"I saw you two going into that coffee shop near your

place. She looks good for an old biddy, but her lifestyle is completely inappropriate for someone her age. She's almost seventy and she's a grandmother, for crying out loud. She should be here baking cookies for her grandchildren and doing church work."

"Baking cookies? Ray is about to graduate high school and Amber's done time. I think the cookie-baking days are officially behind us," Andrea said, letting herself feel the sting of talking about her daughter's trouble.

Charlotte didn't speak for a second as if reading Andrea's thoughts.

"Scary as hell, isn't it? Your babies aren't babies anymore."

"Tell me about it."

The two paused again as if the thoughts were too heavy to turn into words.

"See, this is why I never wanted children."

"You never wanted children because you're a selfish, egotistical nymphomaniac," Andrea said.

"Yeah, and there's that," Charlotte said and slapped Andrea a high five.

Andrea paused again before going to her next heavy topic. She had wanted to venture into these waters with Charlotte for years, but had never gotten up the nerve. Ever since she had met Juan, started openly dating such a young man and then married him, Andrea had wanted the inside scoop. No time like the present, she told herself, and then dived in.

"Charlotte, do you love Juan?"

"Do I love Juan's what?"

"Not his what. Do you love him, the man?"

"You're asking me this question because you can't make your brain accept that it's possible."

"That's not true."

"It is more than true. You cannot wrap your cerebral lobe around how a fifty-year-old woman and a thirty-year-old man could be in real love."

"Well, maybe you're right. So, are you?"

"What answer do you want Andrea?"

"The correct one. Or I wouldn't have asked."

"When Daddy died I got a huge inheritance, one that you may not know about."

"You didn't get any money. Daddy didn't have anything. I was there, remember."

"Not money. Inheritances can be something other than money. What I got was a clear picture of me. Who I really was and what I really wanted out of life. Worth much more than money."

"And who are you?"

"The woman you see in front of you. I'm unconventional, Andrea, and I'm okay with it. I like sexy men with loads of cash to buy all the things I want, and I like to feel like I'm wiser than most, so I may seem slightly arrogant, but I mean well."

"Yep, that about sums you up in a nutshell."

"The problem for you is that you're too concerned about what everyone else will think of what you like, or want to do with your life. I, on the other hand, really could care less."

"So you love Juan."

"So I love everything about my life, especially my

husband. And if I don't love something, I am honest with myself about it first and foremost. And then I do something to change it."

"Sounds extremely selfish to me."

"Of course it does. But then again you have different dynamics. You have kids, everyone on the East Coast knows you, and you care about that woman that birthed us. I don't have that baggage."

Charlotte inhaled the rest of her sandwich and slurped down her cola. High-calorie everything and not a bulge on her body to show for it.

"For your information, Andrea, I've never wanted your life—kids, and a man so old and bogged down with responsibilities and pressure that he needs a little blue pill just to make things happen in the bedroom."

"Juan will not be young forever. That little blue pill just might be in your future."

"And by the time he's old, I'll be dead. Dropped to the floor in a whirlwind of heated passion that slams my heart into overdrive until it just stops. And I'll have a big-ass smile on my face. Matter of fact, you can put that one on my headstone, if you'd like."

"You are ridiculous, Charlotte."

"Andrea, you want things, but you're afraid that if you get them, and they're not just right in everyone else's eyes, then life won't be perfect anymore."

"You said yourself that I have kids, others to think about."

"And you're a wonderful mother. A damn good anchor-woman and your body is still tight enough to turn a few heads. Even if they are old guys like Maxwell."

"He's your age."

"Yes, which is too damn old for someone your age," Charlotte whispered and then took the rest of Andrea's sandwich.

"Listen, kid. Figure out who you are and what you want and stop copping out and do your thing. And forget about Ronald and his half-your-age wife. You'll never be twenty-five again, and your life with him is over. He's moved on. When are you going to?"

Andrea couldn't speak. If she so much as opened her mouth, the tears would flow and she wouldn't give Charlotte the pleasure of knowing she'd hit a nerve.

"You and Ronald both wanted something you couldn't give each other. And now he's found someone who can give him what he wants."

"He wanted a doormat, that's what he wanted."

"And Charity is not a doormat. She's good at all that crap she does and that's okay. So you had to hire an interior decorator, and a housekeeper, and you eat out every day. And things are shaky at work and you're raising teenagers and running over a few bumps in the road."

Andrea was fighting the tears with all her might. A battle she wasn't sure she'd win if Charlotte continued.

"You're not perfect, Andrea. You can't be everything to everybody. You're divorced, you could lose your job, your son is leaving home in a few months for college and your daughter has a criminal record. So you're not some perfect cardboard cutout who spouts off the news every night."

Despite the crowd of people gathering in the deli,

Andrea let the tears flow. By the time Charlotte continued, Andrea was sobbing.

"You're a living, breathing woman who cares. Why the marriage didn't work, that crazy job of yours, is Amber okay, will Ray be able to accomplish all his dreams, and of all the crazy ideas, me chatting with that woman. You care, Andrea. And some days that's the best you can do."

The restaurant was full and Andrea noticed a few eyes lingering extra long on her. She could hear the questions floating around in their minds, "Isn't that the TV lady?" and "Why is she crying like that?"

But none of that stopped Charlotte, who was on a roll.

"In the overall scheme of things, I suppose caring is what matters most. With everything as screwed up as it is, it doesn't change who you are inside, little sister. You're not the hard-ass you pretend to be. You're all heart, Andrea."

Since Andrea couldn't control the sobs, Charlotte leaned her sister's head into her own breast and then gave her attention to the gawkers. "At least have the decency to look away. We're in the middle of some heavy shit here."

Andrea's tears turned to chokes of laughter at her sister's straightforwardness. But she kept her head down, leaning into her sister's chest, hoping to avoid the looks they had been getting from their display.

"Inside, you got everything you need, kiddo. Well, except some heat in the sheets, but I'm working on that."

"So, you think I should date Maxwell?" Andrea asked, regaining her composure. "I mean, I know nothing about him, and besides, how could I start a relationship with all this mess I have going on in my life?"

"I think you should date whoever floats your boat. And why not now. You don't have anyone better to do. It's obvious you like him. And there must be something sensual about him if he can get you hot by just driving a car and looking at you in the rearview. Imagine if he laid a hand on you."

"Gosh, sometimes I have to look twice to see which one of you I'm talking to... Is it Charlotte, or is it Chloe?"

"I try to help you and all you have to offer is insults. Be selfish for two seconds, Andrea. Get this man if you want him. And give me the damn number."

"Are you serious? Her number... You're going to call her?"

"Just give me the number and go get laid. And then we'll both have benefited from this conversation," Charlotte said as she grabbed Andrea's drink and polished off the rest of it, to wash down the rest of Andrea's sandwich.

CHAPTER 20

After Andrea left Charlotte, she stopped at the café near her apartment for a quick cup of coffee before heading to work. She took her place in line and spotted Maxwell as soon as he walked through the door.

"I was sure our coffee date was tomorrow," she said as he took his place in line behind her.

He smiled and scanned the menu as if running into her was no mistake.

"I swear I come to this café at least a couple of times a week and I have never run into you. You aren't by any chance following me, are you?" she asked, her tone flirty and full of innuendo.

He gave her another slow smile before responding, "I come to this café a few days a week, too. Must be the days you aren't here. I guess we just got our signals crossed, that's all. And you can't back out of our date tomorrow just because we're both here today."

Andrea gathered her coffee and sauntered toward a table at the back of the café, where she pretended she wasn't waiting for Maxwell to join her. She glanced in his direction a couple of times and caught him staring at her. She could feel the heat rising from under her jacket. She looked overhead at the ceiling fan that was twirling and wished for a cold burst to bring her body temperature back to normal. But that wouldn't be possible as long as he was anywhere around.

"May I join you, ma'am?"

She scooted her newspaper to the side and pretended to be surprised by him wanting to sit with her. Even though she would have been disappointed if he hadn't.

"How's work?" he asked as she noticed that he was a white mocha man.

He had gotten a "to go" cup and the letters *wm* were scribbled on the side. Since Andrea had enjoyed more than her fair share of white mochas she automatically knew what the letters meant. She did not, however, want to talk about work.

"Some things going on with the management types. Not sure what it means for the rest of us. And you? How are things in the world of…" She was lost for words.

"Driving people around for a living?"

She giggled at his description. She hated to giggle. She made a mental note to stop with the schoolgirl antics and just talk with him, one adult to another. But there was something about him that made her feel young and flirty and desired.

"Work isn't bad. I actually enjoy meeting people."

She had a hard time believing that he actually liked driving because it gave him an opportunity to meet people, since for the few times that she had ridden with him, he had never so much as uttered a word of conversation.

"But you don't talk when you drive, not like the cabbies, anyway."

"I didn't talk to you. I usually talk a pretty good deal especially if I find that I have something in common with the client."

"So it was just me? You didn't want to talk to me?"

"Not that at all. You had a strange effect on me. Still do," he admitted, and she felt a blush run across her face. She hoped he hadn't noticed the effect he had on her.

"I'm sure you know that in this city, newspeople are like celebrities. It can be kind of exciting and intimidating to have a celebrity in your backseat."

Oh, the times she had dreamed about him having her in his backseat.

"I deliver the news, that's all. Hardly what I call celebrity," she said as she flipped her newspaper over to see her face on the front cover.

"What the…?"

"Is everything okay?" Maxwell asked as the blood drained from Andrea's face.

There she was on the front cover of the newspaper with a caption about Baltimore's news leader on the opposite side of the camera. She scanned the first few lines of the story and felt the breath leave her body.

"Andrea, is everything okay? You look faint. Are you feeling well?"

"Oh God, not this, not now," she said, still not answering Maxwell's inquiry.

Before she could read further, or answer Maxwell, her cell phone chirped in her purse. She yanked it out to see the number on the screen. The station, Nancy's desk to be more specific.

"Yes," she said instead of the traditional hello.

"Have you seen it?"

"Two seconds ago. I usually read the paper as soon as I get out of bed in the morning, but I decided to work out, have coffee, and run over it at the café down from my apartment."

"Well, I just got out of a meeting. Daniel Tate from the Claxton Public Relations department is on his way over to meet with you. They need to decide what spin we plan to put on the story. And, oh, Ted got into real trouble for not running Christy's story yesterday."

"I'm on my way, Nancy. Keep your eyes and ears open for me, will you?" she asked, knowing that Nancy would do nothing else.

To Maxwell, she said, "I gotta run, trouble at work."

"Okay, but are you okay to drive? My car is right outside, I could take you."

She thought for a quick second. She would have to walk two blocks back to her apartment garage to get her own car. It might be quicker if he gave her a ride, but then how would she get home after the meeting?

As if reading her thoughts, he said "I'll get you to the station and keep my schedule clear this morning so I can come back and get you. Midday is not a busy time for us anyway, so it won't be a problem." He tossed his cup into the trash.

She followed him outside and slid into the backseat of his car.

"You don't have to ride back there."

She didn't want the onslaught of questions. She needed time to think. The station was only a few blocks away, so she only had the few minutes in his car to prepare herself for the Claxton spin mobile.

"This is fine," she said.

But the churning in her stomach and the ache in her head as she glanced back down at the newspaper let her know that nothing about this was fine.

CHAPTER 21

She had missed at least two opportunities to meet with Daniel Tate, Public Relations Director for Claxton, but there was no getting out of this confrontation. As soon as Andrea walked into the room, Mr. Tate began speaking. She was given little room to tell her side of the story or tell anything for that matter. Mr. Tate had the plan laid out and Andrea was plain and simple being told how she would handle the situation.

"We're slightly behind the eight ball on this because we didn't have a heads-up. It's always better to come forward first with news like this. Anything else looks like you're hiding something. In the future, if something like this happens you must let us know so that we can take the lead in handling it."

"This is my daughter, not just some issue that could make the station look bad," Andrea said, but as soon as the words were out of her mouth, she was certain that Mr. Tate did not appreciate her take on things.

"Ms. Shaw, I would expect that a woman in your journalistic position would realize that a hot-button issue like school violence is very much a public issue."

"Yes, sir, I am aware of the importance of the issue as a journalist, but I am also a parent in this particular situation."

Mr. Tate didn't bother to look at Andrea or acknowledge her words. "At any rate, we can bring this back around and keep things under control. Here's what I have in mind."

Mr. Tate went on to pull out a flip chart with detailed color diagrams that had Andrea confused since he couldn't have known about the newspaper article for more than a few hours.

"We're going to let Dave do the newscast solo tonight. We feel that it will be best if you're not there when this full story is told. Based on court records and information from the school board, I've already written the story."

So he writes news copy, too, Andrea thought. Why not just let him do the damn news?

"Dave will mention this once more on the late-evening news, again without you present and then by tomorrow it will be a thing of the past. We will have done our duty to present a fair and honest assessment of the situation."

Mr. Tate flipped his chart down and smiled at Andrea as if waiting for applause.

"So, what do I do with the rest of my day?" she asked.

"I'd steer clear of other media sources. And ask your family to do the same. They may target your husband, son, or even your sister since they were all mentioned in the newspaper article."

Andrea was disturbed at how much this stranger knew about her personal life. He knew the players that were closest to her. She hadn't thought about anyone going after her family to get questions answered, but she should have known that could be a problem. How many times had she chased down a source and come up empty, only to then fall back on a distant relative willing to spill the beans?

She couldn't think of anyone in her family crazy enough to talk to the media about this, but she would call them and put them on alert just in case.

"Is that all, Mr. Tate?"

Andrea suddenly wanted to put lots of space between herself and this man. She needed time to get herself together and process what she had been told. But she didn't want to just rush out when they were overdue to discuss her future at the station.

"That should cover everything, Ms. Shaw. As I said, in the future, please make us aware of problems like this first, not as an afterthought."

He sat in front of her with a syrupy smile that made her want to slap it off his face. She had the highest-rated show in the city, but somehow she knew that meant little to the Claxton Company. So far, she had not been treated like a high-ranking news personality. At the moment, she felt more like a scolded child.

"It was a judgment call to not go with the story," she said, her hand resting on the doorknob.

"A poor judgment call, Ms. Shaw. Ted allowed his friendship with you to cloud his news judgment. A crime was committed, there was sentencing and we cannot ignore something like that as a news outfit. Nothing personal."

That was the key to it all. There was nothing personal at all about Claxton and their dealings. Sure, Andrea could see the point of mentioning the charges and they had been wrong for not doing that, but at least Nancy and Ted had cared about her as a person and the fact that this was her life, her family that were falling to pieces.

Did covering the news have to be so impersonal? she asked herself as she exited the conference room, leaving Daniel Tate and his charts to themselves. As she walked down the long hallway toward the stairwell, her mind ventured near the dangerous territory of questioning her own tactics for news gathering. Had she, too, done news stories with no regard for the people left behind in the wake of her revelations?

CHAPTER 22

Ronald flopped down on one of the bright red leather sofas and tossed popcorn at Amber. The two of them were in for the night. Charity was having a Friday girls' night out with women from her church, while Ray was practicing with the band for the Myrtle Beach competition. It was the first time Ronald had been completely alone with Amber since before she was arrested.

"It's been a tough week. I'll bet you're looking forward to the summer," he said.

Amber nodded and grabbed a handful of popcorn. Ronald wanted her to open up to him. He felt that she might need to talk. But then again he wondered if he was the right person for her to talk to. He was just about ready to let it go when he noticed tears running down Amber's cheeks.

"What's up, kiddo?"

She sniffled and wiped her nose on her sleeve. Ronald looked around the room for a box of tissue. When he reached into the box, it was empty. He wanted to pitch a fit. It was one of his pet peeves. A bare trash can, waiting for whoever had taken out the trash to complete the job.

An empty toilet paper roll, left by the inconsiderate person who didn't think someone might come behind him and desperately need a few sheets. Ronald could feel his face getting hot as he tapped the empty tissue box into his hand.

"It's okay, Dad. I'm done."

"Amber, what was up with that list, baby?"

The words were out of Ronald's mouth before he could get them back. Amber's eyed bucked wide, her mouth dropped open. It was the kind of conversation they'd never had.

"I just get so mad sometimes. I just want to scream and hit something."

"What makes you this angry?"

She was crying again. Ronald toyed with the tissue box, but forced himself to focus on Amber.

"It's not just one thing. Everything is so different. I come here and there's you and Ms. Charity and your rules. And then at home, Mom has this big board in the kitchen that she calls the brain of the home. And at school, I had this one teacher who was like, 'parents get divorced every day, what's the big deal.'"

By the time Amber was done spouting off, her whole shirtsleeve was wet. Ronald hated looking at the mess. He wanted to tidy it. To make her take off the shirt and get some tissues and dry her face. But he just sat there and made himself look directly at her hurt.

"That's the teacher you put on the list?"

"I didn't want to hurt her. It's not even about her."

"Then why did you write those things down?"

"I thought it would make me feel better. Like a diary,

except not with stupid stuff about boys and stuff. I was just writing about how I really feel sometimes. Like I just want to hit something."

"But you know our family won't be back like it was even if you do everything you wrote on that list, right?"

"I was so scared when they put me in that place, Daddy. I couldn't sleep. I just cried all night."

Without thinking about the new eighty-dollar shirt he was wearing, Ronald grabbed her and before long he, too, was wet with her tears. He tried not to think about what was dripping from her nose. He laughed within himself at the fact that he wasn't grossed out and couldn't care less about the empty tissue box.

From the beginning, when Ray and Amber were born, Ronald had watched Andrea deal with the dirty diapers, runny noses, thrown-up meals and everything in between. And he had only come behind her to replace the trash bag, or refill the toilet paper roll. And that had its place, but as he held on to Amber and listened to her sniffle into the soft fibers of his shirt, he realized what he had missed out on. Touching them. He had never closed his eyes, looked beyond the mess, the imperfections…and touched his kids.

"Daddy, I messed up your shirt. And look, you spilled the popcorn."

Amber left the room to wash her face. Ronald looked around at the popcorn pieces littering the sofa and the floor. One side of his shirt was stuck to his upper body and shoulder, and felt cold under the breeze of the ceiling fan. Amber returned with a roll of toilet paper that he was certain she had swiped without putting one in its place.

All he could do was smile and munch on popcorn from between the sofa cushions, and think that in a crazy sort of way, something good had happened, and he didn't mind the mess so much.

CHAPTER 23

The last thing Andrea wanted to do was watch Dave deliver stoic news copy about her personal life, so she had called Maxwell and moved their date to Friday night. Despite all the personal ups and downs, she had been anticipating the date ever since he had called and she didn't want to put if off any longer. She hoped a drastic change in her plans would snap her out of the funk her life had fallen into.

There had been so many things going on at work and she hated being in the hot seat with a new company taking the reins. As much as she needed to concentrate on how to put herself back in good standing with Claxton, she had to admit she needed a break from all of it to relax and let her hair down. Hopefully, time with Maxwell would be just the thing she needed.

There was something about him that made her both excited and afraid. She was waiting for the really awful thing to pop out and say "Hey, here I am. I've done prison time," or "I'm on the run from a crazed baby mama." But so far, he was clean.

He was handsome, intelligent, and she felt more comfortable around him than she did around people that she'd known for years. She was sure something horrible would happen on the first date to wake her up from the bliss that she was slipping into concerning him.

Andrea had switched their harmless coffee date to dinner, and Maxwell seemed all too glad to oblige. Instead of meeting him at midday on Saturday, he had pulled up to her building at three minutes till seven on Friday night. Perfect timing, since she had just stepped out and started a conversation with the doorman.

As she slipped into the seat of the silver Toyota Camry, she noticed he was not wearing a suit. She hadn't expected him to, but couldn't help but wonder all day what kind of clothes he wore when he wasn't on duty.

She was nearly spellbound by the crew neck white terry sweater and natural-colored linen pants. Casual, but nothing short of high class. A brown pair of leather slides covered what appeared to be clean, well-groomed feet.

"Is Jamaican okay?" he asked as they sped through downtown toward the interstate.

Andrea hoped he hadn't been aware of her checking him out.

"I love Jamaican," she said, although it was what she and Ronald ate just about every Friday night since they first met.

Once they had gotten separated, one of the things she had looked forward to was Friday nights eating a different cultural cuisine.

"Great, so do I. Doesn't seem like there's much we don't have in common."

"I am not too crazy about my ex-husband. I think that would be something."

"You're right. I like him quite a lot actually."

Fear froze in her chest as she hadn't considered the idea of Maxwell knowing Ronald.

"Calm yourself, I am kidding. I don't know him, not personally, anyway. But everyone in the city knows a little about your family. I was joking about liking him because whatever he has done is making this possible. So hats off to the guy."

A portion of her crazy brain was still wondering if secretly he knew Ronald, and was just waiting to shock her with the knowledge of their close and longtime friendship. But she let it go and decided to enjoy the evening regardless, that is, until something slammed into the back of the car and nearly tossed her out the front windshield.

The seat belt snatched her back so hard, she was sure it had stripped her shirt off her body. She could hear tires squealing and glass breaking, but then all she felt was pain. All over her body.

"Are you okay?" she heard Maxwell ask from her side.

She was afraid to turn her head. It felt as if someone had tried to snap it off, and movement would complete the process.

"I think, I'm... I don't know."

Before she could gather her words to form a coherent sentence, there was a man standing at the passenger-side window staring at her. She stared back. She wasn't sure what he wanted her to do. She wondered if she was going into shock because she still hadn't done a thing that made sense.

She could roll down the window, she thought. But that would have required her to move a part of her body. She decided not to do anything.

"I think she's hurt," she heard Maxwell say as he reached across her and rolled down the window.

"We called 911. They're on the way. Sounds like I hear them now, but that doesn't mean they're coming this way. In this city, I'm sure there are plenty of these going on right now," the man said.

Andrea wondered why she hadn't yet moved. Oh God. She was paralyzed, she thought, and immediately started wiggling her fingers and toes.

"Do your hands hurt?" Maxwell asked.

He was leaning across her, staring down at her wiggling hands. He was close enough to kiss, had they been on the date they were supposed to be on, and not in the middle of the highway waiting for an ambulance.

"Yeah, a woman. She's pretty banged up. Don't think she can move," the man from the window said to someone else.

"I can move. I think I'm okay, just dazed from everything."

"But don't move. You never can tell," Maxwell said.

"But you can move and I'm sitting right beside you. Tell them I'm okay."

Before Maxwell could stop the emergency workers, they were yanking on his door. They couldn't budge it, and before Maxwell could hit the button to unlock it, they yanked it open anyway, breaking the lock.

"Dammit," she heard him say, trying to motion

toward the emergency workers who had their eyes locked on Andrea.

With the door open, several hands reached in and started poking and prodding at her. One of the men asked if she was okay, the other if anything was hurt. She said yes, but she was not sure to which. That was enough to signal someone else to bring the board.

Yes, a flat board that they commenced to strapping her body to, securing her head in the event of a spinal cord injury. The sound of it all made her very concerned even though she knew she was fine.

"I think she's okay, just shaken up," Maxwell said as they were rolling her toward the flashing lights.

They stopped. The men looked at each other, then at Maxwell, then back at each other again.

"You don't want us to take her in?" one of them asked.

"I don't know. She was wiggling her hands in the car and said she was okay."

"So, you don't think she needs transport?"

"I don't know, you're the emergency workers. How should I know?" Maxwell added.

"Sir, the car is pretty banged up. She was in restraint, but there could still be some injury."

"What do you recommend?" she heard Maxwell ask.

She wanted to yell for someone to ask her what she thought about all this, but they were too involved with what they were doing to check with the potential patient.

"I'd say get her checked out. If she's okay, then at least you'll know."

"Then let's go," Maxwell yelled, just as a very concerned first date would do when involved in a car accident en route to a Jamaican restaurant.

At the hospital, Andrea was poked and prodded some more. Finally someone talked to her and came up with a quick assessment that she was shaken up and very sore, but other than that, she would definitely live.

They gave her a prescription for some strong pain medication and suggested she take a day or two to recuperate and if she had any other symptoms, to call her regular doctor.

With that they were released and she and Maxwell rode back to her apartment in a rental car he had secured while doctors and nurses were coming to the conclusion that she was okay and they could attend to the gunshot victim behind the partition next to her. Somehow her celebrity status had gotten their attention over the guy bleeding to death just inches from her bed.

"It's not Jamaican, but it's food," Maxwell said as he jumped back into the rental car with take-out pizza.

"It smells great. Just get me home in one piece so I can have a slice."

"Please tell me I haven't blown it. I mean of all things, a trip to the emergency room has to rank up there on the list of bad first dates."

"This just means you have to take me out again. We'll scratch this one and try later, when my body has had time to heal."

He nodded to that and then drove her home, never going faster than thirty-five miles an hour at any given time. The pizza was cold when they got there. But somehow it didn't matter.

When Maxwell was gone and Andrea had popped a pill, she called Charlotte for a date report. After giving her the play-by-play of the accident, all Charlotte could say was, "You could have saved yourself the trouble if you just slept with him, but you never listen to me. You'll learn."

CHAPTER 24

After his date with Andrea had gone so badly, Maxwell was excited when Wayne suggested the two of them do something with Tim. Although Maxwell had talked to Tim almost every day since their baseball outing, they had not gone out and done any kind of activity.

Wayne had suggested getting something to eat, bowling and then perhaps a late-night movie. Something with lots of guns and a few fight scenes. They would have normally just gotten a few beers and talked about a bunch of nothing, but for a teenager that was not only inappropriate but probably extremely boring, as well.

Maxwell had taken off early to pick Tim up before rushing to gather Wayne. He watched as Tim took note of the care involved in getting Wayne in and out of the car and into his wheelchair. The moving around had become second nature to Maxwell since Wayne's accident. For Tim it was all new to see that his uncle, who had been so strong and vibrant, needed to be carried almost like a child.

Wayne had had the accident a year before Maxwell's divorce, but just like his relationship with his father, Tim had no contact with his uncle during the last five years, either. A few times Maxwell caught his son staring at his uncle's legs and then when he realized Maxwell was watching, he ducked his head away as if in shame. Maxwell wanted to ask his son what he was thinking, but decided to leave well enough alone.

Dinner had gone normally, and then it was off to bowling. When Wayne had told Tim that they were going bowling, Maxwell noticed the shocked look on his son's face. He hoped he hadn't suggested another sport that his son hated.

"You do like bowling, Tim? We used to go when you were younger," Maxwell said more as a question than a statement.

Tim stuttered as he spoke. "Sure, I like it, all right. But if you guys want to do something else, that's cool with me."

Maxwell had seen Tim's eyes divert to Wayne while he was talking. Wayne didn't give Maxwell time to answer Tim's concern.

"Listen, nephew, don't worry about me. I can do a lot more than sit in this chair and tell your father what to do all day."

"You wouldn't think you could do anything *but* that," Maxwell said in jest.

Before the accident, Wayne had been a shorter, stockier version of Maxwell. In the chair, his height wasn't as apparent anymore, but his buff upper body was enough to draw a second glance. His arms and chest muscles doubled the size of those in his legs that were no longer of use to him.

"Bowling is one of the things I do quite well since the accident. I'd be glad to whip your butt in a game or two," Wayne said, rolling toward Tim to signal the challenge.

Tim didn't back away or seem uncomfortable anymore, even though the man challenging him dwarfed him in size. Instead he appeared to like the dare of his uncle's words. And just like that, Wayne had done it again. He had made his handicap a nonissue.

Tim leaned over the wheelchair coming face-to-face with his uncle and said, "Then it looks like we're going bowling. And I'll have you know, Uncle Wayne, I'm not that little boy you used to help hold the ball. I do pretty well on my own."

Maxwell couldn't add a word. He loved spending the time with his son and including Wayne. Although Wayne had sounded like the all-around kind of guy, Maxwell knew that his brother hadn't gotten out nearly as much as he had before the accident. He could see that Wayne was going overboard to have fun with his nephew, and Maxwell hoped that this was not only good for his son, but his brother, as well. The more he thought about it, he knew that this outing was good for all three of them.

Tim ended up winning the bowling match but not without plenty of trash talk from both Maxwell and Wayne. Tim had been right. He was no longer that little boy who needed help. If Maxwell had any doubts about that fact, they had been erased by watching his son's expert handling of the bowling ball.

They decided to skip going out to a movie in exchange for renting one to watch back at Wayne's house. The three of them gathered their snacks, drinks and kicked back for the end of their action-packed guys' night out. Before the movie got going, Tim started with the questions.

"Uncle Wayne, can you have sex?"

Maxwell was taken aback by his son's forwardness.

"Tim, that's a little personal," Maxwell said, but was cut off by Wayne rolling toward his nephew, ignoring Maxwell's attempt to defuse the situation.

"I'm sorry, I didn't mean to say anything wrong."

"You're okay, kid. You're sixteen, what else could you possibly have on your brain except sex," Wayne joked.

Maxwell forced himself to laugh, but there was nothing funny about any part of this conversation. Tim having sex or Wayne not being able to.

"Little man, as you'll probably learn someday, there are all kinds of ways to please a woman."

"Okay, Wayne, that's enough," Maxwell interrupted.

"I know all about sex, Dad. You keep acting like I'm still ten. I was just wondering how much he can do with his legs."

"Nothing except use my arms to move them from one place to another," Wayne said and demonstrated by lifting his right leg and then lowering it back onto the chair. "There's nothing below the waist, kid. But there's plenty above. I'm all heart. And that's really what women want, anyway," Wayne added with a mischievous grin.

Maxwell also knew that Wayne had not been in a serious relationship with the opposite sex since the accident. But he had never had the courage to ask about it.

"So, your girlfriends are okay with just doing other stuff?" Tim asked, and Maxwell felt himself wince.

"There's no one serious right now, but I can guarantee one thing, any woman would be blessed to get a piece of this," Wayne said, lifting both arms and flexing his raw upper-body strength.

Maxwell wondered if Wayne really believed his own words. He knew that any woman would be blessed to be with his brother because Wayne was, as he had said, all heart.

"Speaking of women, you know your old man is dating the TV lady?"

Tim's head spun around to Maxwell. "For real? The hot one here in Baltimore?"

"The very same one," Wayne said, not giving Maxwell room to speak.

"That's cool, Dad. She is fine, you know, for an older lady."

"We've been out once. I wouldn't say that's dating, but we'll see."

"And they were in a car wreck during the date," Wayne joked.

"Oh, man, that's not so good, Dad. I hope she wasn't hurt."

"Nothing hurt but my ride, and my pride," Maxwell added, then let the two have their fun teasing him about his dating disaster.

Just as the movie previews started playing, Tim opened another can of worms that Maxwell wasn't ready for.

"Since you're dating the TV lady, I guess that means you and Mom won't be getting back together?"

Wayne took the cue and made up some lie about needing

something from the kitchen. As he rolled out of the room, so did every intelligent thought in Maxwell's brain.

"I mean, she's not dating anyone, and I'm sure she hasn't since you left. I was just thinking that maybe you two would talk."

"Listen, Tim, you remember how much the situation hurt you?"

Tim nodded and stared down at his shoe as Maxwell explained what he knew his son already knew, but needed to hear his father say.

"I hurt your mother, too, and sometimes it's just too hard to bounce back from something like that. She lost faith and trust in me. A marriage is nothing without those things."

"But I forgave you. Maybe she could, too. The accident was five years ago. Maybe she isn't so disappointed anymore."

Maxwell wasn't comfortable talking with his son about such adult issues, but then he remembered his run-in with Ray Grimes. He had sung the praises of parental intention to Ray, but did he possess those same qualities with his own son?

"Tim, things were not so great between your mother and I before the accident. In fact, she had almost left a couple of times. And I talked her out of it and we patched things up and moved on but it was never really better. And then the accident happened, and it was like the final draw. We didn't break up just because of the accident, but because of that and a bunch of other things."

"It's fine, really. I wasn't trying to make you uncomfortable. I was just wondering," Tim said, still looking down at his shoe. And then he raised his head as if a thought had just grabbed him.

"I like hanging with you and Uncle Wayne. It's cool just us guys."

"I'm glad you like it, son. I'm having a good time, too, and other than the sex talk, I think Uncle Wayne likes being with us."

"But I'm going to stay with Mom."

Maxwell had never thought of it any other way. But obviously, it had crossed Tim's mind. Maxwell would never come between his son and his mother.

"You don't have to leave your mother, son. I don't expect that."

"You don't?"

"No, what gave you that impression?"

"Some guys were talking at school and they said that when their folks split, their dad and mom fought all the time about who they would live with. I need to stay with Mom. I do stuff around the house for her. And I need to look out for her."

"And you should. I would never put you in that kind of position, son. You should be with your mother if that's what you want, but that doesn't mean you can't still hang out with Wayne and I whenever you like."

"Like I don't have anything else to do on the weekend than be with you two knuckleheads," Wayne said as he rolled back into the room.

"And you have done worse if memory serves me correctly. What was that girl's name. You remember the one with the ugly feet?"

"And the ugly face. But that girl could cook," Wayne said and slapped his brother five.

One bad date story turned into another until the guys were too tired to watch the movie. Maxwell finally turned the TV to the late news, and as Wayne and Tim dozed in and out of the broadcast, Maxwell wondered what Andrea was doing. He had wished their first date would have gone better, but fate would not have it be so. His comfort rested in the fact that they had agreed to see each other again.

One minute he wanted things to move faster with her, the next he was glad for some time to work on his relationship with his son. Perhaps fate was right in this case. Had his date with Andrea gone the way he had planned, he probably would have been with her tonight instead of hanging with the two guys that needed him most right now. He had to trust that things always have a way of working out for the best.

CHAPTER 25

Ronald and Charity had put their vacation plans off until Amber finished her community service and first round of counseling. The counseling part was the portion of her sentence that the judge insisted on.

After a couple of sessions, Ronald and Andrea were called in to talk with the counselor. So, instead of dropping Amber off for an hour at the office, it was the parents who were sitting in the waiting area in hopes that Dr. Anderson hadn't uncovered anything too troubling that they would not be able to handle.

A receptionist pointed the way as soon as the good doctor was ready to see them. The thought that their family was in counseling didn't weigh too heavily on Andrea's mind, but it did trouble her enough to keep her from telling anyone what was going on.

"Have a seat. It's a pleasure meeting both of you," the counselor said, not bothering to get up from behind her desk.

Andrea thought that was rude for starters. Since she saw no need to greet them properly, Andrea didn't see the need to rush over and shake hands with her. Ronald, however, rushed right over like the typical teacher's pet. He was trying to get in good with her already. Get her on his side.

"Sorry for keeping my seat, but for some reason my walker is in the corner across the room," she said, pointing to the walker.

Ronald promptly grabbed the contraption and placed it beside her desk.

"Might as well keep it close. Never know when you'll need it."

"Thank you. That is so kind of you."

Andrea simply took a seat, too embarrassed at this point to do anything else.

"One of the reasons I called the two of you here today is to commend you on your effort to help Amber sort through her issues. You may be surprised how many parents cannot, or choose not, to take these vital steps in assessing their child's behavior and then doing what's necessary to see the desired result."

In a nutshell, Andrea thought, she was kissing up to them and giving compliments because she was about to lower the boom.

"However, there are a couple of things that have come to my attention while talking with Amber and I'd like to discuss those things with you."

Just as Andrea had suspected, the counselor's assessment...you're great parents, but then again, you're not.

"Amber mentioned an older brother, Ray."

"Yes, Ray is our sixteen-year-old," Ronald stepped in to clarify.

"And has he shown any signs similar to Amber's?"

"No, Ray has been perfect," Andrea added since she would know Ray's behavior better than his father.

"Perfect?"

"Well, not perfect, but you know what I mean," Andrea stumbled.

"Please explain."

"He's been great at school, no discipline problems. Grades have gone up, and he plays the saxophone, even that's improved. He's going to Myrtle Beach next week for a competition."

"You're right. It sounds like he's adjusted quite well to the divorce."

"The divorce? You think that is the cause of Amber's problems?" Ronald asked.

Until now, he had been sizing up the doctor. He had come in playing his Good Samaritan role and she didn't seem moved by it. Appreciative, but it hadn't appeared to gain him any points over Andrea.

"According to her records, Amber was an honor student, with no discipline problems, until about six months ago."

"That's correct. It started with small things, and then just got worse, regardless of how much we'd talk to her," Ronald went on, he being the expert on their daughter.

"I'm not going to insult your intelligence. I realize both of you are professional people, so I'll just cut to the chase."

At one hundred fifty dollars an hour, Andrea appreciated that line of thinking. She could sue someone at a better rate than that.

"I think that both Amber and your son, Ray, are showing some signs of adjustment problems stemming from the change in family life."

"But Andrea just said that Ray's behavior has been darn near perfect."

"Precisely," she said, tipping her glasses down on her nose, glaring at Ronald.

"So good behavior is a problem, too," Andrea said more sarcastically than she had planned.

"No, but the changes either good or bad are a sign that something is going on. In my professional opinion, your daughter's problems are easy to point out and even treat because when a child misbehaves, we know what to do."

"But in Ray's case?"

"In Ray's case, his behavior is more subtle, but just as dangerous. I haven't talked with him, but taking an educated guess, I would say that he may be overcompensating to gain approval from one or both of you."

"I've read that children often blame themselves for their parents' divorce, but Ray is old enough to know he's had nothing to do with what's going on between Andrea and me."

"You may be right, Mr. Grimes. However, he may be acting in protective mode. He's seen the downside of what the separation and divorce did to you both, and he wants to do anything to help it hurt less. He's trying to put a Band-Aid of good behavior on his family situation."

"I haven't witnessed anything like that," Ronald said, laughing at the idea of Ray doing anything that complex.

"Well, I have," Andrea inserted.

Both of them looked at Andrea.

"Explain, Ms. Shaw."

"He's always doing things for me. As soon as you moved out, Ronald, Ray started doing things. Things he should have been doing all along, but hadn't. The trash. Pumping gas for me. And two nights ago, he rubbed my feet. The second time he's done that."

"Damn, I need to switch kids with you."

They all laughed. The humor lightened the mood, but only for a second. Andrea couldn't remember the last time she had laughed in the presence of Ronald. She had laughed at him and behind his back plenty, but not with him.

"So, he's in mommy-protective mode. He sees your pain, struggle, apprehension. And he wants to do anything he can to make it better. So, he goes overboard to do the things that will please you."

"And the problem with that is?"

"The problem is that he will never be able to heal the issue, because it is not his problem to heal."

The last thing Andrea wanted to do was get into a conversation about anything she was dealing with while Ronald was sitting right there. True enough, being a single parent was tough. The decisions were always so much larger than they used to be. And dating, oh God, she wouldn't dare go near that.

"Ms. Shaw, do you date regularly, or are you seeing someone seriously?"

She went there anyway.

"No, not really. Work keeps me on my toes, not much time," Andrea lied.

"And you, Mr. Grimes?"

"No, I don't date...well not anymore. I'm remarried."

"I see. So, your son perceives you as being okay since you have someone, but he sees a void with you, Ms. Shaw, and he's trying to fill it with good deeds."

"What should we do?" Ronald wanted to know.

Andrea just wanted them to get away from the discussion of her void.

"The judge ordered Amber to meet with me for the duration of the summer. That is all that is mandated. However, I would suggest additional sessions for Amber, not weekly, but at least monthly. And something for your son, as well. And a few family sessions wouldn't hurt."

"But that's the problem, Ms. Anderson, we're not a family," Ronald threw at her, his tone bitter and in direct contrast to the sweet demeanor he had come into the office with.

"Mr. Grimes, I beg to differ. You are a family. Your family dynamic has changed. You no longer live in the same house, you have relationships with other people, and even the possibility of having more children...which brings in an additional dynamic. You are very much a family, you just need to come up with a new system that works for the type of family that you are now. You could take some cues from the type of family you used to be."

With that statement both Andrea and Ronald had tuned her out. Their nice family had not been so in years and neither of them could remember a time when things worked between them.

So the counseling session had given them two things: less hope that they could make things better, and the knowledge that Ray was probably in just as much trouble as Amber. And they had no idea what his problem might be.

CHAPTER 26

It was almost a month since the Claxton folks took over, and the last thing Andrea expected that Monday morning when she got to work was change. But it nearly hit her in the face as soon as she pulled the back door to the newsroom open. She yelled as she came face-to-face with the large square object. And by the time she got herself together, she realized she had knocked a box out of Ted's hand. Their eyes met and words were not necessary. The nature of the box was clear, his emotion crystal.

"No, tell me they didn't."

"Sorry, kiddo. They made me an offer I couldn't refuse."

"Did they?"

"Yeah, get out, the sooner the better."

"Oh, Ted, I'm so sorry. Let me help with that."

She slid the box from his hand. He juggled his briefcase and the two of them went back out the door.

En route to his car they got distant glances from others. No one would make direct eye contact. No point in getting caught in awkward conversation where saying you're sorry seems so inadequate.

"Retirement, or are you gonna try to find another shop?"

"Another shop? Fifty-nine years old. I've had a good run. Trained the likes of you and a few others that aren't as grateful. I have no reason to hold my head down."

"That's the right attitude."

Andrea wanted to ask about anyone else getting the boot, but she didn't want him to think she was just concerned about herself. She slid the box into his backseat and waited while he opened the front door to leave.

"So this is the last of it?"

"Amazing how it works. You come with nothing, and you go with pretty much that same nothing."

"Oh, you have so much more than nothing."

"I'm just being a spoilsport. I slip back and forth from being relieved about this to being pissed off. At least now I don't have to keep looking over my shoulder wondering if I'm doing a good enough job."

She knew the feeling. That's exactly what her life had been reduced to. Survival each day, trying to second-guess what the powers-that-be were going to do next. When Ted was officially out of the loop, that job had become more difficult, and now with him gone for good, it would be damn near impossible.

"Margaret wants to travel."

"Let me guess. First stop, Michigan, for some serious grandkid time."

"You got it. She's probably already made the flight arrangements. Listen, Andrea, don't let this thing get to you. You're one hell of a journalist. And I hope at least one person at Claxton is smart enough to see that."

It sounded as though Ted knew more than he was letting on. Were they really going to replace her with Leslie? Andrea had noticed that she was pretty good. She had seen her doing some on-set sessions. Young and eager. Perfect situation for a new management group to grow with.

When Andrea had gotten the anchor gig, it was because someone older had been put out to pasture. She had to assume it was her time now.

"You know me. Fight till the end. Just hope I got the steam to finish it out."

"You've got everything you need. And I don't just mean here at work, but with those kids, too."

"What do you know of that? I've been tight-lipped. Even when those jerks tried to plaster my face all over the news. It's not that I didn't want you to know what was going on, but there have just been so many uncertainties here, I didn't want to worry you with my personal stuff."

"I don't know the whole story and I don't need to. I know you're a darn good mother. You love those kids and will move mountains on their behalf. Trust me, you have everything you need to make the right choices."

"You may be right, but I also have an ex to deal with. He doesn't always make things easy."

"Just remember, they are his kids, too. And in the end, when it comes to them, both of you probably want the same thing. You're just coming from different angles."

Andrea grabbed him and hugged him. Just as she had so many times over the years. When she had gotten promoted from reporter to anchor. When she had won the Peabody. When he had lost his oldest son to cancer. The hug felt like a combination of all the years. The good, bad, and every feeling in between.

"It's been good."

"Keep in touch, Andrea. Love ya, kid."

Her emotions got the best of her. So many things in her life were either kick-starting or coming to an abrupt end. Too much drama and not enough in-between stuff. High-stress issues were all around her as she watched Ted drive off and she truly prayed that she would have the strength to ride the waves to calmer waters.

CHAPTER 27

Ted's retirement had put quite a damper on Andrea's mood. Nancy suggested going out and getting drunk after the late news, but somehow Andrea didn't want to avoid the emotion altogether. She just wanted to go home alone and sulk.

Amber was of course at Ronald's, and Ray had mentioned that he might be out late at band rehearsal and then grabbing a bite with the guys. The phone had started ringing as soon as she got home, but she didn't recognize the number on caller ID and chose to ignore it and sulk about her miserable life and uncertain future.

She had slipped into a wool nightgown despite the fact that it was July. It was clean, and seemed to echo her mood. Heavy and dark. She couldn't find the ratty bunny slippers that she usually wore with it, so she tossed on a thick pair of Ray's socks. When the doorbell rang, she yanked it open expecting a teenage boy delivering the pizza she had ordered.

"Well aren't we just the sexiest thing happening," Maxwell said before she could slam the door in his face.

She tried anyway.

"Oh, no, you don't. I've seen you now."

"You should have called. Do you have any idea what time it is?"

"I do and I did. The phone rang and rang."

"Oh, that was you."

"It was indeed. I decided to come anyway just in case you were still in pain or perhaps just avoiding civilization."

She was in pain and avoiding civilization, but she didn't want to get into it with him. They had only been out once and she didn't want to seem as if she was always sulking about bad news.

"I'm waiting for pizza."

"Any idea how I might be able to get you out of that getup?" he asked as he followed her into the living room.

Andrea blushed at the notion. A glimpse of Chloe and her all-men-want-sex speech slid across her mind.

Maxwell laughed at Andrea's strained expression. "I'm not sure we're on the same page. I was talking about a decent dinner. There are quite a few places that are open late. Something other than pizza, and perhaps dressing for the occasion, not that I don't love that outfit."

"It's late, Maxwell, and I'm not really in the mood. Bad day. My news director got canned."

"Ooo, sorry. Were you close?" he asked as he rubbed his hand gently over her shoulder.

The spark she felt from it made her want to go on pouting just so he would keep touching her like that.

"He was the one who gave me my first shot at big-time," she said as she pretended his touch was not changing her mood.

"Then you definitely don't need to be alone. Okay, we won't go out. We'll stay here and do pizza, but you have to put on something besides my grandmother's nightgown."

Andrea couldn't help but laugh as she excused herself from the room and slipped into her bedroom to change. She tried to be casual, all the while fighting the schoolgirl butterflies that were fluttering in her belly. Completely out of the blue and spontaneous, he had just stopped by. Although she had thought she wanted to be alone, she just adored the idea of him sitting in her living room waiting for her.

Once Andrea was back in the living room, sitting beside him waiting for pizza, the apprehension returned.

"Is everything okay?" he asked.

"There are just so many things going on. Are you really sure you want to get involved in this madness?"

Maxwell slumped back on the couch and stared at the ceiling before speaking. "Honestly, some days I'm not sure what I want. But tonight I wanted to see you. And I know it's late, but I still had to see you, so here I am."

Andrea slumped on the couch, as well, only her eyes were glued to him. She wanted to gauge his reactions to her questions. She wanted a relationship, but first and foremost she wanted honesty.

"Another thing, you know all my issues, well most of them. Too many of them, honestly. What about you? I know so little about you."

Maxwell squirmed in his seat and sat up straight. He searched for the words to start the speech he had rehearsed since their disastrous dinner date. He knew he would have to tell her, but he had wanted more time to win her over. To show her that he really was a good guy. But the day of reckoning was upon him.

He opened his mouth at the exact moment that Andrea's front door opened. Maxwell had thought he felt sick about letting Andrea into his past, but the look on Ray Grimes's face brought on an all-new feeling of dread.

CHAPTER 28

Shit, shit, shit, Ray screamed inside. He had no idea why the man he had met on the subway was sitting on the couch all cuddly with his mom. It was almost midnight and he had rushed home from the rehearsal so she wouldn't worry. And of all things, he had to walk in on her with a man. And not just any man. The only adult who knew his situation.

"Ray, I thought you were going out to eat after practice," Andrea said to Ray, who was trying to pull his eyes from Maxwell to answer his mother.

"We finished up early and when I talked to Amber, she told me that Mr. Baxter lost his job, so I thought you might want some company."

Ray still couldn't keep his eyes off the man. His mother didn't seem upset with him, so obviously she didn't know about the pregnancy. So why was he here? Ray asked himself as he shifted from one foot to the other.

"Your father called and said you left some of your music at his house. I hope it's not anything you need for the competition."

Ray hated the fact that his mom was still just talking

and not telling him what that man was doing in their house. Were they friends? Did he know who Ray was when they met on the subway?

"I'm heading to Dad's now. I know it's late, but I need that music, and I just wanted to stop by and check on you," Ray mumbled.

Andrea stood and moved toward the door where Ray was still dumbfounded.

"Ray, I'd like for you to meet Maxwell Leonard. Do you two know each other?" Andrea added, looking back at Maxwell.

Ray assumed she had gotten suspicious because as much as he had tried, he couldn't keep his eyes off the man. Even when he had been talking to his mother, his eyes had drifted back to him.

"No, but it is my pleasure to meet you, young man," Maxwell said, moving quickly toward the doorway where Ray was standing.

The two shook hands and looked at Andrea as if wondering what to do next.

"Ray, if you're going to your father's you should get on over there. I don't want you out too late on a school night. And you know how I feel about you being on the subway."

The mere mention of the word *subway* had both Ray and Maxwell squirming again.

"Andrea, could I trouble you for a glass of water?" Maxwell asked.

Andrea took her attention off trying to get rid of her son, and gave Maxwell a confused look. Ray knew that his mother was smart and could see that Maxwell was trying to get rid of her.

"Sure, just a minute. Be on your way, son," she added, giving Ray a kiss on the cheek.

Ray reached for the door as his mother left the room. When he heard the clinking of glasses in the kitchen, he stepped away from the door and closer to Maxwell. His voice was a low grumble as he spoke. "You didn't say you knew my mother."

Maxwell whispered back, "I didn't realize who you were at first. Then when you told me your name, I put two and two together, but it was too late."

"You could have said, 'hey man, I'm making moves on your mom, but don't freak, I'm not going to tell her you got some girl pregnant.'"

"Well, I'm not going to tell her. It's not my place. But it's obvious you haven't told her."

"And it's obvious that that's my business," Ray's voice was getting louder and he really wanted to get out before his mother returned. He also wanted to make sure that Maxwell wasn't going to ruin everything.

"You're right, and I have no intention of getting into it. But I do think you should tell her. It would be much better coming from you."

Ray stepped closer to Maxwell, almost in his face and said, "Listen, you just worry about yourself. I got my situation worked out."

Maxwell stepped back and glanced toward the kitchen to make sure Andrea was not eavesdropping.

"That little pamphlet, huh. I suppose you've come to a conclusion?" Maxwell asked.

"Again, not your business, man."

"I see you two are getting acquainted. I'm sorry I didn't tell you about Maxwell, Ray. We've only been out once. And that ended up in the emergency room."

Ray and Maxwell stepped away from each other. Andrea approached, laughing about the emergency room incident. Maxwell took the glass of water from her hand. It had been a ploy to get her out of the room. But now, he really did need the water to help ease his nerves.

"I'm outta here," Ray announced, then spun on his heels and shot out the door.

When he was gone, Andrea turned to Maxwell and said, "Teenagers. Please tell me your son does not give you that kind of grief."

Maxwell drained the glass before speaking.

"Not really. We're not real close."

"Oh, yeah?" she asked, moving back to the sofa.

"But we're working on it," Maxwell added, and set his glass down on the table.

He knew the next line, but he couldn't form the words, or make them come out of his mouth. It was the perfect opportunity to tell her. But he reasoned that she'd had a tough day. There was enough on her plate already.

"Your son doesn't look much like you. He must get his height from his father."

"Actually he gets his height from my father. Ronald, my ex, is almost as short as I am."

"What happened with you two, if you don't mind me asking?"

"You're going right to the heavy stuff, aren't you?"

"You don't have to talk about it if you don't want to."

Andrea thought back to the conversation she'd had with Charlotte and felt good about letting Maxwell in on her woeful life. At least she could find out eventually if he was interested in getting mixed up in her crazy out-of-sorts life.

"Typical story. He wanted Martha Stewart and I'm more Barbara Walters."

Maxwell thought about the irony of their situations. His wife had been Martha Stewart and he had hated it from "I do." Deborah had swept him off his feet with the attention and home-cooked meals. He never imagined that that was all she really wanted out of life. Once they were married and he spoke of riding the corporate ladder straight to the top, and strategic moves to put himself on the right career path, she had criticized him for not being stable.

"So, Barbara, is he married to Martha now?"

"In the flesh. I think his wife could give ole Martha a run for her money."

"And what is it that Barbara wants in a man?"

"I love what I do. I mean really. It's not just a job to me. I feel like I was born to do this. But now, there are so many things going on at that station, I wonder how long I'll have a job. And then what will there be for me? Maybe Martha was my best bet all along."

"Not a chance. Never question who you are. Jobs come and go, but you can't be somebody different just on a whim or because it works for someone else."

When Maxwell spoke, his words reminded her so much of her father. He had known it, too. Andrea belonged in that anchor chair, and that's where she was going to fight to stay. If not at the Baltimore station then somewhere else, but she would not give up what she loved. While Andrea floated on her personal revelation, Maxwell had stood to leave.

"I don't want to keep you up too late. I know it's been a tough day. But…you have to let me take you out again. I need redemption."

"Yes, you do. But just what did you have in mind?"

"Believe it or not, I've never done the tourist bit down here at the Harbor. I transport people around all the time, and I know all the shops and restaurants, but I've never really gone into any of them, except coffee shops, so how about you give me a tour?"

"That's simple enough."

"And we can walk so there's less chance of a trip to the emergency room."

"You must admit that was a classic. I can't say I've ever had a date take me there."

"So the Harbor it is. The weekend sound okay?" Maxwell asked, even though he didn't want to wait an entire week to see her again.

"It's a date, sir."

There, it was settled. They had scheduled a second date, and that's when he'd tell her. He'd tell her why he looked so familiar and how one wrong move had destroyed everything. He'd make himself tell her. And then let the chips fall where they may. And, oh, how he hoped they fell in his favor because he knew Barbara was just perfect for him.

CHAPTER 29

When Andrea went to work later that week, she was shocked to see Leslie and Dave huddled in the corner. When she walked past them, Dave only glanced at her then shook his head. They appeared to be going over the rundown for the evening newscast from what Andrea could see in passing.

Nancy buzzed through the door nearly knocking Andrea over. "Great, you're here. Wanna take a smoke break?" she asked.

"I don't smoke."

"That never stopped you before," Nancy said as she pulled Andrea toward the back door.

Once outside, Nancy didn't waste time getting to the point, which was one of the things Andrea loved about her producer.

"They're doing a dry run with Leslie and Dave in about fifteen minutes."

"A dry run? Why would they do that?"

"Carol Manning called in sick and they're letting Leslie do the five-to-six show."

Carol was the anchor for the show just before Andrea

and Dave went on. Whenever she called in sick, Ted would usually get Andrea or Dave to fill in. Andrea had always suggested they get the weekend anchor or perhaps a reporter to do it. But it had always been easier for her or Dave to fill the spot.

"But Carol calling in sick has nothing to do with a Leslie-Dave dry run."

"That's all they told me. Just to prep a dry run. The production folk are in place and Dave is going over copy with Leslie now. We're taping for a meeting tomorrow morning."

"What kind of meeting? Is this what I think it is?"

"God, Andrea, I hate that they're doing it like this. They have absolutely no tact. I wish I had options. I would tell them where they can shove all this crap. With Ted gone…"

Nancy couldn't go on. It was the first time during their years of working together that Andrea had ever seen her get emotional. She had always been passionate and operating at a notch that bordered on panic, but never tears.

"Do you think this has anything to do with what happened with Amber? Could they be punishing me the way they did Ted?"

"That would be my guess, but who knows with these people."

Andrea sighed and rested her weary body against the side of the building.

"Okay then, sounds like you have work to do, Nancy. And so do I," Andrea said as she pulled herself together and strolled back into the newsroom.

As Leslie and Dave left for the news set and their dry run, Andrea sat at her desk pretending to be busy. But there was nothing to do. Another anchor was sitting at the news desk gunning for her job, and there wasn't a thing she could do about it. Or was that what Claxton had wanted her to think?

She decided that if she was going to be bumped or terminated altogether then she might as well find out what was really going on. She made her way upstairs toward the business office and then toward the executive suite where the Claxton boys were rumored to hide out each day.

To her benefit the secretary was not at her desk, which left nothing between her and the door leading to the new general manager of WVTR. She could hear his voice along with a few other male voices as she pushed the door open.

"Excuse me, gentlemen, I was wondering if I might have a word with you?"

If they had been about to lie and say that they were busy, their game was busted. Each of them sat casually with ties loosened, and one of the men had the nerve to have his feet propped on the GM's desk. The feet came down and Andrea stepped into the room giving them all her sternest and most in-control look.

"Ms. Shaw, have a seat, please," Richard Messner, the new general manager, said as his hand punched at the power button on a monitor feeding the dry run of Leslie and Dave directly into his office.

Andrea was glad she didn't have to make her speech while watching what might very well be the future evening news team. As Andrea took her seat, she recognized the man who had removed his feet from the desk as the PR spin guy, Daniel Tate, who had helped her handle the story of what had happened with Amber.

"I see that Leslie is filling in for Carol today."

"Yes, as you know Leslie has anchor experience. She worked at our station…"

"Yes, in Milwaukee. I heard," Andrea interrupted.

She could see the men shifting in their seats. She tried to remain professional and not let her emotions get the best of her.

"And I also see that Leslie is doing a taped dry run with Dave. Is Dave going to be working the five-to-six show, as well, or is Leslie filling in for me, too, permanently?"

No one answered immediately. Andrea hadn't expected them to. She had thought about beating around the bush with her inquisition, but decided to take a page out of Nancy's playbook and get right to the point.

"Andrea, you have been in television long enough to know that we like to cover all bases. Your show with Dave is our highest-rated show. If you were out for some reason, we want to know that all the bases would be covered," said Mr. Messner.

"And I've been out in the past, and so has Dave. And the show went on without a hitch. I don't understand why you think there might be a problem suddenly."

Before either of the men could speak, Andrea continued. "Please tell me that this has nothing to do with my daughter. I thought we had covered that and moved on."

This time PR guy spoke up. "Ms. Shaw, our desire is to make this transition as seamless as possible. Claxton has quite a reputation in the business and we want the fine people of Baltimore to know that they will get nothing short of the quality journalism they have always gotten."

"I'm listening. I still don't see where you've answered any of my questions."

Mr. Messner chimed in, "Our sincere hope is to make as few waves as possible. Our job is to deliver the news, not become it."

Andrea nodded her head as if her suspicions were confirmed. "So, I was right. This is about my daughter."

"This is about public opinion, Ms. Shaw. The public wants fair, honest and accurate news coverage from a person they feel they can trust."

"And they can't trust me all of a sudden because my daughter got into trouble?"

"Not because she got into trouble, Ms. Shaw, because you covered it up. Not only you, but Ted and Nancy, also. That is not in the best interest of the public, in my opinion," Mr. Messner said, rising slightly from his seat.

Andrea paused before she spoke again. She knew she had gotten him riled. She didn't want to press her luck. She really did not need to lose her job on top of everything else.

"So, now I'm out, just like that?"

No one spoke, so she continued. "It all happened so fast. She's my daughter. My concern was for her well-being. I'm sorry that I didn't think of my journalistic obligation first and foremost."

"Oh, it seems you were quite concerned about her well-being and making sure that this didn't become public knowledge," Messner added, this time popping the power button to turn the dry run of Leslie and Dave back on.

Andrea could feel the tears pooling. She would not let them fall. By turning the monitor back on Messner was telling her just how he felt about the situation.

"We covered the story. And it's done now. Except the counseling and community service, it's over," Andrea said, her voice almost a whisper.

On the screen in front of her, she could see Leslie chatting with Dave and then turning to a single camera shot to read a story. She could not hear the sound, but from previous experience, Andrea could quickly see that Leslie's delivery was near perfect.

"And our viewers have reason to believe that when it is not in our best interest, we may not report the news accurately. This is not at all personal," Messner said, pulling her attention back from the monitor.

"It certainly feels personal. Perhaps that's because this was me, my daughter, my livelihood. Those things are personal to me. I would think our viewers would understand and empathize with a parent in the position I've been in."

PR guy jumped back in with his two cents. Andrea felt as if she was watching a tennis match.

"You didn't give the public that opportunity. Instead you chose to act as if it didn't happen, Ms. Shaw."

When Andrea left the office she had no idea what would happen with her job. Would Leslie swoop in and replace her? Would she be sent back to beat reporting and investigating full-time? She had no idea, and if she had wanted to get answers from the men upstairs, all she had gotten was the stern reprimand that might be the beginning of the end.

CHAPTER 30

Andrea had very little time to sulk over Ted's retirement or her devastating meeting with the boys upstairs. She had to nail down several decent story leads before she started her vacation, which would take her to Myrtle Beach for two days longer than she needed to be out of town with so much turmoil.

Amber had started her counseling and her nursing home work. Ronald had volunteered to handle getting her back and forth since he had the most flexible schedule. Ray had already left for South Carolina and Chloe had called to say that she would meet them there at the end of the week.

That left Andrea and Charlotte, who were loading their car when Charlotte mentioned stopping off in North Carolina for the night.

"And why would we stop in North Carolina? We can split the driving and get there today. It's only Myrtle Beach."

"Sure we can, but since Juan wasn't able to go, I decided to schedule a little girl time for us."

"Oh dear God, please tell me this girl time does not include near-naked men and dollar bills."

"Girl, that was a year ago. You should be over that by now. And nobody told you to try to put that dollar there," Charlotte added, tossing the second of three large suitcases into the rental car.

"You have two kids, so I cannot figure out why the confusion with the male anatomy, Andrea."

"Just tell me what we're doing in North Carolina."

"You know I will not, because you'll only back out."

"This should tell you that you've planned something that doesn't interest me. Or rather, frightens me. It's got to be one of the two."

"A night at a wonderful, quaint bed-and-breakfast. I met the owner a few months ago at a B and B convention."

"What were you doing at a B and B convention?"

"I don't remember. Juan was at a meeting in some ritzy hotel. The convention was next door and I was bored."

"Just like that, huh? You just walk right into a convention that you have no business attending."

"Says who. I visit lots of B and Bs. So there."

A night at a bed-and-breakfast did not sound so bad. Andrea thought it made perfect sense. It would break up the trip just enough so that neither of them would be worn-out when they got to the beach. And Andrea loved B and Bs. That did not, however, stop her from being suspicious. A quiet night in the country did not sound like her sister Charlotte.

Andrea took the first leg of driving, just as she suspected she would. Traffic wasn't bad going down Interstate 95 toward North Carolina where Andrea really hoped her sister had planned a quiet evening at a nice country inn.

While Charlotte dozed, Andrea reflected on the past few weeks. Although things had been rough, she and the kids had come through without too many bumps and bruises. Not to mention the potential relationship with Maxwell. They had managed to squeeze in a few small dates here and there. She still didn't know as much about him as she would have liked, but she had met his brother, Wayne, and he seemed normal enough. She would assume that the rest of Maxwell's life was also normal.

Charlotte rejoined the land of the living in time to give Andrea directions to the bed-and-breakfast. As she sped down the winding country roads, she noticed Charlotte drumming her fingers against the dashboard. Her sister's sign of uneasiness.

"What is it?"

"There is this one thing about our stay tonight."

"I knew it. Please, no naked farm boys. I cannot take this, Charlotte."

"What is it with you and naked men? You really should get yourself some, so you can put something else on your brain."

"What on earth is waiting for me in the backwoods of North Carolina? Tell me now."

"The innkeeper is Marge. She's wonderful. You'll love her. She's vegan, so dinner and breakfast will be no-meat meals."

"I have no problem with vegan. You know that. Now the bad news."

"Great. So it's settled. We have separate rooms since you like to sit up late and read. Dinner should be ready as soon as we get there. So, we'll wash up and eat before the psychic arrives."

The right wheel of the car dipped off the road just enough to make Andrea lose control. She corrected and regained control just as Charlotte said, "Oh, right here. This is the place."

Once they were safely in the driveway, Andrea killed the engine and turned to her sister, who had apparently lost what little mind she had.

"I don't do psychics. You know I don't believe in that kind of stuff. This is too much. After a few drinks, I could handle the stuffing dollars into underwear."

"Correction, sweetie. You did not handle that very well. But even with your fumbling hands, if memory serves me right, that dancer had nothing to be ashamed of," Charlotte whispered just as a rail-thin white woman zipped out the front door, headed toward their car.

"You should be ashamed, though, Andrea. For not being more open-minded. You've been through so much. And don't you want to know what's going to happen with your job?"

"Charlotte, you are not telling me that a psychic in the backwoods of North Carolina knows a damn thing about my job."

"No, probably not, but I just thought this would be fun, okay?"

Before Andrea could answer, Charlotte's door was ripped open and the wiry woman yanked her out of the car.

"Andrea, this is Marge."

Andrea wanted to ask where the fire was, but she

wouldn't get the chance since Marge had now sprinted around the car and grabbed her by the arms.

"It's so nice to meet you. Charlotte has told me so much about you. You have your own room with a nice recliner for reading. I have some nice cucumber sandwiches to get you girls started. You do like cucumbers, don't you? Charlotte said you did," Marge said without taking a breath.

Almost before Andrea could answer, get the trunk of the car open and grab their bags, Marge was already dashing across the yard carrying all three suitcases.

"Come along, ladies. You got lead in your feet or something? Oh, Lord, you Northerners."

Andrea was tired from the drive and afraid of both the innkeeper and the pending psychic. When they got inside the house, the kitchen table was decked out with all kinds of food, several bottles of wine and a crystal ball. Andrea thought she would drop dead on the spot.

"It's a joke, Andrea. Marge found it at an antique show. I told her to put it out just to mess with your head."

Freaked out just about summed up the emotions Andrea was feeling.

"We're doing tarot cards," Charlotte corrected.

Great. The most Andrea knew about tarot cards was that there was a death card. She was certain to get that one. Well, at least the timing wouldn't be so bad. She was probably going to lose her job and the kids had gotten accustomed to spending more time with their father, anyway.

"Okay, bring it on," Andrea said and drained wineglass number one.

CHAPTER 31

The condo Charlotte had rented in Myrtle Beach was perfect. They arrived early enough for Andrea to grab a few minutes of rest before Ray's performance. Much-needed rest since Andrea had driven every mile of the trip.

As her head fell back on the soft down pillows, she thought back to the psychic experience and the fact that it hadn't been painful at all. The evening had started with dinner, just as Charlotte had said. A main course of three-bean casserole, surrounded by stuffed portabellas and roasted marinated vegetables. Andrea would have enjoyed that combination had she not been waiting for a psychic.

Marge had invited her other guest to join them. He declined, as any well-meaning business traveler should when offered a chance to have his future spilled from tarot cards in front of complete strangers.

Charlotte had volunteered to have her reading first, to give Andrea time for a second glass of wine and determine whether or not to run out of the house, yelling and scream-ing. From what Andrea could remember, the psychic said a bunch of mumbo jumbo and Charlotte and Marge grinned at each other endlessly. Marge did not have her reading done, since it would have required her to sit still for two seconds. Which Andrea didn't think was possible.

Andrea had pretty much lost herself in the very delicious red wine, when she noticed everyone's eyes glued to her. She could care less about Charlotte glaring at her. That was pretty much normal. However, seeing Marge's eyes immobile for longer than a second was a bit unnerving. The worst part was clearly the slanted glance from Madam Librarian. That was not her real name, but the name Andrea had given her without her knowing.

The middle-aged white woman could have doubled for someone's conservative, Republican-voting mother, or the city librarian. But certainly not the tarot card-toting psychic that she proclaimed to be to the three women in front of her.

With the librarian's eyes held steady on her, Andrea assumed it was her turn to watch the woman flip cards that were a tad larger than playing cards, and tell her life-altering things that would dazzle them all.

What actually happened was a series of cards arranged in an order that only made sense to the card flipper. There were cups and saucers and various other kitchen items. And there was a card with a rather frightening-looking man on it. Andrea was sure it was the death card. But the psychic assured her that because the card came after the cups, it was not bad. It would have been bad, however, had it come after the diamonds, or clubs, or maybe it was the spades. Andrea couldn't remember which. Too much wine.

In the end the woman had informed Andrea that she

had a child, no, two children. One child making a change, a big step in the right direction. The other child not so good. Child number two had a dark aura, with change, as well, and a crossroad that could lead to good, or evil.

When Andrea asked about her job situation, more cards hit the table and of course the frightening-man card was one of them. Madam Librarian's brow furrowed a little as she informed Andrea that her answers lay within. What the hell did that mean? To Andrea it sounded like a safe way to say that the psychic had no idea what would happen at her job.

Since Charlotte was paying this woman big bucks, Andrea thought she should confirm the reading by letting Madam know that she did in fact have the two children. A daughter at a crossroad, and a son planning his collegiate future. And that she would listen deep inside herself for answers to her job situation. Yeah, right.

So, when the night had ended, Andrea was no worse for the wear. The psychic had pretty much told her what she already knew. They could have saved a few dollars and the time, but she would have never met Marge or been introduced to the wonderful bed-and-breakfast in the middle of nowhere. All in all, the experience was surprisingly wonderful. Typical Charlotte.

The arrival at the House of Blues in Myrtle Beach was not so wonderful. They had all agreed to meet in the lobby and Andrea was excited about the event until she spied Ronald and Charity decked out in matching outfits. The good feeling turned to nausea and she wanted to puke all over the matching cobalt-blue rayon short sets.

Say nothing for the fact that Ronald couldn't keep his hands off Charity's rear end. It didn't surprise her that the two of them were happy together, but she hated when they flaunted it right in front of her.

"Please be civil, Mom. Promise," Ray said after noticing the scowl on Andrea's face.

Andrea thought back to what the psychic had said. She was happy for Ray. This competition was just perfect for his goals to get into a strong music program in college.

Andrea and Ronald had held off on getting Ray into counseling. They both thought the counselor was jumping the gun on her diagnosis. Ronald insisted that she was just money hungry and they'd make anyone have a problem to bill another hour. So, Ray was not in counseling and Ronald and Andrea had only gone that one time. Amber had seemed better adjusted after her visits, so they had left well enough alone.

"You thought any more about what that counselor said when we were there?" Ronald asked.

Charity had gone inside to powder her nose, for real this time. Andrea hoped it was just an expression and the woman was not in fact standing in front of the bathroom mirror powdering anything.

"We said we weren't putting him in."

"Not about Ray. About coming up with a plan. I think she's right. We need to do something. Next year this time, this family may have grown by one and that changes everything," he added, glancing toward the door that Charity had gone through.

It was the first time Ronald had ever mentioned having

children with Charity. Although Andrea knew there was a distinct possibility that it could happen since Charity was still in her childbearing years, to hear it come out of his mouth brought a whole new reality to the situation.

"And what brought this on?" she asked.

"That's not the issue. We really need to establish some things or this is just going to get worse with each new piece added to the puzzle. And I hear you're dating."

Of course he had heard that she was dating. She knew the night Ray met Maxwell that he would run straight back to his father with the news.

"I'm not saying we need counseling or anything. But we need something. What are your thoughts?"

"I've been a little busy at work. Haven't had time to give it much thought."

"Of course you haven't," Ronald whispered and started to walk away.

"Oh, no you don't. You act as if you are the only one with an important job to do, and the moment I mention my work, you get that smug look. You have always had a problem with what I do."

"Listen, Andrea, this is not the time for this. The program is about to start."

"But you brought it up. And now you want to end it. But I'm not done."

Charity had returned from the bathroom, giving Ronald reason to walk away from Andrea. She watched as the two of them, arm in arm, strolled into the House of Blues.

She followed. Not because she wanted to be anywhere near them, but Ray would be disappointed if she missed his performance. She had to get her mind back on the real issue and forget Ronald's slanted accusations.

The lights went dim before Andrea could find a seat. She stumbled around, reaching for a table, a chair, anything. She had touched at least one man in perhaps a location she should not touch a stranger, but it was dark, he had been sitting alone, and no one else saw it. She moved on and flopped in the first empty seat, just as the lights came up again.

To her horror, she was sitting with Ronald, Charity, Amber and Charlotte. It made sense that they would all sit together since they had all come to see the same young man play. But the sight of this unlikely-ever-to-be-happy family made Andrea's blood boil. As much as she tried to keep her mouth shut and enjoy the concert, Ronald's accusations kept ringing in her ears as if he'd just spoken them.

"Besides, if it's not important enough for you to put work aside for a moment, there's no point in making a scene about it now," Andrea whispered, picking up the conversation from outside, all the while hating herself for being so juvenile.

"What the hell are you doing?" Charlotte said, leaning close to Andrea.

Since Charlotte had not been privy to the near argument between Ronald and Andrea earlier in the lobby, she was thrown by her sister's out-of-the-blue temper tantrum.

"He started it," Andrea answered.

"And are you suddenly two years old? Ray will have your head if you ruin this for him. Now stifle," Charlotte whispered.

Andrea tried again to ignore the anger rising in her breast. She really did. But in the end, anger won out over good judgment.

Pointing toward Charity, Andrea said, "Having kids. You finally want to play daddy. Well, a fine job you did with our kids. Leaving them for me to raise. That's why you didn't want me to work. Because it might require you to be a real father. Well, maybe you'll have better luck with her."

"Who the hell are you pointing at!" Charity screamed at Andrea.

It didn't take much to get a rise out of Charity. In the past, whenever they had all been in the same room, the tension had been unbearable and harsh words inevitable.

While caught up in her battle with Charity, Andrea didn't notice her mother walk in wearing a tight-fitting dress that looked absolutely great on her. Not to mention the eye candy on her arm. Chloe was walking side by side with a man who was at most Charlotte's age. And although Andrea had not seen her mother, Charlotte had most definitely noticed her. While Andrea, Ronald and Charity were screaming about present teens and pending babies, Charlotte and Chloe were fighting without words. Their glares and eye rolls weren't complete until Charlotte finally addressed her mother as a trifling bitch and stormed out.

On stage, the song ended and the group promptly started another as a group of ushers tugged at the arms of everyone at Andrea's table. The simultaneous outbursts had gotten them all thrown out. Even Amber, who got a real kick out of it. The adults, however, were basically still very pissed and a little embarrassed for not controlling themselves better.

"See what you did," Andrea heard Ray yelling from the doorway of the building.

"Me? Your father started it," Andrea said.

"You're like a child, Andrea," Charity screamed, directing her anger at Ronald and Andrea. "You can't figure out what to do with the kids because you act too much like one yourself. And so do you."

"Charity, how dare you," Ronald said, but Charity was long gone.

Andrea put her two cents' worth in. "See, that's just the problem. You didn't want a wife, you wanted another kid. Someone you could control. You should have learned when that didn't work with me."

By now tears were pouring down Ray's face.

Ronald hadn't noticed as he yelled back at Andrea, "Asking you to put your family first was not about my control over you. It was about avoiding all the things we're going through now."

"So, all of this is my fault?"

"You are impossible."

"But I am no longer your kid, your doormat. If I want to work seven days a week round the clock, that's exactly what I'll do, Ronald. I am not your mother."

A second after it came out of her mouth, Andrea remembered that it was never a good thing to mention someone's mother in the middle of an argument. Especially if they loved said mother and she was deceased and he had never gotten over losing her.

Andrea just knew Ronald was going to slap or punch her or something. But he didn't. His eyes filled with tears, and he walked out. And she didn't have the good sense to go on her way and leave it alone. She followed.

"I didn't mean it in a nasty way. It's just that you knew I never wanted to just stay at home and take care of the house. You knew I wanted a career in journalism. You just thought that since I put it off for a few years, that I would never pursue it. And then you were sure I would never be good at it."

"You're right. It's all about you. Not about anyone else. Not about my expectations. My life was good because my mother was there for me growing up. When I got home from school, she was there. The house was warm and alive when I walked into it every day."

"But is that what your mother wanted?"

Ronald pulled a tissue from his shorts pocket and dried his eyes.

"We are not having this discussion, Andrea."

"Why do you think she went inward? Why the depression? She sank so deep inside herself that she just never came out again. Why, Ronald?"

"I don't know, but do you think that's what I wanted for her?"

"No, but all your life, neither you nor your father ever found out what she wanted. She spent her life revolving around the two of you. And maybe, just maybe, she wanted more. Maybe she had a dream."

"She never talked about anything."

"That doesn't mean it wasn't there. Sometimes dreams

are so huge and impossible sounding that you can't talk about it. But it's not that they aren't there. I would have never thought I'd win a Peabody, or be one of the top paid black female anchors in the country. And I'd hate to imagine my life had I not stepped out and tried all those years ago."

By the time Andrea had finished baring her soul to Ronald, Charity, Charlotte and Chloe had all gathered around them. Ray was still standing near the doorway, his cell phone in his hand, tears pouring from his eyes like a rainstorm. Andrea wanted to run to him, but Charity grabbed her arm.

"I would really appreciate you not cornering my husband like this, ever again."

Andrea assumed Charity was mad and jealous. It had to upset her that Ronald and Andrea were discussing, with such passion, issues that had happened long before her time. Poor clueless lady, Andrea thought. Charity didn't seem to understand that divorce doesn't erase all the years, all the happenings, or the hurt and history.

"You couldn't just wait until I was done. You had to mess this up," Ray said before Andrea could address Charity.

And before she could apologize to Ray, he was gone. She wasn't upset because she really didn't have the strength for one more fight. Until she noticed, just across the parking lot, Charlotte's index finger just inches from their mother's nose. And then she saw the man again. The same man who had ushered Chloe into the concert. A tall, rather classy-looking Latino gentleman. His close-cut wisps of gray hair were perfectly trimmed around a mocha face. He would have been drop-dead gorgeous in his heyday and added new meaning to the term "hot Latin lover." Those were terms she wasn't prepared to use describing her mother and a man. A man that, at that very moment, would have been right at home on the cover of a magazine, that is, if he didn't look as if he feared for his life.

"Mother definitely has a man, and it's just about to hit the fan between those two. Damn," Andrea said, and walked in the opposite direction of that fight.

CHAPTER 32

Ray was angry with his parents for being so insensitive, but they were not the total reason for his outburst. While he was trying to tell them off for ruining his performance, Tammy had called. The same Tammy who was not at a hotel recovering from an abortion, but rather running through scenarios of how she would tell her parents.

"I don't want to go through with this, Ray. If you disagree and decide not to be involved, then that's your choice, but I do not want to have an abortion," Tammy had announced.

Ray had tried to conceal the shock of the news, but it was too much. Fortunately, everyone was so caught up in their own mess that he was able to lose his cool and fit right in. He had pretended to be angry about his parents finally having the conversation they should have had two years ago. But he had pulled it off, played the role of disappointed son and they had left him to himself.

Since his parents' divorce, he had become pretty good at hiding his real feelings and masking trouble. When he had hung up with Tammy he was angry that, again, all of the adults in his life were behaving as if they were the only ones in the family with issues. Even if he had wanted to confide in one of them, they were too distracted to help him. They acted as if he were self-sustaining and never in need of anyone or anything. In recent weeks, that had been so far from the truth.

"Cut them some slack, buddy," his grandmother, Chloe, had said after catching up with him.

He had seen her going toe-to-toe with Aunt Charlotte about God only knows what. He assumed she had only sought him out to get away from her issues.

He wanted to tell her that, for once, he was the one in need of being cut some slack. But no one was acting in his favor. Not his family and now not Tammy. Everyone seemed to be looking out for themselves and it was all tumbling in on him.

Did any of them ask themselves how their decisions would impact him? He assumed not, even as he walked with his grandmother to the car. She had her arm around him and her hand caressing his shoulders, but she had no idea of the tension building inside his chest. And he wondered if any of them ever would.

CHAPTER 33

While Andrea had been in Myrtle Beach, Leslie had her chance to step into her shoes. She had filled in as coanchor with Dave. When Andrea returned, she wasn't sure whether she would be preparing for the newscast, demoted, or terminated. She knew that whichever the case, she would be able to see it written all over Nancy's face as soon as she walked into the newsroom.

"God, I'm glad you're back. She's awful."

"Not a good anchor?" Andrea asked.

"No, great anchor, lousy person."

Not exactly what Andrea wanted to hear.

"Do I still have a job?"

"Dave and I are both looking forward to having you back in the seat tonight. There was a rumor that Claxton was considering Leslie for Carol's slot, but of course Ms. Leslie said that if she couldn't have the main gig, then she didn't want anything."

"Oh, she does sound pleasant," Andrea joked.

Jumping right back into their old rhythm, Nancy and Andrea were having lunch at her desk, flipping through old leads to find a new hot piece to investigate. Andrea updated Nancy on all the particulars, her outburst at the band competition, her feelings for Maxwell, and the fact that her sister and mother were back on speaking terms.

"How long have those two been at odds?" Nancy asked, referring to Chloe and Charlotte.

"Too long. They fought like wild women right in front of mother's new man. But at least they were talking. After I had ruined the event for my son and sent my ex off crying, I decided to do some good and referee for my sister and mother."

"So they're all chummy now?"

"Oh God no. Chummy and those two women may never be in the same sentence, but I think they have agreed to chat at least once a week if nothing more than an extension of the argument that started at the beach."

"Well, at least it sounds like things are progressing well with the mystery driver."

"They are..." Andrea sighed.

"But..."

"I didn't say *but.*"

"You didn't say it, but I heard it. In what you didn't say."

While Andrea had been away, Nancy had gone from her usual ragged, ill-fitting attire to business suits. She had informed Andrea that she had only bought three suits because that's all she could budget for with four kids to feed and clothe. She had also mentioned that Mr. PR had suggested she make her attire fit the position. She had been insulted because to her taking care of her kids was a better use of the money, but not insulted enough to lose her job.

Andrea made a mental note to pull at least three more suits from her own closet to add to Nancy's new wardrobe. Andrea was just glad that instead of predicting her doom, Nancy had resorted to trying to prevent it.

"Maxwell is a great guy. And I really enjoy his company. So please tell me why I'm waiting for someone to lower the boom and tell me that it's all a lie?"

"Because you've slumped into a negative place where you wonder if anything good can happen for you romantically."

"Oh, goodness. Look who's been watching one too many talk shows."

"I'm serious, Andrea. Divorced, and a series of bad dates. And you're not getting any younger."

"Are you related to my sister, Charlotte? She has the uncanny ability to insult me right to my face and avoid being slapped or cursed out. So the bad feeling is all my fault, huh?" Andrea said, and tossed the used Chick-fil-A bag into the trash.

"No, everything that has happened is adding to the feeling. You just need to remind yourself that you have every reason in the world to be able to attract and deserve a wonderful man who wasn't formerly an ax murderer."

"Okay, so I'll let it go and just enjoy the ride."

"No, you will not. This is Baltimore. There are some crazies out there. You can't completely dismiss your feelings."

"You're talking out of both sides of your mouth, Nancy. And it's not very attractive, especially when you're eating. I've had a trying weekend, so one line of thinking at a time is all I can handle. What do I do? Dismiss him or continue to be paranoid."

"Neither. Background check."

"I will not. That is sneaky and borderline despicable."

"And the only real way to find out what you want to know about this guy."

"Do you want to do it or shall I?" Andrea said with a sly grin.

She had given Maxwell ample opportunity to tell her more about himself. But he had only been vague and un-revealing. She didn't think it was fair, considering that she had told him all of her troubles, and the fact that she really wanted a relationship with him.

Nancy started with the calls. As a representative of the station she could get information pretty easily. And most of what she came up with was useless, somewhat boring, and things Andrea had already assumed about him. Age, socioeconomic status, rents rather than owns, etc.

Just when Andrea was about to conclude that Maxwell was a nice guy and she should never listen to Nancy again, she ran his name through the station files. And there on the computer screen in front of her, it popped up on two-and-a-half pages of news copy story headers. Andrea ran down the list and lost her breath as she opened the first one and watched the video play on the monitor.

It all came back in a rush. The investigation, and then the fallout and the arrest. Nancy stood over Andrea's shoulder for a couple of the playbacks, but then left her friend to watch the rest alone.

It was not a pretty picture. She hadn't recognized him

because he had hair back then. Plenty of hair, so she couldn't assume he was naturally bald. The only thing she was left to think was that he had altered his appearance with hopes that she or someone else wouldn't recognize him.

She hit the Stop button on the playback machine after a couple more pages passed. As she sat there staring at the blank screen, she knew it wasn't just what he had done, but the fact that she had asked why he looked familiar and he had not divulged one piece of information.

Once she could get herself together and breathe again, she exited the program, turned the computer off and slumped down in her seat. Her greatest fear had fallen into her lap. It had seemed too good to be true, and it was.

He had not been convicted of anything, but there was evidence that he had a good bit of involvement. However, the Feds were gunning for the big guys. He was a nobody compared to the men who took the fall. But most importantly, he hadn't breathed a word to her, knowing that she had been the reporter to break the story.

There had been countless opportunities and he had said nothing. Would she wait to see if he would bring it up, or confront him head-on with what she knew? She wanted to be crafty and slick, but all she felt was hurt and betrayed. Crafty and slick worked in nailing down a good news story, but in matters of the heart, they didn't do her much good.

CHAPTER 34

Andrea had visited Maxwell at the office a couple of times since they had first gone out. He had been glad to hear from her when she called to ask if they could talk. The entire time she had been in Myrtle Beach, he had thought about how much he missed her. As she strolled into the office this time, there was something about the look in her eyes that told him to be on alert.

"This is a pleasant surprise," he said, hoping his suspicion was wrong.

She was upset. That much he knew. He wondered which it was. Ray and the pregnancy, or had his eyes given him away as his mother had always said.

"A surprise, huh. Nothing like the surprise I've had today," Andrea answered.

Wayne had been smiling and wheeling from one end of his desk to the other, until Andrea spoke. It was her tone, not the words that Maxwell assumed made his brother excuse himself to one of the back rooms.

Andrea didn't have to say anything else for Maxwell to know to what she was referring. It was not her son, but rather his tight lip that she was angry about.

He had hoped he would have more time, and that he would find the right moment before she put the pieces together. But now it was in front of him, and he was not prepared.

"Did you not think I would eventually put two and two together and get scandal?"

Before Maxwell could utter a word, the phone rang. He reached to grab it even though he knew Wayne could answer it from the other room. Which he did. One ring and then nothing more.

"If you could please give me a minute to explain. I assure you I have a reasonable explanation for why I haven't said anything."

She didn't appear to want explanations. She paced around as if she had come to her own conclusions, and Maxwell wondered if anything he could say would help her understand things from his perspective.

"Maxwell, I hate to interrupt, but everyone else is already out and this one is one of our regulars," Wayne said from the doorway.

Andrea sighed and rolled her eyes at both men. Maxwell was seeing a different side of her. The one he remembered from when she was running across the lawn of his former employer yelling questions at men who had no intention of answering her. She could be hard when she needed to.

"I have to take this one. No choice, but if we could get together after you get off work…" Maxwell offered.

"Can't he take it?" Andrea asked, referring to Wayne.

Maxwell knew that Wayne had not driven since the accident and he wasn't likely to do so now, even though one of the cars was equipped for him to drive. As much as Maxwell didn't want to rush out in the middle of this conversation, he really had no choice. Part of Maxwell wanted to let Wayne take the call, but then he knew the last thing Wayne wanted to do was get back on the mean city streets.

"I could take it if you need," Wayne offered.

Maxwell was touched by the fact that his brother would risk losing an important client as well as possibly wrecking a vehicle to help him out. But he couldn't let him do it. He was caught in a hard place, but if there was one thing he had learned in the past five years, that was to own his decisions, right or wrong.

"I can talk with you after my shift, but I really need to go now," Maxwell said and he knew from the popping and clicking of her head and mouth that she felt put off and that he was avoiding the issue yet again.

He might not get an opportunity to make it right, but that was a chance he had to take. He had a responsibility and a commitment to his brother and he would honor that. If Andrea didn't understand or didn't want to hear him out later, he would have to live with that.

She stormed out of the office, with Maxwell following to get into his car and do his job. Wayne rolled out and met him on the sidewalk.

"She'll hear you out later," Wayne said.

"Maybe so, maybe not. Thanks for offering to take this, but we both know that would not be in your best interests. If you want to practice sometime, I don't mind. I just didn't think you'd want to drive."

"That'll be fine. I'm not really interested in driving. I'm just thinking of your best interests, too."

"I'll be fine. If it's meant to be, then it will be," Maxwell said and drove off, relieved by the opportunity to let out some of his aggression on the busy streets.

He honked his horn and swerved about the streets from lane to lane toward his client. He put the thoughts of Andrea and what might come of the two of them out of his mind as best he could.

He had set himself up with false hope. He knew that it would be tough for anyone to see past his indiscretions, and see the real man who had just made poor decisions. And he had steered clear of relationships because of it. But she had made him want to venture out again. And he had. And look where it had landed him.

CHAPTER 35

When Andrea got back to the station from her less-than-one-minute fight with Maxwell, Leslie was sitting at her desk as if it was her own. Andrea walked in and moved around so that Leslie could see her, but the girl didn't bother to scamper away and offer apologies this time. She simply sat there, chewing gum and yapping away on Andrea's telephone.

Andrea walked around the room again, stopping at Nancy's desk to tell her what had happened with Maxwell. Nancy, however, didn't want to hear about Maxwell, but rather how Andrea planned to get Leslie out of her seat.

"She's really pushing it, isn't she?" Nancy asked.

"I suppose not. She's been getting more and more territorial lately. Feels like the end is near. Looks like you were right. I guess I'm next."

Andrea made her way to her desk for the inevitable. Leslie still hadn't spotted her. Instead, her head was bent over bobbing up only every few seconds so Andrea could see the wad of gum in her mouth. Leslie's eyes were closed as if she was really enjoying the conversation, or perhaps just the gum.

Andrea stood right in front of the desk, hoping her presence would cause Leslie to look up, see her, and then get her tight little rear out of Andrea's seat. Andrea had resolved that if they were going to get rid of her, they'd have to actually do it before she let some rookie just take over things.

Andrea rushed back upstairs and right into the executive suite, storming past the waving index finger of the secretary sitting in front of Messner's office.

"I'm sorry to barge in on you again, but I absolutely need two, three minutes tops."

The same players were again in place. This time ties were not hanging loose and they did not seem relaxed.

"Welcome back from your vacation, Ms. Shaw. We're glad to have you back," Messner announced, and the others all nodded their heads.

When Andrea stepped toward his desk she spotted the front page of a talent contract on his desk. Even upside down, she could read the name in bold print and the position. "Leslie Shore" and "6:00 and 11:00 news coanchor," were glued to Andrea's eyes even before Messner snatched the paper away and tossed it onto the credenza behind his desk.

Andrea couldn't breathe. They were offering Leslie her job. They had probably been waiting for her to return before they did the deed. And Leslie knew, that's why she was lounging at Andrea's desk.

She didn't know if she should just leave and let it happen or continue with the speech she had planned. She had nothing to lose, it was now or never. If she was out of a job, then what difference would it make anyway?

"Thank you, sirs, and I'll get right to the point. I've given some serious thought to what you said about journalistic integrity as well as my claim that viewers really want to know that we're not just newsreaders but real people. I think that both are true and there is a way to accomplish both and redeem ourselves from any negative publicity this station may have incurred due to my indiscretion regarding my daughter's legal trouble."

"Ms. Shaw, you really don't have to..."

Andrea threw up her hand to stop Messner from speaking. She had to get this out or she was as good as gone. She loved investigative reporting, but working as a beat reporter would be harder on her with the kids. She already spent less time at home than she would like, and if she were tossed back to reporting, it would only get worse.

"Please, just one more minute of your time."

Messner nodded and Andrea continued. "I'm proposing that we take the situation with my daughter as a jump-off point and lead into an all-out exposé on school violence. I have people lined up that are experts on dealing with the issue, not to mention my firsthand experience with how the school system and our legal system handles these cases. The public should be made aware of how substantial this problem is."

Andrea saw no response on Messner's face, but when she glanced at Tate, the PR guy, she could tell that she had his undivided attention. So she continued.

"But it doesn't just end there. Some of my daughter's problems have been the result of my divorce and her trying to come to terms with how that has changed our family and what that change means to her. My ex-husband recently remarried and now we are a blended family with even more opportunity for things to go wrong. I could give you a rundown of the numbers of single-parent households and blended families in this country, but I'll spare you the details and just let you know the numbers are staggering."

Andrea really didn't have the numbers, but after several years in the news business, she had learned the art of fast-talking and selling her point. She had spent too many days coercing people who did not want to talk into spilling their guts to her with a camera shoved in their faces.

"So, I propose then leading into a report on blended families, with experts who handle these issues every day and the families who make it work. Gentlemen, I really believe that our viewers want to believe that we are perfect, articulate and talented people, but at the end of the day they know we are just like them. We face problems, our kids get into trouble—for Christ's sake, we get into trouble. But where we can make a difference is in presenting real-life solutions to these real-life problems, allowing our viewers to feel more like friends, peers, if you will."

Andrea was out of breath when she was done speaking. Still no response from Messner. Tate had lowered his head as if in thought. Or perhaps he had tuned her out and they were all just waiting until she was done so they could kick her out and make Leslie's day.

"Ms. Shaw, this is not an altogether bad idea, but we will talk this over and let you know our decision. For now, we'd like for you to…"

"I think she's on to something," Tate interrupted.

"We can talk about it later, Daniel," Messner said, standing to usher Andrea to the door.

Tate went on talking as if Messner hadn't said a word. "My son and a few of his friends were hanging out at the house one Saturday. Just kids watching movies and playing video games. I had a six-pack in the fridge and I guess one of the guys took it upon himself to have a few.

"When he left my house to go home, he was involved in an accident. No one was hurt, but his parents wanted to blame me. Said that I was providing alcohol to minors, setting a bad example. I couldn't believe it. I had my beer in my fridge. If anything, their little brat stole my beer. And then they wanted to press charges and everything."

Andrea wasn't sure what was happening. She had never been privy to the executive meetings, but she was sure this was not the kind of thing that they usually discussed. Claxton was not a "get personal" kind of company.

Still, no one spoke, but Tate continued. "I think she's right. If we can show that our talent, Andrea and Dave, are just normal parents like the rest of us, trying to do our best without screwing up too much, I think viewers will appreciate the honesty. It may mean being more transparent than you'd like, Andrea. Could you handle that?"

Andrea noticed that for the first time he had used her first name. She had connected with him. She did not get an opportunity to answer before Messner spoke again.

"Ms. Shaw, thank you for your time. We appreciate you sharing your thoughts with us."

Messner then opened the door and ushered her out.

Andrea would just have to leave it at that. She had done all that she knew to do. The rest was out of her hands.

When she got back to the newsroom Leslie was no longer at her desk. She looked at Nancy for answers.

"She was called upstairs to the GM's office," Nancy explained as Andrea flopped down at her desk.

No sooner than Andrea could breathe a sigh, Cara, the receptionist, was motioning toward the phone on her desk.

"I'm transferring the call. Your daughter," Cara said.

Andrea smiled, although she wanted to just walk back out the door and not deal with one more problem. Instead she picked up the beeping phone.

"Mom, you need to come right now."

"Amber, what's wrong, baby? Are you okay?"

"It's Ray. You just need to come now."

"Amber, tell me what's going on. I'm at work and it'll take me at least twenty minutes to get home."

"Not home. Dad's. We're at Dad's and she's bleeding," Amber said before the phone went dead.

CHAPTER 36

Who could be bleeding? Andrea wondered as she flew out of the station parking lot and punched in the number at Ronald's house. It was a wonder she didn't crash into something since her mind was all over what might be going on there instead of the roadway she was soon barreling down.

The phone rang until the click for the answering machine. Andrea didn't bother with a message. She tossed the cell phone aside and ran over scenarios.

Amber had said "she was bleeding," which might mean Charity. But why would she call Andrea about that?

She couldn't make any sense of it. And why had the call ended so suddenly? Had someone broken into the house? Were they being robbed and threatened? Andrea hoped Amber was smart enough to call the cops and not just her.

She reached for the cell phone again, hit Redial and waited as the four rings lingered through her eardrums. The answering machine again. Andrea drove faster.

Amber had also mentioned Ray. Had Ray and Charity gotten into an argument, a fight even? Or maybe Charity had fallen and hurt herself. And Ray was trying to help her. She hoped Amber had called the ambulance. And where was Ronald?

The traffic light gods were on Andrea's side and she made it to the house in record time. Not that the seventy in a forty-five-mile-per-hour zone didn't help.

As Andrea rounded the corner to Ronald's house, she could see the flashing lights. An ambulance was in the driveway, so Andrea pulled the Porsche along the curb in front of the house.

Before she could make it across the yard and into the house, Amber was by her side tugging her along.

"Is she okay?" Andrea asked, assuming something had happened to Charity.

"The ambulance guys are with her. They're taking her to the hospital," Amber announced as the two of them nearly ran head-on into the stretcher.

Andrea had expected to see Charity laid out with blood coming from some part of her body. Instead a pale, almost greenish-looking Tammy was the patient.

"Tammy, what's wrong? What happened?"

"Are you the mother?" a paramedic asked Andrea.

"She's my mother," Ray said from behind the paramedic.

"What's going on here, Ray?"

The paramedic answered instead of Ray, "She's bleeding ma'am. It's not as heavy now, but we still need to take her in. We've put in a call to the doctor she's been seeing for the pregnancy."

Andrea heard the word, but she could only blink. No words, only blinking.

"I'm sorry, Mom," she heard Ray say, and just like that the blinking stopped.

No more confusion. Tammy was pregnant. By Ray. And she was bleeding and could be in trouble. Andrea watched as the paramedics stood by as if waiting for her to say something. So she did.

"Well, get moving already. She needs to get to the hospital. We'll take care of everything here."

The paramedics bumped down the front steps toward the ambulance.

"Have you talked to your parents, Tammy?" Andrea yelled toward the stretcher.

She could no longer see Tammy, but only the men lifting her into the back of the rescue vehicle.

"They don't know yet," was Tammy's faint response.

Great, Andrea thought. You're leaving me to jump that hurdle for you.

When Andrea turned to look at the confused faces of Ray, Amber and Charity, she felt as though she was back in her old crime-beat reporter days. She would get a sudden call to respond to an accident scene and had to be prepared at a second's notice to gather information and be ready to spout it off, live, to television viewers.

Even now on this scene, she drew on those skills and shoved the others into gear.

"Okay, she doesn't need to be by herself. Ray, go with her. Charity and Amber, you can follow in my car." Andrea tossed her keys in the direction of a very frightened-looking Charity, who caught the keys and nodded. She was pale. And kind of green as Tammy had been.

"You okay?" Andrea asked Charity as she and Amber scooted past to get into the Porsche.

"No, not really. What do I do?" Charity asked.

"Just be there. They feel better when an adult is with them even if you have no idea what you're doing. I'll be on my way as soon as I talk to her parents. Although I'm not sure what the hell I'm going to say."

Again, Charity nodded and continued toward the car. Andrea watched Ray jump into the back of the ambulance and the doors shut. With sirens and lights flashing, the ambulance sped down the street with her Porsche following. It was only then that she noticed that neither Charity's nor Ronald's cars were in the garage.

Andrea went inside to do the tough job that she had stayed behind to do. Make the call every parent must dread. How can you form the words to tell a mother and father that your son had knocked up their sweet innocent little girl? And that she is now on her way to the hospital where anything could happen.

Since she didn't have transportation, she didn't rush herself. In the lemon fragrance of Charity's kitchen, she looked up the number for Tammy's parents in the phone book. She had never met them. They had an unfair advantage here. They knew who she was, along with everyone else in the city. But she wouldn't have been able to pick them out of a lineup if her life depended on it.

She ran her finger down the list of Wainwrights until she got the street address she remembered from Ray. Dr. and Mrs. Clay Wainwright.

"A doctor. Good, then maybe he's already at the hospital," Andrea said into the empty kitchen.

And even if he wasn't, he could probably get there before she could with no transportation. A ride. She'd need to figure that part out. But first things first, she thought as a woman's lively voice sang *hello* into her ear.

CHAPTER 37

At the Professional Auto driving service, Wayne nearly knocked Maxwell over as he walked through the door.

"You should keep your cell phone turned on, man," Wayne yelled, still blocking the doorway.

"Okay, I will, but could I please get inside?"

"No. She called. Said it was an emergency. I told her you were out and I couldn't get hold of you. She needed a ride to the hospital. I asked if she needed an ambulance, but she just got aggravated and hung up."

"How long ago? Do you know where she was?"

"Slow down, man. Ten minutes ago and sort of."

"Where is she, Wayne?" Maxwell yelled, moving back toward his car.

"She was at his house. The caller ID said Ronald Grimes."

Maxwell stopped in his tracks trying to figure out why she would be calling from her ex-husband's house. Nothing he could think of made sense, so he jumped into the car and speed off to the tune of Wayne yelling for him to turn on his cell phone.

Maxwell sped toward the hospital, hoping he had

chosen the right one. He didn't know where Ronald Grimes lived, so he wasn't sure which hospital she would be going to. When he had met Ray on the train, he had mentioned going to his dad's house, and both he and Maxwell had gotten off at the same stop. So Maxwell picked the hospital closest to his own house.

The more he thought about it, he knew it was one of the kids. He hoped her daughter hadn't gotten into more trouble. He knew Andrea had been stressed-out about her. Then he couldn't help but wonder if something had happened with Ray's girlfriend. Maxwell had assumed from his last conversation with Ray that they were planning to have an abortion. Perhaps something had gone wrong.

When Maxwell got to the hospital, he parked the car in the emergency parking as close as he could get to the section where the ambulances were coming and going. He jumped out of the car and shot down the sidewalk toward the sliding doors. It occurred to him that he may not be at the right hospital, but the faster he got inside the faster he could determine if he needed to speed across town to the other hospital.

Once inside, his eyes flew from one side of the long room to the other. He was just about to approach the registration desk when he spotted Andrea. She was talking fast and hard. He scanned the room again, this time spotting a young girl and another woman just a few feet from Andrea, but clearly grabbing at every word of the conversation that they were not supposed to be part of.

Maxwell assumed the girl was Andrea's daughter. Still

not sure what was going on and why she had called him, Maxwell did not want to just leave without at least getting her attention. He slid to the other side of the young girl and woman, and tried to blend in with the crowd. And hear what was going on, without them knowing he was there.

CHAPTER 38

"Oh God, I can't believe this is happening. My baby. Where is that doctor?" Mrs. Wainwright said, while Andrea shuffled from one foot to the other, dodging wary looks from emergency room personnel.

Her last concern should have been what these people were thinking of her. Why was the TV news lady in the emergency room? She had to block it out of her mind and attend to the personal crisis that had nothing to do with what she did for a living.

Tammy was frightened even though she was out of danger physically. And Ray was too afraid to face her parents. So, that left Andrea to deal with it alone. Besides a wide-eyed Amber and Charity, who hadn't said a word since she arrived. Andrea had wanted to ask her about the cars, and why there were none in her garage. And where Ronald was. But Charity didn't look as if she could breathe, much less carry on intelligent conversation.

The thought crossed her mind that having Ronald beside her would have at least taken some of the pressure off. But she blinked that thought away quickly. That had been the last thing she had wanted.

"I have to get back there to my baby," Mrs. Wainwright continued.

"Honey, you have to wait until they say it's okay. Trust me on this one," her husband offered.

He had been at the hospital and was called away while seeing a patient. If anyone knew hospital protocol, it was him.

"Then why does he get to be back there with her," she said, referring to Ray.

Although the doctor had come out to let them know Tammy's condition, that had happened before the Wainwrights arrived. When they had rushed in demanding to see their daughter, they had been put off since only one person could be with her while they were assessing her condition and stabilizing her. That person had been Ray, and as much as Andrea wished Ray could come out and be replaced by the Wainwrights, the doctors were doing what they thought was best.

"How long have you known about this?" Dr. Wainwright asked Andrea, contention edging his words.

"I just found out. I'm as shocked as you are."

"Of course you are. Are you clueless about what's going on with both of your children? Trust me, we heard about that one," he said, his eyes pointing to Amber.

Andrea sucked in a breath and tilted her head to the side, ready to give Dr. Wainwright the "what for," but she didn't have to. Charity had somehow gained the courage and strength to speak.

"How dare you? She is not a 'that one.' She's a teenage girl who's faced huge family changes, changes most adults don't even adapt to well…but we expect a child to just roll with the punches and be okay. Her name is Amber, and if you choose to refer to her, I suggest you use her name."

Charity had moved from Amber's side and was standing toe-to-toe with Dr. Wainwright, her voice never rising, but her intent growing stronger with each word.

"And what right do you have to question another's parenting skills since you didn't even know your own daughter was pregnant. And you can cast blame on our children and target Ray as much as you like, but he was not the only one who lay down, Dr. Wainwright."

When Charity was done, she tugged the bottom fringe of her blouse and strutted back to join Amber on a couch nearby.

Damn, Martha has balls, Andrea thought as she stared at Charity and then back at the Wainwrights.

Mrs. Wainwright was now leaning on her husband crying. Andrea watched the couple for a second then diverted her attention back to Charity who was no longer in a lethargic state, but rather confidently chatting with Amber. It was then that Andrea noticed the dark suit, bald head and compassionate eyes.

CHAPTER 39

Ronald could not believe his ears when he listened to the message Charity had left on his cell phone. He had put the phone on vibrate during his meeting, and when the call came in, he had looked down to see his home number, but it was the worst possible time to excuse himself to take a call. So he waited and waited.

Twenty minutes had passed, then thirty. By the time the clients were done grumbling and complaining, nearly an hour had passed since the phone had started jerking on his hip.

"Ray's girlfriend is pregnant, and she's in the bathroom bleeding. She had said her stomach was hurting, and then the next thing I knew, she was yelling from the bathroom. Oh, God, Ronald. I called the ambulance and I think Amber called Andrea, but what else should I do? Ray is pacing around...."

The message ended and Ronald had hit the button to play his second message which was a continuation of the first.

"I know you're in a meeting, but you have to call me. What should I do? What if Andrea can't come? I don't think Tammy's parents even know she's pregnant."

There was a pause and Ronald could hear voices in the background.

"Andrea's here, I'll call you back," Charity had ended.

Sweat was running down Ronald's brow by the time the message had ended. There were no other messages, so he assumed they had gone to the hospital.

"I gotta go. Emergency at home," Ronald yelled to the clients as he yanked at his briefcase and rushed for the door.

The clients were already disgruntled about the progress of their project. Ronald had planned to meet with them, give ear to their complaints and come to an agreement to continue the job. But now, he was running out.

Before he reached the parking garage, he had gotten Charity on her cell phone.

"I just got your message. I was in the middle of the meeting, but I'm on my way," Ronald said as he hit the button and waited for the double chirp to signal that his car alarm was disengaged.

"We're at the hospital. Are you done with the meeting?"

"Not really, but I'm getting into the car now. Hang on, I should be there in less than an hour. Which hospital?"

"You don't need to run out on those guys, Ronald. Everything is okay here. Tammy's okay. The bleeding stopped. Her parents are in with her now. The doctors are keeping her on bed rest for a couple of days. She had been stressed because she was planning to have an abortion, but then decided against it."

"An abortion. What? But, but…"

"But, Ronald, you need to finish what you're working on. We have this under control."

"We?"

"I'm taking Amber to the nursing home for her work session, and Andrea is with Ray."

"Good, Andrea decided to show up this time. Well, what about Tammy's parents? I know they are beyond pissed."

"They're fine. We took care of it."

"You keep saying we. Who's we?"

"Andrea and I. And Andrea's boyfriend is giving her a ride since my car is in the shop."

"Oh, man, that's right. Your car. I forgot it was in the shop. What are you driving?"

"The Porsche."

It would have been just as believable if Charity had told Ronald she was driving an army tank. No one drove Andrea's Porsche. Not even him. What had happened to his once completely dysfunctional family while he was away on business?

CHAPTER 40

"Thanks for coming. You didn't have to, especially with the way I acted earlier," Andrea said after Ray had gotten out of Maxwell's car.

He had given them a ride home from the hospital. She hadn't said much to him at the hospital or during the ride home. She had chosen to ride in the front seat instead of the back as she had when he had normally picked her up in one of Wayne's cars.

"I met Ray on the subway almost two months ago."

Andrea's brain did some quick calculations. Two months ago, they hadn't started dating. Yet, he had met Ray and never mentioned it. Her mind went back to the night Ray had come home while Maxwell was there. She had noticed something between the two of them. But she passed it off as just Ray being annoyed that she was dating.

Maxwell continued. "I didn't know who he was, but he looked like something was troubling him, so I struck up a conversation and he told me."

Andrea couldn't speak. Once she had seen Maxwell at the hospital, she had thought back to his involvement in the case with his manufacturing company. She felt bad for letting that come between them, at least prior to hearing the whole story of why he had kept it from her. But now, what she was hearing brought all-new feelings of anger and disappointment. She couldn't bring herself to look at Maxwell even though he was still talking.

"Before our conversation ended, he told me who he was and it wasn't until that moment that I realized he was your son. Of all the people I could run into on a subway, with a huge secret, it had to be him."

Andrea felt the tears. She would not let them fall. She had been on the brink of crying too many times today. She would eventually give in to the feeling. But not right now.

"There I was carrying my own secret, and now I had another one just dropped into my lap. So, I decided to stay out of it and let him handle it for himself. The night I saw him at your place, he begged me not to say anything."

"Of course he did. He was trying to hide it. But you're an adult, Maxwell, with a son of your own. You know the right thing to do," she yelled.

"Yeah, the right thing. There are always clear-cut lines. Perfect choices. And I'm just an idiot for not making the right one. Is that it?"

They both went silent. The car windows were fogging. The doorman had glanced in their direction a few times. Andrea knew if she didn't get out soon, they would have company. All of the men who worked the front door at her apartment building were protective over the women, especially her. She had always appreciated their concern and tried not to give them too much to worry about. But this time, she had to deal with Maxwell.

"I didn't say that," she retorted, still not looking at him.

"But that's what you're implying."

"I need to get inside," she said, reaching for the door handle.

"Let me finish, Andrea. I made a huge mistake five years ago. And I've paid dearly for it. And then I met you," he said, turning his head toward her for the first time.

His eyes drew hers. His stare held her eyes locked to his own as he continued.

"We didn't talk at all at first, but just being around you, made me want to make it right. It made me go back and mend my relationship with my son, and apologize to his mother for ruining her life. And I guess I got hooked on the me that I was becoming around you. And I didn't want it to end. I told myself that if you got to know this new guy, the man I've become…then when I got the courage to tell you about that stuff, you wouldn't hold it against me."

Andrea could see the doorman walking toward the car.

"And if you don't forgive me, I'll be okay. But he won't," Maxwell said, referring to Ray.

"I'd appreciate it if you would leave him out of this."

"Okay, I will. But he's afraid. He messed up and everything inside him is telling him how bad it is and how bad he is. And if that's all he listens to, then he'll wind up running and hiding like I did."

He pulled his eyes from her and looked forward again. She did not stop staring at him.

"But there's something about you that infuses people. You make good people better and fallen people get up again. So, I came to the hospital because I was concerned and then when I realized you had everything under control…I stayed because I wanted to thank you."

Emotion caught in Andrea's throat. But she didn't pull her eyes from him, even though the doorman was now standing beside the car.

"I'm leaving the driving service. I just wanted you to know in case you call sometime in the future. But don't worry, Wayne will make sure you get someone good."

He turned to her and smiled. She smiled back and didn't bother to hold back the tears. She got out of the car and stood at the doorway to watch him drive off. But he didn't. She followed the doorman to the front of the building, assured him that she was okay.

Maxwell still sat there staring at her. No longer in the rearview, but up front and personal. It was an epiphany for Maxwell. She had been the one to pull back the covers on his poor ethics, and yet she had also been the one to restore him. She walked into the building and he drove away, his heart full of hope for a bright future despite the fact that Andrea Shaw would not be part of it.

CHAPTER 41

Ray wanted to sleep, but he couldn't get his heart to slow down enough to relax. He had been on edge ever since he found out that Tammy hadn't gone through with the plan. And then the bleeding and her screams, and there was nothing he could do. He had wanted to help her, and stop her at the same time. He didn't want anyone to know what they were dealing with until he could come up with another strategy, but it had come out anyway. In a big, loud, grand way, it had all come out.

As he and Andrea sat in the living room, he thought about how reasonable the adults had been. He would have never guessed that Tammy's father wouldn't want to hurt him. Or that his mother wouldn't curse a blue streak when she found out. But something had happened. They all just wanted to make sure that he and Tammy and the baby were okay.

Was he okay? He couldn't be sure yet. He was still waiting for the bottom to fall out. He was afraid to speak and almost to breathe for fear that it would all come crumbling in on him.

"Your dad is on his way over," Andrea said, her words so soft he nearly missed them.

Ray knew what that was all about. He hadn't talked to his dad since everything happened. But he had heard the speech before. His dad would talk to him about responsibility and the future. He would make him go to the Wainwright's house and face them. He would tell him how hard life was going to be and what separates the men from the boys and all that. Ray had grown up with minisermons about right and wrong. That was his dad's way.

"I asked him to wait until tomorrow, but he insisted," Andrea said, and then moved onto the couch beside him.

She pulled his head over onto her shoulder and rubbed his back as she had when he was a little boy and couldn't sleep. As she had when he had a cold and couldn't breathe well enough to find rest. As she had done so many times, for no reason at all.

"This is going to be hard," she whispered.

"Yeah, well, I know all about hard. When you and Dad got divorced, I thought it was the worst possible thing and my life was over. But then it turned out not to be the worst thing after all. We don't all live together, but I still have both of you and now, Ms. Charity."

Andrea felt a twinge of jealousy at the mention of Charity's name. Then her mind went back to how Charity had stood up for Amber and Ray at the hospital. She had even referred to them as their kids.

"And when I found out Tammy was pregnant, I was sure my life was over. You would kill me, or Dad, or Dr. Wainwright. But Mr. Maxwell told me I wasn't giving you enough credit."

Ray went into the kitchen, leaving Andrea alone with

her thoughts of what Maxwell had told her earlier. She hadn't given him one bit of credit. Had she been too hard on him for not handling everything so perfectly? She didn't have time for further reflection since the doorbell was now ringing. Ray returned from the kitchen in time to open the door for his father.

"Are you okay?" Ronald asked as he draped his arms around Ray.

Andrea was sure it wasn't the first time Ronald had hugged his son. There had to be other times, but she couldn't remember any. Still, seeing this was good. She smiled as Ray started gushing information to his Dad. "I swear, I used one every time, Dad. Every time."

"You used what, Ray?" Andrea asked from the sofa.

"I gave him condoms a while back," Ronald announced and turned his attention back to Ray.

Andrea stood back in shock, watching a relationship between father and son that she had not been aware of until now.

"Dad, I know you're pissed, but I did exactly what you told me to do."

Andrea thought of the condoms in the trunk of her car. Doing absolutely no good to anyone. At least Ronald had tried to offer protection. She had been too embarrassed and confused to do anything.

"I have no idea how this happened," Ray rambled as his father pulled him toward the door, away from Andrea.

The two were whispering, but Andrea leaned toward them and listened harder.

"Did you use all of them?" Ronald asked.

"Tam didn't like the ones you gave me, so I bought some different ones. But they were the same name brand."

"And where did you keep them?"

Ray glanced back at Andrea, who pretended to be picking something off her pant leg.

"In my closet. Inside my old sax case," Ray whispered.

Ronald closed his eyes and nodded his head back and forth, pulling Ray farther toward the door. "Did you check expiration dates?"

"Expiration dates? No, I just used them and then bought more."

Andrea wasn't sure what to think about her son running through boxes of condoms right under her nose. And if he was, then how could Tammy be pregnant? she wondered.

"The ones I gave you are probably too old by now. You didn't use them lately, did you?" Ronald said, and Andrea nearly fell off the sofa trying to hear Ray's response.

"Mom, could you get Dad some tea or something?" Ray asked.

Trying not to let her shock and disappointment show, Andrea slid to the other end of the sofa and turned her back to them. She was not leaving the room without finding out what had been going on behind her back.

"Did you use one of the old ones, Ray?"

"One night when Mom was running late. I didn't have any so I got one of those out of the sax case. But I would have known if it broke, right?" Ray asked his dad, his voice so low he had to stand right next to Ronald's ear to be heard.

"Not if you were rushing and didn't check," his father responded.

"I'm sorry, Dad. I know I need to talk to Dr. Wainwright, but I was too nervous tonight."

"You might want to give him a day or two. I'm sure you're not his favorite person right now."

Andrea could hear the two of them laughing. She had heard most of what they had said and was still reeling over the fact that Ronald and Ray had such an open relationship, especially about sex.

"Like I told you, son, if you're man enough to do it..."

"Gotta be man enough to face the responsibility. I know, Dad, I know."

After Ronald was gone and Ray had gone to bed, Andrea couldn't help but think about if she had had to handle the situation with Ray alone. There was no way she could have had the condom talk with him. She realized at that moment that she needed plenty of help raising her kids. Not just Ronald, but Charity had helped defend them when she was lost for words. And even Maxwell had given Ray sound advice when he learned of the pregnancy.

"I guess there's something to that, 'it takes a village' stuff," she said into her empty living room.

When she looked at her watch, it was not yet ten o'clock. She had two calls to make before she could rest for the night. She logged into the WVTR database and found Daniel Tate's home number. When he answered, he sounded as businesslike as he did each time she had spoken with him at the station.

"This is Andrea Shaw. Sorry to call you at home, but I rushed out this afternoon and wasn't able to do the newscast again."

"Andrea, I'm glad you called. Nancy said you had another family emergency. What gives?"

"My son's girlfriend is pregnant and she started to bleed, so we spent a few hours in the emergency room and no, I didn't know she was pregnant until today."

"Damn, and I was worried about a few beers. What's that saying about 'when it rains'?"

"Tell me about it. Anyway, I just wanted to let you know what happened and find out how my dog-and-pony show went over with Mr. Messner."

"I think you're on to something with your proposal. If anybody knows how hard parenting is, you are the lady. Messner offered Leslie the weekend shift, but she turned it down. I think she's going back to Milwaukee. Find me tomorrow when you get to work and we'll go over a PR strategy for your proposal."

Andrea wished Daniel a good-night and thanked God that she was still employed. With everything that had happened, if they had let her go, she wouldn't have had the strength to fight it.

And then call number two. She dialed his number, hoping it wasn't too late to call. His voice punched through after only two rings.

"Hello."

She could hear the sounds of traffic in the background. He was still in his car. Perhaps on his way home.

"I need a ride," she whispered without identifying herself.

"I don't drive for Wayne anymore."

"I know. Maxwell, I'm sorry."

With those words, he changed lanes, popped his signal,

and turned the car around heading back toward the Bal-timore Harbor.

"Give me five minutes."

"Take your time. I'm not going anywhere."

EPILOGUE

Eleven months later…

Andrea Shaw never expected a knight in shining armor to ride up and sweep her off her feet. So it never happened. What she expected was a relationship, with challenges and misunderstandings and wonderful times in between. And that's what she got. The unexpected came almost a year later, in a tiny box from Tiffany & Co. that she was almost afraid to open.

"Someone told me women like these things," Maxwell said as they dressed for Ray's high school graduation party.

"Tiny boxes often freak women out. What is this, Maxwell?"

"You have to open it. And don't play naive with me. You knew this was coming. Now open it, so I can ask you and get over this sick nervous feeling."

She held the box tight to stop the shaking. It didn't work. Fumble after fumble finally revealed a two-carat princess-cut stone set in a platinum band.

"Now you've transferred the sick feeling to me. This is

beautiful, Maxwell. But we've both done this before. We already know there's no promise of a fairy-tale ending."

"You're right. So, that takes some of the pressure off. We can just live and be happy and work hard to love each other. To hell with fairy tales. Real life is much more exciting," he said and kneeled down to make his pledge to the woman of his dreams.

Later that evening at Ray's party aboard the *Princess Pride* yacht, Andrea did everything she could to stop staring at the ring on her finger. This was Ray's big night and she didn't want to upstage it with her personal euphoria. Ray had graduated with honors and gotten the music scholarship he had been working hard for.

Andrea had moved from the lower deck to the upper for some time alone. She had only been there a second, taking in the fresh night air when Charlotte interrupted her moment of peace and quiet.

"Is everything okay with you?" Charlotte asked as they both grabbed the rail to steady themselves.

The night was gorgeous for a cruise with only a minor sway here and there to remind them that they were on water.

"I saw you and Mother yapping away earlier. And I could have sworn she has earrings just like that. I thought you were too selfish to let anyone borrow your jewels," Andrea said, teasing her sister's earlobes.

"Your mother could only dream of earrings like this. And, yes, I am quite selfish, but we're going to Barbados for a week this summer, so perhaps I can buy her a pair."

After Ray's performance at the House of Blues in Myrtle Beach, Charlotte and Chloe had fought long and hard about Chloe's new man. The fight, albeit ugly, had led to conversation, which was what the two women had been missing.

The distance between the two had been because of all the things they had in common, but the most important of those things was their love for one man…Andrea's father. Charlotte and Chloe had used their time at Myrtle Beach to go back in time to where Daddy had been their world, and then come back to the present where they both had longed for men who would fill the gap. Charlotte had found everything she dreamed of in Juan, and finally allowed her mother to feel those same things for a man of her own.

"I suggest you don't eat or drink. No point in spending the entire night in the head, again," Andrea joked, as Charlotte sipped from her wineglass.

"That's taken care of, ma'am," Charlotte said, holding up a pack of seasickness pills.

When Andrea reached to take the pills from her, Charlotte grabbed her sister's hand and screamed.

"Jesus H. Christ. I see what's wrong with you. When did this happen?"

Andrea tried to pull her ringed finger away from her sister, but Charlotte was not about to let her brush over an engagement of all things.

"Right before we came here. But keep quiet, I don't want to ruin Ray's night."

"I heard my name," Ray said, stepping behind Charlotte with Kenya in his arms. "I've been looking for the two of you."

Tammy had delivered a healthy baby girl. She and Ray were no longer an item, but they were still friends and planned to do their best raising three-month-old Kenya Lashaye Grimes.

"Auntie Charlotte, you haven't held my little girl yet," Ray said, nudging Kenya toward his aunt.

"And I don't plan to. They leak from too many places at that age. Don't worry, you won't be able to keep me away from her once she's old enough to shop," Charlotte said, brushing her hand over Kenya's head, and strutting toward the bar.

Andrea didn't have any problems taking Kenya from Ray. She adored her granddaughter, although the idea of being a grandmother would take some getting used to.

"Thanks, Mom, this boat is awesome. And everyone's here. Tam and her parents are in there with Dad and Charity. And guess what?" Ray asked, but then answered before Andrea could guess. "Ms. Charity is gonna have a baby."

"Are you serious?" Andrea said, feeling pleased, to her own surprise.

She had thought that when Ronald and Charity finally got pregnant, it would bother her. But she wasn't at all troubled by it.

"They just told everyone a few minutes ago. Isn't that cool?"

"That's great. I'll go in and congratulate them."

Since what had started out as a dreadful summer last year, Andrea and Ronald had gone into counseling. Individually and then as a group including Charity. It had been an unconventional move, but one that they all benefited from.

Andrea kept her job as news anchor and watched a pouting Leslie Shore make her way back to Milwaukee. As promised, Andrea had done a series of news reports on school violence using Amber's personal story as well as reports on blended families and how to handle the ever-changing dynamics. And she had won another journalism award for the effort.

"Ray, Maxwell asked me to marry him," Andrea blurted out before she could stop herself.

"Mom, that's great, right? You are happy, aren't you?"

"Yes, I'm ecstatic. Still trying to adjust," she said, holding up her ring finger.

"Damn…"

"Ray, watch the language in front of the baby," Andrea said, juggling Kenya so Ray could see the ring.

"Mom, did you hear?" Amber yelled, nearly knocking Ray out of the way, as they rejoined the others on the lower deck.

"Hear what, honey?"

"Dad and Ms. Charity are having a baby," she yelled. "This is so exciting. A baby. I'm going to be a big sister. And I was thinking, when the baby comes, I could move in with Dad for a little while and help out," Amber rambled.

By the time she was done, the rest of the crowd had quieted to hear the ruckus going on between Andrea and Amber. After the kind of year their family had been through, the slightest sign of raised voices immediately got everyone's attention.

"Honey, I think that would be a great idea. If it's okay with Dad and Charity."

Charity nodded and Ronald hugged his wife against him, a look of pride aglow on his face. Andrea hated the fact that all eyes were on what she had felt was a somewhat personal family moment. Before she could move out of the line of sight, Maxwell stepped forward and took her hand into his.

"Sounds like the perfect opportunity for us. Ray will be in college in California on a full music scholarship and if Amber is with Ronald and Charity, we could do our thing," he said, and you could have heard a pin drop on the luxury yacht.

Andrea was on the spot. All eyes were on her, even the DJ and the waiters, who had previously been moving around the room keeping them full of delectable treats. She had to speak. So she did. "Looks like we have a baby and a wedding to plan for."

The clapping and cheering led to a round of toasts and then a second round. The DJ and waiters finally got back on the job and Andrea retreated to the upper deck again where she could get a better view of people she knew well, and a few newcomers twirling and spinning on the dance floor. She had been so into watching those below, she hadn't seen her mother come up the steps to join her.

"I'm so proud of you," Chloe said, stepping close to Andrea and sliding her arm around her daughter's waist.

"You don't say," Andrea leaned into her mother and kissed her cheek.

"Seriously, and not just because of this," she said pointing to the ring. "But rather because of that," she added, nodding toward the crowd on the lower deck.

"That motley crew?"

Chloe spun Andrea around and looked directly into her eyes as she spoke. "Andrea, anyone can do husband, wife, two point five kids, house, two cars, stable careers. But it takes a special talent to juggle the imperfect. An ex-husband, his somewhat-timid wife, a gorgeous fiancé… and teenagers, his and yours."

Andrea glanced down at Maxwell's son Tim, dipping Amber so close to the floor, she slipped out of his arm and lay sprawled out at his feet. The music was too loud for her to hear the laughter, but the gaping mouths told the story.

Andrea scanned the crowd as her mother left her to join the others. The group was all that Chloe had described and more. The best word she could find to describe what she saw before her was *family*.

Not picture-perfect by conventional standards, but a good thing just the same. In some strange way or another, they all belonged to each other. Andrea smiled out over the horizon at that notion of belonging. When it all boiled down, she had what really mattered. To love, and to be loved.

SPECIAL NOTE FROM THE AUTHOR:

At the core of *Changing Lanes* is the struggle of the blended family. Although there are times I feel like the poster child for the blended family, when I set out to write this story, I in no way intended it to be personal.

When I turned the final draft in to my editor, I realized that no matter how different the names, locations, occupations, etc, the issues are the same...divorce, remarriage, birth children, stepchildren, biological parents, and stepparents...all walking that tightrope to keep a delicate balance between harmony and utter chaos.

When it works, the blended family can be both rewarding and enriching to everyone involved. When it doesn't, it can lead to heartache and disappointment.

My hope is that inside the pages of *Changing Lanes,* you will find that just shy of perfection, you too can find richness and joy in the unique characters that are blended into your life.

Cassandra Darden Bell

CHANGING LANES

By Cassandra Darden Bell

ABOUT THIS GUIDE

The questions and discussion topics that follow are intended to enhance your group's reading of *Changing Lanes*. We hope the novel provided an enjoyable read for all your members.

DISCUSSION QUESTIONS:

1. Andrea Shaw is a career woman to the core. In the opening chapter, Andrea receives troubling news concerning her teenage daughter yet due to job responsibilities, she is forced to sideline the issue until after her newscast. Discuss the difficulty women face when juggling high-profile careers and family.

2. Ronald Grimes is out to ruin Andrea's goal of having a rewarding career and solid family. What is at the core of his actions against Andrea and what is he willing to risk in order to bring her down?

3. Andrea's two teenage children are having adjustment problems since their parents' divorce. Discuss Amber's trouble at school and what Andrea and Ronald can do to help her better adjust to their new life.

4. Ray Grimes is carrying a heavy and burdensome secret. After working hard to be the "good kid," his efforts have backfired. Discuss his handling of his parents' divorce and his pending role as a teenage father.

5. Maxwell Leonard has a secret of his own. What event or series of events propels him to reconcile with his son?

6.   Andrea's sister Charlotte and mother Chloe are an interesting and colorful pair. What role do these two women play in Andrea's life as her perfect world unravels?

7.   Maxwell and Andrea are trying desperately to get on the same romantic page, yet for both of them, past demons and present-day struggles make a relationship seem like an impossible dream. Discuss the difficulty of single parents getting back into the dating game while maintaining their many other roles.

8.   Ray's band competition at the House of Blues seems to be the boiling point for everyone. Discuss Andrea, Ronald and Charity's confrontation and why each of them is so passionate about his/her point of view. Charlotte and Chloe's private battle finally comes to a head. What is at the source of their years of tension?

9.   The miscarriage scare with Ray's girlfriend, Tammy, seems to be the catalyst for the family working together toward a common goal. If you are part of a blended family, what makes your dynamic difficult? If your blended family is a healthy one, what makes it work?